WOLF BOUND

GREYSTOKE WOLF PACK
BOOK 1

TERRY SPEAR

PUBLISHED BY:

Wilde Ink Publishing

Wolf Bound

Copyright © 2024 by Terry Spear

Cover Copyright by Rainy Day Art

Discover more about Terry Spear at:

http://www.terryspear.com/

Print ISBN: 978-1-63311-103-5

Ebook ISBN: 978-1-63311-102-8

Thanks to Eileen and Blake Grimsley, this book is dedicated to both of you. My prayers are with you Blake as you fight your battle with cancer. May your Airborne strength help you to overcome your trials. Thanks to you both for your friendship and I'm grateful you're enjoying my books!

SYNOPSIS

Red wolf Kira Westwood is on a mission with the United Shifter Force where she's trying to track down kidnappers who are gray wolf shifters. What she doesn't expect is to find a wounded gray wolf—shifter type—who's an innocent bystander and the boy who has been taken hostage. Now her mission is complicated by leaps and bounds.

Fisher Greystoke can't believe a walk in the national park has led to nearly being killed and meeting the prettiest red she-wolf he has ever met. But there's no time for anything but helping her go after kidnappers and joining the United Shifter Force so he can get to know the red wolf a whole lot better while ensuring the rogue wolves don't take them down first--permanently.

PROLOGUE

Red wolf Kira Westwood had just turned eight years old and celebrated her birthday by staying overnight at her girlfriend's home, who was also her age and home-schooled, except Sally was a gray wolf. Kira's own family lived only a couple of blocks away. They'd had a blast while running in the woods that evening with Sally's twin brother and her parents as wolves, and then having a pizza party. They'd watched their favorite movies, and then the girls talked most of the night before finally falling asleep, making for the perfect birthday sleepover.

That morning, Kira had eggs and toast with Sally. Sally's twin brother had gone out to meet up with his friends. Sally's dad had gone off to work, and her mother, who had a cake baking business out of her home, was busy making cakes for an upcoming birthday party and a wedding. So Kira said goodbye to Sally and her mother and headed home.

She was tired and hoped her parents weren't going to push her to go someplace she didn't want to go. She was ready to chill on the couch and watch TV the rest of the day. But she hadn't made it a block before a white van pulled up next to her. Wary, she glanced in its direction. As soon as she did, a guy with a short haircut—

wearing black pants and a black T-shirt with a skull on it—got out
of the van. Before she realized what he was up to—she smelled his
anxiety right away—he grabbed her arm and yanked her toward
the van. Her heart racing, she screamed and kicked and hit him like
her parents had always told her to do if anyone ever tried to grab
her. As much as she wanted to, Kira couldn't bite him, or she would
chance turning him into a wolf shifter like her.

"Shut her up," the driver of the van said, and she knew she was
in terrible trouble. She wasn't big enough to fight off one husky
man, let alone two.

Her blood ran cold. Going against everything she'd always been
taught she knew she didn't have any choice. She bit the man's arm
hard. He was holding her wrist tightly and there was no yanking
free of his iron grip so she figured it might be the only way to
escape them. Maybe she hadn't turned him, but she tasted his
blood in her mouth. Once the bite registered in his brain, he cursed
a blue streak and immediately lost hold of her. She scrambled to
get out of the van and fell to her knees on the pavement. Terrified
he would grab her again, she got to her feet and dashed back
toward her friend's house, terrified, screaming and shouting. She
hoped someone would witness the van and record the license plate.

What she couldn't believe was the van kicked into reverse and
shot backward toward her. The vehicle was just about in reach
when she dashed up her friend's walkway. She pounded on the
door, screaming and crying. She was so panicked that she just knew
the man was going to grab her again and shut her up for good.

The van just sat there for a moment, and she figured the man
she had bitten would grab her again if she didn't get inside any
second now, figuring she had just gone to a random house and no
one was home to save her. "Sally! Come on, come on! Open the
door!"

He yanked the van's panel door open, and she screamed, "Help
me!" Everyone in the neighborhood was probably working or

running errands. She didn't see any other cars on the street, so she didn't believe anyone would come to her rescue.

Sally suddenly opened the door, frowning, her mouth hanging agape. "What...?"

Out of time to explain anything, Kira jumped inside, slammed the door, and locked it. "They tried to kidnap me. I bit one of the men. I had to." Tears filled her eyes and ran in rivulets down her cheeks.

They peered out the window and the van peeled off down the street. The girls ran outside and memorized the license plate number and then tore inside and Sally got her mom. "Mom! Mom! Men tried to kidnap Kira!"

It would have been easy just to report them to the police, but not after Kira bit the one man. She was so upset, knowing her mom and dad would be distraught that she might have turned him. He might not shift for a while, but they couldn't leave things as they were.

Sally's mom asked, "Did you turn wolf?"

"No," Kira said, then realized what she was getting at. She could only turn someone if she had been a wolf. She gave a sigh of relief.

But her mom got on the phone to call Kira's parents and then she called her husband right away instead of the police. They were part of a small wolf pack, none of them in law enforcement—baker, butcher, construction workers, a chef, and a nurse. What made them the perfect people for the job to deal with the kidnappers was that they were all wolves with a common driving goal—protecting their kind and maintaining their secrecy. They took care of their own. She thought they might have worried the men would try to grab her again since she had seen their faces, now that it wasn't an issue that she had bitten the one guy.

Everyone who could leave their jobs for the emergency mission did. Kira's mom was a nurse, and her father was a chef, and both arrived at Sally's house to coordinate the effort. Several men were armed with guns and drove in their own vehicles, headed the way the van had gone. Since Kira knew the van the best and which man she'd bitten, she had to go along with her mother. Sally stayed home with hers.

"This is a learning experience," her mom said. "If we bite someone as a wolf, we have to either take them into the pack or eliminate them. But you bit him as a human. Still, we're concerned they could come back for you or come after Sally, and the police might never catch them or they might get off. We can't let that happen."

"I'm so sorry," Kira said through her tears.

"No, darling. Oh, sweetheart. You did what you had to do. We're so proud of you. We always told you not to bite anyone, but in this situation, you were human. They could have killed you and that was the only way for you to save yourself. You had to do what you did. Even if you'd managed to shift into your wolf, we would have been behind you all the way. Your dad and I would have done the same thing at your age if we had been in your shoes. Even if we were grownups, given your situation."

Kira still thought her dad, or even the other wolves in the pack, might feel differently. They all had to leave their jobs to deal with this and she could imagine they would be mad about it.

"Are you okay?" her mom asked. "They didn't hurt you, did they?"

"Bruises on my arms. But I'm okay otherwise." Then Kira saw the van up ahead. "There it is!"

"Okay." Kira's mother called her dad on Bluetooth. "The van is traveling north on Live Oak. They just turned right onto Pine Street."

"Are you far enough away from them?" her dad asked.

"Yes. There's another car between us. It just turned off, but another car pulled in front of me, so there's still a car between us and the van," her mother said.

"I'm near your location. I'm going to call Rutherford to let him know where the van is."

Rutherford, who owned his own butcher shop, was their pack leader.

"The van just drove into a driveway. Four-ten Pine Street," she said.

"I'm right behind you. Just park on the street a few houses down from there. I'm parking behind you."

"Alright, dear."

Her dad ended the call and Kira knew he was calling the pack leader to coordinate everyone's efforts. She was scared, worried that the men might try to get her again or hurt her parents or the others in their pack.

She glanced out the back window. But her dad was staying in his car while Kira and her mom stayed in hers, watching the house as the men climbed out of the van, shaking their heads. The driver shoved his finger at the chest of the man Kira had bitten, pushing him back.

"Which man did you bite?" her mom asked.

"The one in the black pants, black sneakers, and shirt with a skull on it. The other man was the driver." Kira could still taste the man's copperish blood in her mouth, smell his body odor—he'd been drinking beers and hadn't bathed recently, his skin sweaty and his black hair greasy. He'd eaten chili filled with onions—which she'd also smelled on his breath.

The van had smelled of discarded fast food hamburger sacks and greasy fries all over the front seats and the back.

The men walked into the one-story house covered in green siding and sporting a gray roof. Big windows were covered in blinds. The neighborhood was older, established, the vegetation— trees and shrubs—overgrown.

Then a black pickup pulled into the driveway behind the van and parked, effectively blocking it in. Kira recognized it was

Rutherford's truck. He got out of the vehicle and then she saw other vehicles pull up and park in front of the house.

That's when her dad left his car and came up to the passenger's side window. "Which man did you bite?" he asked Kira.

"The man wearing black pants, black sneakers, and a shirt that had a skull and crossbones on it. He had black hair and a beard and mustache."

"We'll get him, honey. Don't you worry."

Her father didn't sound angry with her either. But what were they going to do with the two men?

Five of the pack members, including her father, went to the door of the house and Rutherford knocked on it.

The driver of the van opened the front door of the house, and Rutherford and the other men shoved their way into the house. Then the door slammed shut.

"What's going to happen?" Kira knew that if her father and the others killed the two kidnappers, they could eventually all be caught and tried for murder. She didn't want any of them to be in trouble for "taking care" of these criminals.

"It depends on how the kidnappers react."

It seemed to take forever before Kira's dad came out of the house. "It's done. Go home. I'll follow you there."

It wasn't until they arrived at home that her dad hugged Kira and her mom hugged her again. He told her what had happened. She had to know. It was the wolf's way. "They committed suicide. Evidence was all over the place, indicating they had kidnapped other children, and none of the kids had ever returned home. So you did what was right. The men felt such remorse that they hanged themselves."

Kira didn't believe they would do it. For all her youth, she recognized what her father was telling her. They had helped them find death.

Shortly after they arrived home, Rutherford showed up to

speak to them. He was a kindly gentleman of sixty in human years, a gray wolf with graying hair, but he was strong and capable and would probably run their pack for several more decades.

They all sat in the living room and Rutherford said, "We can't know how terrified you truly were without having been in your place, but what you did was the right thing. From all the evidence we found in the house—for over a decade, those two men had kidnapped children, and they were never punished for it. They felt so badly for their sins, knew they were going to prison, and decided to hang themselves."

"You helped them." Kira was known to be tenacious at times.

Rutherford cast her a hint of a smile. "They might have needed a little persuasion. Not that they didn't deserve it."

"But will anyone find out you were all involved?" That was what concerned Kira the most.

"They left suicide notes. Both wrote their own. They confessed to the kidnappings they had committed. With their confessions, the police will be busy looking into cold cases that they had never been able to solve," Rutherford said. "Okay, I'm headed back to my shop before my mate sends out the police looking for me. Just know this, you not only saved yourself, you saved other potential victims." Then he patted her on the head and left the house with her father.

That's when Kira decided she wanted to do something when she grew up where she could protect their people and others who might be harmed by men like these.

1

The youngest of quadruplet brothers, Fisher Greystoke, was having pizza with his brothers before he took a run as a wolf through the Rocky Mountain National Park near the pack's territory in the town of Greystoke. "Are you sure none of you want to go with me?"

He didn't mind running as a wolf alone, but it was more fun going with one of his brothers or cousins or one of the other wolf pack members.

"I've got a couple of patients to keep an eye on." Heath was drinking soda with his pizza instead of a beer because of it.

A fourteen-year-old wolf teen had been driving his car without his parents' permission or a driver's license——had veered off the road and hit a tree. He had broken both legs and his right arm and was in traction at the moment, but he was wearing arm and leg casts and would stay that way for a while. Heath was on call if anything happened that required his immediate attention. The teen's friend had been luckier, wearing a seatbelt and the car's impact with the tree had given him whiplash, but at least he was at home with his family. At times, wolf teens were no different than human teens at getting themselves into trouble. Though Devlyn, their pack leader, had given them hell for it. Bella, his mate, was more the good guy this time and much more comforting, though she could be just as growly a wolf when it came to it. Of course the teens' parents were pretty steamed about it too and let both boys know it.

Fisher glanced at Shawn. He shrugged. "I've got a date. No one you know. We might go running later, but it'll be just the two of us."

Tanner smiled. "Serena and I are spending some quality time at home. The only reason I'm even here is that she pushed me out the door, telling me to go have a slice of pizza on her. Right now, it gives her heartburn, but she knows how much we like having our weekly pizza dinner."

"Yeah, it won't be long, and you'll have little wolf pups yapping at your wolf heels," Fisher said.

Serena and Bella were twin sisters, and both were expecting twins in six months.

"Devlyn and Bella are busy tonight too," Fisher said. Devlyn was their cousin. "And so is Aaron with his mate Angie. They're taking a nighttime ride on their horses." Aaron was another of their cousins and he owned a horse ranch. "And you know Brock. He's up to his eyeballs on a PI case." Yet another cousin. But his brother, Vaughn, was with the United Shifter Force and currently on a mission with his mate. Brock was also mated. So it meant Fisher, Shawn, and Heath needed to get on the stick and find mates. Fisher was curious about who Shawn was dating on the sly.

"I hope you're no longer on that dating site," Shawn told Fisher.

"Nope. We need a wolf shifters' dating site."

"There's not enough need for it," Heath said.

Fisher rolled his eyes. "Like we're swimming in single she-wolves around here."

"Right, but if you found a wolf you liked, and corresponded with her, but she's in Florida or Oregon, then what would you do?" Heath asked.

"Go see her," Fisher said, though he agreed for the most part with his brothers. They really needed to spend some time with the she-wolf to know if she was the right one for them.

"Let us know when you return home." Of the four brothers, Shawn had become the worrier of the bunch.

"Yeah, sure. I should be gone for about an hour. Two at the most." Fisher hadn't run as a wolf in so long that he really felt the urge to be one.

They all finished their pizzas and then everyone said good night and went off to do their own things. Heath was checking on his patient at the shifter clinic. Shawn was off to pick up his date to take her to dinner and a movie. Tanner went home to his mate and Fisher drove off to the Rocky Mountain National Park.

When he arrived at the trailhead, he noticed a brand-new red Yukon like his and he smiled. The owner had good taste. He parked next to it, then grabbed his bag. He had water in it and a first aid kit, but also, he would throw his clothes in it once he reached a place perfect for him to shift into his wolf. Then he locked his car, yanked his backpack on, but as he walked past the other car, he smelled the scent of a red she-wolf, and he raised his brows. He smelled three gray male wolves in the area which meant they could be with her, though it smelled like their scents weren't as recent as hers.

Maybe she wasn't with them, and he could catch up to her. He hurried off down the trail. Were they running as wolves? He didn't recognize their scents, so he knew they weren't members of the Greystoke wolf pack.

The forest appeared as magical as always, the sun setting, glowing yellow and orange through the trees, birds chirping before the sun finally set. He loved the fall and this time of night because he didn't normally encounter hunters, though it was illegal for them to kill wolves in any event. He quickened his pace—eager to find a spot to strip and shift and see if he could catch up to the red wolf, just in case she was truly on her own.

Kira Westwood worked for the United Shifter Force as a special agent, tracking down shifters who were rogues. She'd been in law enforcement for years, but when she had gotten a call from Martin Sutherland, the director of the newly formed United Shifter Force, she knew that was her calling and she'd given notice at her work as a homicide detective in Loveland, Colorado where her family lived and joined the USF team.

With the case she was working on now, gray wolves had kidnapped human kids and ransomed them for money and left them at locations that were safe. The only reason she had gotten the mission and known the kidnappers were gray wolves was because she had been near the crime scene when they had stolen the most recent child and she had smelled the wolves' scents. The USF took the case on right away because they couldn't allow one of their kind to get locked up. What if they shifted in prison? They would out their whole kind.

Thankfully, the three men didn't have a clue that a USF agent was tracking them through the national forest. She had learned the three men had the same MO as in other kidnappings in Colorado and she was sure they had done all of them. Learning the men had been stopped for a traffic violation near the national park and then seeing their black Chevrolet Suburban parked at the trailhead, she hoped to get lucky and locate them.

She had to find them and turn them over to the USF. Unfortunately, her partner in this case had been in a car accident and broken both legs right before she had left to track these three men down. Everyone else in the USF was working on an important case so there was no one left to spare.

She quickly called her boss to inform him about what she had discovered. "I'm at the Rocky Mountain National Park and I've located the kidnappers' SUV."

"You're in the Greystoke wolf pack territory then. Call Devlyn or Bella Greystoke who are the pack leaders. They will send you help if you need it." Martin gave her their phone numbers. "Keep me informed when you can but keep yourself safe."

Devlyn's cousin, Vaughn Greystoke, and his mate Jillian were fellow USF special agents out on a case in Oregon. But Devlyn and the rest of the pack were well aware of the USF and the good that they did.

"Okay. Thanks. Out here."

She wasn't wearing her wolf coat as she tracked the wolves' scents. She knew the three men had guns and she couldn't very well approach them as a wolf. What worried her the most was that she'd smelled Billy Forsythe's scent, the human child, who had been kidnapped. She was glad she was getting close to them, but was concerned she wouldn't be able to rescue the boy on her own.

Then she heard talking and laughing deeper in the woods—a man and a woman, who eventually reached her on the trail and greeted her as they walked on past.

She planned to just track down the kidnappers first, and if she found the three men and the boy, she would ask Devlyn to send reinforcements. There wasn't any sense sending anyone here until she could actually give them coordinates of the kidnappers' location. What if they had already left the national park and she ended up sending the Greystoke wolf pack on a wild goose chase? The boy who cried wolf came to mind.

As a wolf, Fisher had been loping through the forest for about three miles when he heard a child crying about an eighth of a mile away from where he was located. The boy was closer to a trail than he was. "I wanna see my mommy. I want my daddy," the boy said.

A man said in a gruff voice, "Shut up."

Wondering what was going on, Fisher headed their way, partially because of his instinctive wolf's curiosity and partially because of a need to make sure the child was supposed to be with whoever the man was.

"Here, kid, have another cookie," another man said, his voice just as gruff, but it was deeper than the other man's.

"Are you sure you want to do it this way this time?" another man asked, his voice younger.

"Yeah. We need to change up our MO or we're going to get caught," the first man said. "We've got the pickup location; the kid stays here."

"But what if someone else picks up the kid? Someone bad?" the younger man asked. There was a significant pause. "Well, badder than us."

Fisher didn't like what he was hearing. As a former Army Ranger, he had some skills he could use in taking down bad guys, but the problem was if they were armed, he wasn't. With his teeth, sure, but if they were armed with guns and at least three of them were involved? The odds were definitely stacked against him. And as a wolf shifter, he didn't want to bite any humans, unless he had no choice.

But if these guys left the kid in the woods and took off to their "pickup location," Fisher could rescue the kid. Well, kind of. He was still in his wolf coat. He could pretend to be a dog and befriend the boy. That's what he would try to do. Any self-respecting wolf normally didn't want to ever be thought of as a dog, but in a case like this, he would do whatever it took to save the kid. If the kid needed saving.

"What if a cougar gets him?" the younger man asked.

"A cougar's not going to get him. Come on. It's time. We leave him here and go. We'll have plenty of time to make the pickup," the first man said.

"I don't know," the younger man said.

Fisher moved in closer so he could see the three men and the boy. The wind was blowing away from all of them so he couldn't capture their scents.

"Okay, well, we'll leave you here with the kid and you protect him. Then you join us in Florida," the brown-haired guy said.

"I won't have a ride out of here," the younger man said.

"Exactly. So make a choice. Come with us or stay here and figure out another way to meet up with us. But you better not get caught." The guy looked similar to the younger man, same narrow jawline, same small eyes, but he was probably middle aged and darker haired.

"Listen, kid," the younger man said, his blond, shoulder-length hair caught up in the breeze. "You stay here and hug a tree. Your parents will come for you. If a cougar comes, you scream and yell at him and throw sticks and rocks at him. Don't go wandering off into the woods. If you do, no one will find you. You gotta stay right here and we'll give your parents this exact location. Got it? If you move, you will be lost in the woods forever."

"Give him that extra water bottle," the brown-haired guy said. "Wipe it down."

Fisher wished they would call each other by their names, but he could understand why they wouldn't if they had kidnapped the boy. It was safer for him not to know them.

"Don't drink all of this at one time. Just little sips every once in a while, because once it's gone, you won't get any more," the blond man warned.

"Stay here," the brown-haired man said to the kid, "just like he said."

Fisher was getting close to their location, moving quietly, sneakily, trying to keep his eyes on the men and the boy without any of them seeing him. If the men saw him as a wolf, they might believe he would kill the boy if they left him alone in the woods. Fisher needed them to leave him so he could take the boy to safety.

Of course, the boy might listen to the men and decide he wasn't leaving that spot no matter what, even if Fisher pretended to be a dog and tried to take him to safety. He observed the three men closer. The younger man looked like he was about twenty, his disheveled blond hair shaggy, his black jacket having a red and white striped collar, his white tennis shoes dirty, his shoe size about a ten. One of the stouter men was about thirty with dark brown hair, his build much more muscular. The black-haired man was about his age, his hair cut short, reminding Fisher of a bulldog of a drill sergeant he'd had while in training in the army.

The brown-haired boy of about seven or so was wearing black jeans, sneakers, and a baseball team shirt. He was quiet as the three men started hiking through the woods to the trail, the younger man glancing back at the boy, as if worried about him. The other two men continued on their way without a backward glance as if they didn't give a damn about the boy. Fisher had to wait until the three men were well out of sight before he approached the boy, a water bottle in his hand, tears streaking down his dirty cheeks.

Just then, the younger man caught sight of Fisher, of all the rotten luck, and ran back to the boy, pulling his gun out and shooting at Fisher. Fisher dashed off, furious the younger man had been watching out for the boy and saw him sneaking through the woods as a wolf, looking like a predator ready to take down his prey. When in truth, he'd just been trying to sneak in without getting caught at it.

Fisher dodged bullets, cursing himself for the mistake. He thought the blond guy would just stop where the boy was and wouldn't pursue Fisher any further, not when they had a "pickup" to make. But the blond guy must have thought if he killed the wolf, the boy would be safer if they left him alone liked they had planned.

Even though Fisher was running as a wolf, the blond guy wasn't that far behind him and kept trying to shoot him, until Fisher came to a cliff. For a second, he thought of going right or left, but he was out of time. He glanced over the edge and saw a ledge several feet below. The blond guy aimed, fired, and hit Fisher in the shoulder. Fisher felt like a fist had slammed into his shoulder, the jolt knocking him backward.

Fisher took a calculated risk and fell off the cliff, hoping he didn't hit the ledge and bounce off. He knew he had a chance at surviving, versus staying at the cliff's edge where the blond guy could shoot him until he was dead. Fisher's greatest regret was that he hadn't saved the boy from the men as he hit the ledge with a painful thud and his vision faded to black.

2

_____

As soon as Kira heard the sound of shots being fired, she was certain it had to do with the men she was after. What worried her the most, besides that they were in a shootout with possibly law enforcement agents, human types, was that they had the young boy as a hostage. She'd begun picking up the boy's scent soon after she had located theirs and that made the case of her finding them even more urgent. But when someone began shooting, she was worried mostly about the boy. If the police killed the wolf shifters, as long as they were in their human form, there wouldn't be any problem for the shifter community. Incarceration was the real problem.

She was running as fast as she could go toward the sound of gun shots, until they stopped and then she paused. She wasn't sure what was going on. No one was saying anything. No one was shouting to the men to put their hands up, if law enforcement was trying to take them into custody. Then a man said, "Did you get the wolf?"

Oh, God, so one of the men was running as a wolf. But that didn't make any sense.

"Yeah, I shot him, and he went over the cliff," a younger sounding man said. "We can't leave the kid here on his own."

One of the men was stocky, wearing camo clothes, black sneakers, had short cropped black hair and a thick black beard. "I told you what we're doing. Like I said, if you want to stay, so be it. Come on. We're going and he can stay behind."

"We can't leave him here. If we do and they catch him and he talks...," the other man said. He had shaggy brown hair, scruffy beard, and he was wearing khakis and hiking boots and a light-weight olive-green jacket.

"All right, I'm coming." The younger, blond-haired guy hurried off after the men. He was wearing blue jeans, sneakers, and a black jacket, his face sporting a light smattering of hair. It appeared he wasn't able to grow a beard yet.

Kira wanted to take down the men. She really, really did so they couldn't kidnap any other kids. But she had to get the boy to safety no matter what. Yet, she had to check on the wolf. Wolves were protected, but what if it wasn't even a wild wolf but a wolf shifter out for a run in the park?

She moved slowly through the woods, ducking down when she saw the three men heading through the woods in the direction of a trail. To intersect with the trail, they would have to hike a good twenty minutes, which meant the boy was a long way from the trail so no one who was just hiking along it would ever see him here.

As soon as the three men were completely out of sight, she hurried toward the boy. At first, he didn't see her, but then he did and cried out. She put her finger over her mouth to shush him. All she needed was for him to alert the men that he was in trouble and for them to come racing back to shoot her.

She quickly showed the boy her badge as she continued to run toward him. As soon as she reached him, she pulled him into her arms and gave him a hug, then spoke low for his ears only. "I'm taking you away from where those men are going and then I'll get you home, alright?" Though they needed to check out the wolf too. She hadn't lied. She needed to keep the boy far away from those men.

He nodded.

"I'm Kira. What's your name?" she whispered, taking hold of his hand, and moving him in the direction that she had smelled the blond guy and the wolf run.

"Billy."

"What's your last name?"

"Billy Forsythe."

Even though she was sure of that, she had to have actual confirmation from the boy's own mouth. "Okay, well, Billy, I was after those men, but I need to get you home safely first."

"The one guy was shooting at a wolf this way," Billy said.

"It wasn't a wolf, just a dog that looked like a wolf. We're going to check on him." If the wolf *was* a shifter, she had to let on he was a dog so she could take care of him.

Billy pulled her to a stop. "What if he's injured and mad and tries to eat us?"

"He won't. The blond guy said he went over a cliff. We just need to check on him and we need to stay far away from the men who took you hostage." Kira was trying to move the boy quickly through the brush, but she realized he must be exhausted. He might not have had anything to eat in a while. She stopped and reached into her backpack and fished out an oatmeal bar for him to give him some energy. At least he had a bottle of water.

"They said I couldn't drink very much of my water."

"I've got more if you need it. You can drink as much as you want now." Then she walked more slowly with him while he munched on the bar. "You're not hurt, are you?"

"No, just tired. My legs hurt from walking so much."

"As soon as we get farther away from the kidnappers, I'll use the satellite phone to call for help."

"The kidnappers' phones didn't work out here."

"Right. They wouldn't. There are no cell towers out here." She kept smelling the younger man's scent and the other wolf's anxious scent. The younger man's scent was more pronounced because he'd retraced his steps and run the other way to meet up with his co-conspirators.

But then the younger man's scent stopped, and she knew he must have fired that final shot right here. The wolf had continued on. Maybe he had been wounded. She sure hoped not. Then she reached the edge of the cliff. "Stay back, Billy. I don't want you falling off the cliff."

She peered over the edge of the cliff. Down below, probably thirty feet on a narrow ledge, lay a wounded gray wolf, his shoulder bleeding. Her heart went out to him. He lifted his head to look at her and lay his head back down as if he was too hurt to care that she might plan to shoot him next.

"I'll call this in first." They were far enough away from the kidnappers, but if she became injured, she might not have a chance to call this into anyone. She brought out her satellite phone and called the pack leader. "Devlyn, this is Kira Westwood. I've found the boy the three men I've been tracking had kidnapped. They've headed back on the Greenhorn Trail in the Rocky Mountain National Park toward the trailhead, but one of the men shot a uhm, a dog that looks like a wolf."

"One of ours?"

"I don't know. He's lying on a narrow ledge below a cliff. He fell about thirty feet. I'm climbing down to him to see if I can give him first aid, but—"

The wolf lifted his head and howled.

"Hell, that's my cousin, Fisher," Devlyn said.

"I told you it's a wolf," Billy said.

"Some dogs howl, Billy," she said. "Okay, Devlyn, I'm climbing down to him. I'll call you back after I've taken care of him." Then she gave him their coordinates. She didn't wait for him to answer. She knew Devlyn would rally everyone he could to help rescue his cousin and the boy. But she had to go to Fisher's aid as quickly as she could and try to stop his bleeding and see if he was injured in any other way.

She took hold of Billy's hands and crouched in front of him. "My boss is coming with a whole bunch of men and women to help the dog and get you home to your parents. But I have to climb down and put a bandage on him, okay?" Even though Devlyn wasn't her boss, and he might not actually show up, she didn't need to tell the boy that.

The boy's eyes filled with tears. "Don't leave me."

She smelled his fear and she completely understood how scared he was. But she had to make sure Fisher didn't die on her.

"You sit right here by this tree. Okay?" She gave him a package of jerky. "If you get hungry for something more just eat this. And this way you can rest your legs. Just stay here. Don't go anywhere. Help is coming." Then she gave him another hug and he didn't want to release her, but she had to go to the wolf's aid. "He's hurt. I have to take care of him. I'll be back as soon as I can."

She didn't want to leave the boy behind because he'd already experienced enough trauma and he was scared to death. But she couldn't chance Fisher dying on her because she hadn't gone down to take care of him. She couldn't risk taking the boy down the cliff either.

Worried about the boy and the wolf, she felt her heart pounding furiously. She took the rope she had with her and tied it to a nearby tree. "You stay here. I'm going to climb down and check on the dog."

"He's injured. He could bite you."

"He'll be fine. I've taken care of them before in a similar situation." She began to rappel down the cliff to the ledge and once she was on it, she hurried over to the beautiful gray wolf, his chin and cheeks blond, the arch above his eyes dark brown and black, very distinguished looking. His eyes were a beautiful golden, his black nose sniffing the air, trying to smell her scent. She pulled out her first aid kit with as much caution as she could use. She didn't want to fall off the narrow ledge in the meantime.

"I'm a red wolf." Though after she said it, she didn't know why she did because he could smell her scent. "I spoke with your cousin, Devlyn, and he said you were Fisher. Don't shift." She was speaking low for his ears only. She glanced up to see the boy lying on his belly, peering down at them from the cliff's edge. So much for him staying safely near the tree. "Devlyn's organizing a party to meet us and help out. Were you shot just the one time?"

Fisher nodded.

She was already bandaging his shoulder, but it was hard to do on a wolf. It was easier to do on a man, but with the human boy watching from up above, Fisher couldn't shift. Though it would have made it a lot easier for her to learn where else he might be hurt if he was in his human form.

"Is he a dog?" Billy called out, as if a wolf wouldn't be this complacent and no one would try to rescue a wounded wolf—way too dangerous.

"Yes. He's a friend's dog who got away from his owner," she said and privately said to Fisher, "I hope you hadn't thought to rescue the boy in your wolf coat."

He grunted. She took that as a yes. She kissed him on the top of his furry head. She felt so bad for him. He whimpered. She let out her breath. She hoped he was going to be alright. Their kind healed in half the time that humans did, but his injuries could be bad. Still, he was keeping her from her mission of maintaining the boy's safety. Yet she knew she couldn't safely move the wolf up the cliff, not if he was severely injured from the fall.

"Did you break any bones when you fell?" she asked.

He moved his left foreleg a tiny bit.

"Sprain or break?" she asked. Shoot, he couldn't answer her again but with yes or no questions. "Sprain?" He didn't answer her. "Break?" He still didn't respond. She was trying to get the bandaging around his chest, and he groaned. She suspected he was badly bruised. Maybe he didn't know if anything was broken or sprained for sure. She knew he was hurting though. His heart was beating fast, and she could smell his pain.

Yet despite that he was feeling bad, he took several more whiffs of her like a wolf would, and she thought he even managed a small smile. Glad she was a wolf too? She suspected so. There was a small shelf above them that stretched out over a quarter of the one they were on that provided a bit of shelter from the chilly breeze. At least the ledge seemed sturdy enough to hold both their weights until someone came to rescue Fisher. She thought of moving Fisher under the shelf, but she was afraid to move him if she ended up injuring him worse than he already was hurt.

"By the way, I'm Kira Westwood, a special agent with the United Shifter Force. I know your cousin Vaughn and his mate Jillian. Both are great to work with, but they never mentioned you before. Just Vaughn's brother Brock because they wanted him to join them in the organization." She glanced up at Billy who was still watching them from the top of the cliff. She didn't want him too close to the edge, but at least he was lying down, and the cliff seemed stable.

Even though she was speaking quietly to Fisher, the boy probably wondered why she was talking so much to a dog. "He's going to be alright," she called up to Billy. At least she sure hoped so.

"Good. Can...can you bring him up here?" Billy asked.

"No. I might injure him more."

Kira suspected Billy wanted them up there to watch over him. She didn't blame him. She worried about leaving Fisher alone, but she didn't want to leave Billy alone either.

But then Billy whispered, "Hey, someone's coming." His voice was terrified.

She only heard him because of her wolf hearing, but she worried that the Greystoke pack members hadn't arrived yet. Just normal hikers traipsing through the woods, way off the beaten path? Or something more sinister like the kidnappers, coming to see where the boy had gone to? If they were, they would know she was a wolf and helping the boy and the wolf they had shot. They would know she was a shifter like them, and that Fisher might be also.

As carefully as she could, she pulled Fisher under the shelf to protect him, and he groaned. "Sorry," she whispered. "I have to keep you hidden from those bastards. I'll be right back."

Leaving her backpack with Fisher, she rushed over to grab the rope and began climbing up to reach Billy as quickly as she could. She had her gun belted at her waist, but she couldn't use it until she made it to the top of the cliff. She just had to reach Billy before the men did. Since he had already heard them coming, it was probably too late. But she had to take the chance. She couldn't allow them to take Billy hostage again. She was halfway up the rope, afraid they might cut it or shoot at her while she was climbing. She couldn't tell the boy to run or to hide because as wolves they would be able to smell him anyway and they would be able to outrun him.

Then the boy screamed. Her heart stuttered. A black-bearded man peered over the cliff, and she knew this was really bad. He sneered at her. "We've got a live one," he called over his shoulder. "Cut the rope."

Her heart in her throat, she felt a vibration in the rope, and she knew they were cutting it. She rappelled down the rope as fast as she could. Once she reached the ledge, she dove under the shelf and straddled Fisher, the only way she could get out of harm's way. Sure enough, the rope dropped to the ledge, and gunfire sounded, the bullets hitting the ledge, splintering rock, and the fragments hit her face and her arms, though she was wearing a long-sleeved, flannel plaid shirt that protected her arms.

The boy was screaming, pleading with them not to kill the lady, and she felt so bad that she couldn't rescue him. And bad that he was so scared that they would kill her and Fisher. She wanted to shout that they were okay, but she kept quiet, hoping the men would leave and not take the boy with them. She was being careful not to press her body on top of Fisher's in case he had broken ribs. She was stuck down here now, unless she could free climb back up to the cliff's edge. Which she thought she could do if no one was shooting at her. She just had to concentrate on her foot and hand-holds and be really careful.

She'd never thought the kidnappers would return for the boy. She again considered that maybe she should have tried to move him down there to protect him, but she felt it still could have been just as dangerous.

"Fisher," she whispered to him. But his eyes were closed, and he didn't wake. He appeared to be out cold.

Then one of the kidnappers said, "Come on. They won't be giving us any more trouble."

They moved off into the brush. The boy was still crying, but he was staying next to the cliff edge. She so hoped that meant the men were leaving him behind. She carefully moved beyond the little shelter she and Fisher had and looked up to see if anyone would attempt to shoot at them again. No one did. Then she saw the boy peering down and he smiled at her through his tears. Her heart lifted with joy to see him there and that he was still safe.

He motioned to her, telling her that the men were gone.

"We're okay and help is on the way soon," she said, her voice soft in case the kidnappers were still close by. She wanted him to know help was still coming and that she and the "dog" were fine.

He gave her a tearful thumbs up. He didn't look reassured though that any of them were going to be rescued any time soon. Then she heard a male voice under the shelf saying, "Where am I?"

She glanced back at Fisher and saw a very naked, very hot male wolf lying on his back on the stone.

"Uhm, Billy, I'm checking on the dog real quick. He's under this shelf. I'll be right back." She said to Fisher, "No, no, no. Turn back into your wolf. Your cousin, Devlyn, is sending people to rescue you." She quickly pulled out a first aid blanket and her parka from her backpack. Even though earlier, she thought it would be good for him to shift and be in his human form so she could bandage him and look over his wounds and speak with him, she realized he would be colder, and it could be worse for him.

"I...heard gunfire." He held his head as if it was hurting.

"The kidnappers of the young human boy, Billy, they're wolves. They came back maybe to finish you off. They discovered I had moved Billy to the cliff and had come to save you. In any event, they shot at you and me, but it was fortuitous that I had moved you under the shelf before that happened. They've left again. But they cut the rope that I used to climb down to take care of you."

"With you on it?" He groaned in pain. "They're wolves?"

She pulled out a cloth from her backpack and wiped his sweaty forehead. "I rappelled down before they could cut the rope all the way. And yes, they're wolves."

He let out a relieved breath as she covered his beautiful, muscular, bruised body with the thermal blanket. "And the boy?"

"He's up on the cliff. I'm going to free solo back up the cliff. The boy is terrified and I'm worried that before we can get help, he's going to get too chilled." She placed her jacket over Fisher's chest on top of the thermal blanket, then pulled out a knit cap from her bag and tugged it on his head.

"Are you sure you can do it without falling? How far was that drop?" He really sounded worried for her, which she appreciated.

"About thirty feet. I don't know how badly you're injured."

"A cracked rib or two, or maybe bruised, I think. And the gunshot wound. I'm feeling cold." Even though she had covered him with the blanket and her jacket, the stone ledge he was resting on would be cold.

On top of that, he was sweating from the pain.

"Shift back." She wanted him to be as warm as possible while wearing his wolf fur coat. She grabbed a bottle of water and helped him to sit up a bit to drink it.

"I can't. As soon as I shifted into my human form, I tried to shift back. It's much more comfortable to lie on the stone as a wolf. But I'm in too much pain to hold my wolf form. You have a red Kia."

She frowned, wondering how he knew that. "Right." Then she realized he must have smelled her scent by her car at the trailhead. "Okay, I've got to go." She tugged a sweater out of her backpack, tied it around her waist, then she left him the bottle of water. "Drink some of this if you need to. I'm going to climb up to the boy to make sure he's not getting hypothermia. Because of the trauma the boy had experienced and now that the sun was setting, he is sure to be cold. Don't you dare move from this spot until we get help here for you."

He gave her a halfhearted smile. She suspected he did because he was in no condition to move anywhere on his own. Which was good. She didn't want him accidentally falling off the ledge and then he would be dead for sure.

Once she was sure he was warmer, she used her backpack to make a pillow for his head. "I'll be back."

But before she could leave him, he seized her wrist. Despite being injured, he had a strong grip—that she was glad for—and he stopped her in her tracks. "Be careful."

"I will be. Or I'll end up joining you on the ledge in the same condition as you are, minus the gunshot wound."

Then he released her wrist, nodded, and she made her way to the cliff and began looking for the best possible handholds.

Her heart beating hard, she carefully picked her way around

the rock face, finding the best finger and toe holds she could use while the boy watched her in silence. As much as her muscles were shaking, she knew she needed to get some extra rock climbing into her work routine. The boy appeared to be shivering though, so she was glad she was returning to him to aid him now. She finally made it up to the top of the cliff. He immediately rose to his feet and hugged her.

She hugged him back, so glad he was safe. She untied the arms of her sweater from around her waist and pulled it over his head and arms. Of course now, she was getting chilled! She was wearing a flannel shirt, but she could have used something heavier as it grew colder this evening and the breeze picked up.

She used her satellite phone again to call Devlyn with an update. "The kidnappers came back and tried shooting us, but we managed to get under a little bit of a shelf that protected us. I'm back topside to warm up the boy. The...uhm, dog might have a couple of broken ribs. Not sure."

"I understand. Heath, Fisher's brother, is a doctor and he's bringing medical supplies to take care of him. All our men are armed. If they see the wolves, they'll take them down. The men should be there in about fifteen minutes."

Fifteen minutes would seem like an eternity.

"We've got twelve men headed your way," Devlyn added. "Some will be looking for the kidnappers also. We can't allow our kind to break the laws."

"Right and they're doing it this time in your...uhm"—she glanced at Billy snuggled up in her olive green wool sweater, sitting on the ground—"jurisdiction." Though they couldn't allow them to break the law in any territory, or places where wolf packs hadn't claimed the locations either. "I'm going to let you go."

"They'll be there soon."

"Thanks." She wouldn't call her boss to tell him all that went down until later, since really nothing had been resolved. Saving the kid, yes, but the three kidnappers were still at large, and Fisher could be seriously injured.

3

Tanner, Heath, and Shawn, Fisher's brothers, and nine other men had been trying to reach the location where the USF agent, Fisher, and the kidnapped boy were as fast as they could. But it was a long hike and they'd also been watching for any sign of the kidnappers, should they have come back this way toward the trailhead.

The men had been quiet, listening for sounds of any other people in the area. They ran across a group of four college-age hikers, and later, a man and a woman in their early forties or so, hiking along the trail they were on. Then Tanner got an update from Devlyn about Kira and what she had done for the boy and Fisher. "Thanks. I'll let everyone else know." He ended the call and shared what Devlyn had said with the other members on his team.

They had to remain quiet in case the kidnappers were about. Tanner knew that everyone wanted to kill the rogue wolves for trying to murder both Fisher and the USF agent and for kidnapping the boy and abandoning him in the woods. Then they began to smell wolves—three unknown gray male wolves, a human boy, a red she-wolf, and Fisher. They knew then, even though Kira Westwood had given Devlyn their GPS coordinates, that the kidnappers had recently been in the vicinity as fresh as their scents were, and Tanner and the rest of the pack members were on the right track.

Five miles off the trail, they heard a woman talking low, and a child's voice saying. "Yes. I want a BB gun for Christmas."

Then the woman said, "Shhh."

"It's me, Tanner Greystoke, Fisher's brother and Devlyn's cousin," Tanner called out, so as not to alarm them, sure it was Kira and the boy.

"I'm Heath, Fisher's brother and the doctor," Heath said.

"We're over here," Kira shouted out. "I hope you brought something with you to carry Fisher on up the cliff face."

"We did. We've got a litter and all the climbing gear we need," Tanner said from some distance in the woods, and then they finally reached the woman and the boy, all cuddled up together on the ground next to a tree. Tanner pulled a warm coat out of his backpack and gave it to the boy to wrap himself up in it and gave him a knit hat to cover his head.

Shawn said, "I'm also Fisher's brother. I'm Shawn." He immediately gave Kira his warm down parka to wear.

"Thanks. Fisher is straight down there"—she pointed in the direction where Fisher could be found—"on the ledge beneath the overhang."

"Hey, Fisher, we're coming," Tanner said, shouting over the cliff's edge as he and the others prepared to tie off ropes so they could make the climb safely and rescue him.

"Why are they saying they're the dog's brother?" Billy asked.

Light dawning, Tanner and the others realized the boy had seen Fisher running as a wolf. "He's like a family member to us," Tanner quickly said, still coming to grips with the fact that his brother had been shot and could be seriously injured from the fall. He couldn't believe that a wolf run at dusk would lead to something as insidious as kidnappers taking a boy hostage and then trying to eliminate Fisher too. Tanner suspected that Fisher had realized the boy was in trouble and had gone to help him. Though what his brother could have done for him as a wolf when the men were armed with guns had Tanner scratching his head. Still, Tanner would have felt the same need to go to the boy's aid even if it had cost him his life.

Tanner glanced at Kira, thanking God that she had come to Fisher and the boy's aid and had alerted Devlyn right away as to the trouble they were in. Devlyn had already told them that they might be helping her with her case, but they'd never expected that Fisher would have gotten into the middle of the mess all on his own just by taking a run as a wolf deep in the national park.

WEARING HARNESSES AND HELMETS, some of the men were lowering a litter while Tanner and Heath were rappelling down to check on Fisher. Kira sure hoped he was going to be okay as she sat on the ground with Billy wrapped up in her arms, fast asleep, keeping him warm. She was too keyed up to drift off, but she was glad Shawn had shared his parka with her. She'd been wishing, if the boy hadn't been an issue, that she could have turned into her wolf. Though if the boy hadn't been here, she would have stayed with Fisher and kept him warm.

Then a dark-haired man showed up, his expression serious and determined, looking like he was in charge and Kira suspected he was the pack leader. He headed straight for Kira and then he crouched down to speak with her. He shook her hand. "I'm Devlyn, and we're all at your service."

"These men really need to be caught and I appreciate any help you can give me. No other USF special agents were available at the time to help me with the mission."

"Which is what your boss told me, and we immediately were ready to help out. How's the boy?" Devlyn asked.

"He's tired, as you can see." Billy looked so angelic in her arms, and it made her want to have children of her own to cherish and raise. "He needs a good meal and a good sleep. We need to locate his family."

"What's his last name?"

"Forsythe. Billy Forsythe. I had to wait until you all rescued Fisher before we contacted the police to locate his parents. I didn't want to reach out to them until we knew the kidnappers wouldn't come back, or at least if they did, you could deal with them. But also, Billy saw Fisher when he was a wolf, and now he's not. So we need to keep that from him. He believes Fisher is an injured dog now."

"Alright. We'll help you with locating the boy's family. We don't have cell phone reception out here, so we can't search the internet to see what FBI office is in charge of Billy's kidnapping case. Do you know what vehicle the kidnappers were using?" Devlyn asked.

"A black Chevrolet Suburban, but I looked its license plate up and the license plate was for another car. I'd lost them for a while, then saw it at the trailhead, parked, and went after them."

"Okay, I didn't see it when I drove up."

"I was afraid they had probably already left the area. Though I'm glad they aren't coming after us any longer." She let out her breath on a heavy sigh. She hated that they had gotten away. What if she was never able to track them down again? Or the feds did this time?

Devlyn stood up tall. "We'll get them."

She sure hoped so. Then she heard Heath talking to his brother down below on the ledge. "Yes, yes, Kira is topside and just fine. And the boy is also. He's sleeping in her arms, completely at peace for the moment."

She smiled. She knew Fisher had to be in pain, but here he was worried about her and the boy? That was so sweet of him.

"Okay, we're going to take you out of here on the litter. The other men have got everything set up. We'll get you out of here in no time. At the clinic, we'll take care of the bullet and x-ray you to see if you've broken anything or have any internal injuries," Heath said.

Then the boy cried out and Kira hugged him and kissed the top of his head. "You're okay, you're safe. We're getting you home soon." She spoke softly and reassuringly.

Billy really didn't wake up all the way and nestled back in her arms. She felt bad that she couldn't get ahold of his parents right away to tell them that their son was okay. That the kidnappers no longer had him. They had to be terrified through this whole ordeal. But then she had an idea.

She said to Devlyn, "We need to learn where Billy's parents are supposed to drop off the money. Then we can have some people meet up with the kidnappers."

"Can you tell me your parents' phone number?" Devlyn asked Billy, waking him.

He rubbed his eyes and gave him their phone number.

"Alright. I'll make the call." Devlyn pulled out his satellite phone. He called the number and when someone answered, he said, "I'm Devlyn Greystoke and my cousin and a friend found a boy by the name of Billy Forsythe in the Rocky Mountain National Park. We're in the process of rescuing my cousin who was shot by Billy's kidnappers. Billy is safe and sound." Pause. "Yeah, sure. Your dad wants to speak with you." He handed the phone to Billy.

"Dad," the boy said and then he just sobbed his heart out.

Kira rubbed Billy's back to console him.

Billy finally managed to say, "Yeah, there were three of them. But they left and a nice lady saved me and then a wolf...I mean a dog got shot and...a man? No, a dog. And then they shot at Kira when she was trying to save the dog's life and then she climbed back up the cliff to take care of me until help arrived."

Kira knew this was going to be a mess. She said to Billy, "Fisher, the man was with his dog, and they shot Fisher."

Billy looked puzzled and rubbed his temple. "I...I got it wrong. Anyway, the kidnappers left, and these men are going to bring me to you. Okay..." He handed the phone back to Devlyn.

"Yeah, my cousin was badly injured after he took a bullet and fell from the cliff. We're getting him up the face of the cliff now. One of our cousins is a doctor, and Fisher's brother, so he is taking him to his clinic. We're about five miles out from the trailhead, so we'll be leaving that way, carrying Fisher out on a litter until we can reach our vehicles. If you want to have your men standing by, we'll be bringing Billy there."

Kira figured when Billy handed the phone back to Devlyn, he wasn't talking to the father, but the FBI handling the case. She hoped that the agents wouldn't think Devlyn or the rest of them had anything to do with the kidnapping.

Kira said, "Tell the FBI that they need to meet them at the drop-off for the ransom because the boy is safe." Though she realized that wouldn't work either because they really didn't want them to apprehend the men. The USF, or other wolf shifters, would have to take them into custody. She suspected the three men might figure they wouldn't get away with the ransom this time and not even try to get it. Not when she and Fisher had interfered with their plans, and they were both wolves. Yet, they might not believe they were anything but wolf shifters who lived in the area and wouldn't have anything to do with trying to apprehend them. That they had just been innocent bystanders, hiking through the woods.

Not all wolves were part of wolf packs and if this situation hadn't been Devlyn's pack territory and if Fisher hadn't been his own cousin/pack member that had been shot, he might not have done anything about it other than take care of Fisher's injuries.

Devlyn nodded and then told the FBI what she had said. "No, we never saw a vehicle," Devlyn said.

Kira suspected the kidnappers had left the trailhead by then.

"No, we didn't see the men either. Maybe my cousin has a description of them. We'll ask him once we're carrying him on the trail as long as his brother doesn't give him a pain killer and knock him out for the long hike to the trailhead. Okay, hold on." He handed the phone back to Billy. "The FBI agent wants to ask you what the three men looked like."

"One had black hair and a beard. The one guy was younger, and he was nicer than the other two. He worried about cougars eating me. The other men didn't care. He didn't want to leave me in the woods. The other guy was about the same age as the dark-haired guy, but his hair was a lighter brown. He had blue eyes. The black-haired guy had brown eyes. The younger guy had blond hair and blue eyes. He was skinnier than the others. They were heavier, more muscular." Billy listened for a minute, then said, "Uh, no, they never said names except just Bud or Bro."

"Tell the agent we're on our way to the trailhead," Devlyn told Billy.

"We're leaving now for the trailhead," Billy said.

"We'll be seeing you soon," the agent said.

"Can...can I talk to my mom?" Billy asked. "Thanks. Mom, I'm so sorry I didn't take out the garbage like you told me to." Then he was crying again. "I love you, Mom." Then he handed the phone back to Devlyn and they began hiking out of there.

Shawn was carrying Kira's backpack while she took care of Billy, but she suspected there was more to Shawn's helpfulness than that. When it came to bachelor male wolves, and she suspected he was one, and they were in the least bit interested in a female, they would do everything they could to get on a she-wolf's good side.

"Can you walk out on your own okay, Billy?" Devlyn asked.

Kira was holding onto Billy's hand and making sure he didn't fall because he was stumbling over roots so much since he was exhausted. Not to mention it was really dark out now. The men had lanterns, though they really didn't need them, but the boy couldn't see as well in the dark like the wolves could with the meager light from the lanterns shining in the woods.

"Yeah, I can." Billy might be tired, but he appeared eager to rejoin his family and his spirits were lifted. Maybe he wanted to be like the wolves too, strong, determined, and independent.

Still, if he was having too much difficulty, she was sure one of the men would carry him to the trailhead. He wasn't a full-grown man, just a slightly built boy.

She was keeping him well ahead of the other men who were holding onto the litter carrying Fisher. She didn't want to have to explain to Billy why they hadn't rescued the dog. Then she heard Fisher saying something to the men carrying him about his backpack.

Tanner said, "You can let us know closer to where you dropped it, and we'll grab it."

That was one good thing about being wolves. Their sense of smell was so good they could easily find it. She just hoped the kidnappers hadn't found it and taken it with them though.

At least Fisher was all wrapped up in a blanket on the litter so Billy wouldn't realize he was actually naked. Devlyn was leading the way to the trail. Three other men were with him, keeping a lookout in case they ran into further trouble. She doubted the kidnappers would want to tangle with so many of them. She had noticed right way that Devlyn and the other men were all armed with handguns and rifles.

She kept wanting to go back to see how Fisher was doing, but she didn't want to take Billy to see him. He would start asking more questions about the dog, and for now, all he was concentrating on was moving one foot in front of the other. When they reached the trail, it was a little easier going. It still had some roots and rocks, but it was clearer than the tangled brush they had been trudging through.

The longer they walked, the more Billy stumbled though.

"Do you need a lift?" Tanner asked Billy.

"No, no, I'm fine."

She suspected that the boy didn't want to look like he couldn't manage since everyone else was hiking through the wilderness without any trouble. "I would take him up on it, but I weigh too much," she said to Billy, smiling.

"I'll carry you," Shawn said to Kira.

She chuckled.

Billy smiled up at her.

After another half mile, Billy stumbled and nearly pulled Kira down. He finally conceded that he needed some help, at least for about a half mile. Four miles later, Tanner was still carrying Billy. A seven-year-old normally could walk about five miles at his own pace. He had already walked at least that far with the kidnappers, and she suspected they hadn't let him go at his slower pace.

Tanner was walking beside her, and she saw that the boy had gone back to sleep. Poor kid. This had been so traumatic for him. She turned around and joined the men carrying the litter and put her hand on Fisher's forehead. He was dead to the world, but his temperature felt fine, thankfully.

Heath said, "I gave him something to knock him out. He would have been in too much pain jostling him through the woods on the litter otherwise."

"Good. I'm glad you were prepared. I had never predicted that the kidnappers would take the boy into the national park, and I certainly hadn't expected them to shoot one of our kind," she said.

"Yeah," Heath said. "We were all on alert in case you called us to help you, but we never thought Fisher would be involved in it too."

They finally reached the trailhead and found several vehicles parked there. Next to her car, she smelled Fisher's car that was a red Yukon also. She smiled to see he had parked right next to hers. Just as they walked into the parking area, two black SUVs and a couple of police cars arrived.

Because of all the police vehicles' lights flashing, Billy woke up, looking startled, his eyes wide. He was going home.

4

After Fisher's brother gave him something to ease the pain from the gunshot wound, Fisher was so out of it. He'd woken once when he had felt Kira's warm hand on his forehead, but then was out again after that. She had left him to walk with the boy, so that when he opened his eyes again, he asked Heath, "Is Kira alright? The boy? Is he okay?"

"Yes, they both are fine," Heath said again, or at least Fisher thought he had because his brother sounded a little more vocal about it, like he was annoyed that he had to repeat himself. Maybe his brother had repeated it more than once. "Close your eyes, go to sleep, and enjoy the ride."

Fisher realized he was being carried on a litter, was wrapped in a blanket, and being jostled around. He was glad he had some pain medication, though he didn't like feeling so out of it. "Can I see Kira?"

"She's with the boy way up ahead with Devlyn and some others. We don't want Billy to see you and then he will be asking about the injured dog."

Fisher sighed. He'd forgotten all about the wolf scenario. "What about the kidnappers?"

Heath was talking to Shawn about having Fisher's head checked out. Shawn agreed.

Fisher frowned. "What about the kidnappers?"

Heath shook his head. "Brother, we really need to table any conversation with you until you remember what we're telling you."

"What?" His brother wasn't making any sense.

"You asked us about the kidnappers already. Are you awake enough to hear again what we already had told you?" Heath asked.

Fisher rolled his eyes. His head was splitting in two, his shoulder and ribs were killing him, the pain medication was taking the edge off, but not all the way. Why couldn't he just answer his questions without giving him grief over it?

"Okay, the kidnappers got away as far as we know," Heath said.

"Why didn't you just say that in the first place?" Fisher asked, annoyed.

"I did!" Heath said.

Shawn laughed.

Then Fisher must have fallen asleep again because the next thing he knew, they were securing him in the ambulance.

AN AMBULANCE WAS ALSO PARKED at the trailhead where the other men's cars were, and Kira learned it was the Greystoke's ambulance and that they had their own wolf shifter clinic, which she thought was great. Then Fisher was loaded into it while the FBI agents talked to Billy. It appeared Fisher was sound asleep again.

The FBI agents also wanted to question Fisher. Being his doctor, Heath told them, "I've got to get him to the clinic and take care of the bullet wound. You'll have to interview him after he's out of recovery."

Then Tanner and Heath went with Fisher in the ambulance, and they left the area.

Before Billy left with a couple of officers so that he could be returned to his family, he gave Kira a hug. "Thanks for coming to save me."

She hugged him back. "I'm glad I was able to find you and get us help." Because without the others, who knew how this would have ended. But Billy was the reason why she loved her job— helping victims while taking down the perpetrators of a crime. Then Billy left with the officers and the agents started to question her.

"What were you doing out here?" one of the agents asked her.

Normally, she would avoid human law enforcement agencies while doing her missions, but sometimes they ended up having to work with them. Human law enforcement agencies didn't know that the USF was a shifter organization. The USF agents had badges that were official looking, but they told other law enforcement agencies they were an undercover organization that took down perps. Most law enforcement officials had never heard of them, and many shifters didn't know about the organization, which had been started by jaguars because of the need to incarcerate their own kind who had been involved in criminal activities. Murderers got a death sentence, normally carried out when they were trying to take them into custody and knowing they wouldn't be getting out of the charges against them and would fight them to the death. For lesser offenses, they incarcerated them in a facility for shifters only.

"I'm with the USF and was searching for the three men who had kidnapped Billy," Kira told the agent as he took notes. "I found their vehicle at the trailhead and started searching for them. I finally heard Billy crying, pleading with them to let him go home to his mother and dad. I heard shooting and it was in the vicinity where the men and the boy were. I hurried to reach the location where the shooting was occurring and saw one of the men shoot Fisher Greystoke. I didn't know him or his name at the time. He was just hiking through the woods."

"So one of the men was trying to kill you and Fisher," the agent said.

She explained just what had happened. "Yes."

Once the FBI agents finished questioning her, four of the men in Devlyn's pack took the investigators with them to show them the site of the shootings and where Fisher had fallen off the cliff. The wolves would have to help the FBI agents climb down to the ledge so they could gather any other evidence.

Devlyn said to Kira, "I know you want to continue to search for these men before they take another child, but it's late. They're in the wind now. If you don't have any other leads, come and stay with Bella and me at our house for the time being."

"Alright." She normally wouldn't want to impose on anyone, but Devlyn would have his men continue to help her, so she agreed to follow Devlyn home and stay with him and his mate.

Shawn said, "Do you mind if I ride with you? I came with some of the other guys, but they went back with the agents to check out the crime scene."

He could have gone with Devlyn, she was thinking, amused.

"In case you lose sight of Devlyn, I can make sure you get to his place. It's out in the country," Shawn tacked on.

"Yeah, sure. We'll follow you, Devlyn, and thanks for all your help," Kira said.

"Of course. They were committing a crime in our territory. Even if they hadn't been wolves, since they had injured one of our kind and tried to kill the both of you, we would have gotten involved. Also, learning a child had been kidnapped, because of our keen sense of smell, we would have helped out." Then he got on his phone. "Bella, we've got company." He climbed into his Suburban and shut the door.

"I hope that the boy doesn't mention the dog/wolf to any news reporters," Kira said as she got into her vehicle along with Shawn. Then she followed behind Devlyn's vehicle.

"I know," Shawn said. "It's too bad he saw Fisher as a wolf in the first place."

"I agree. Then you guys are all mentioning being brothers or cousins to Fisher—the dog, which didn't help the situation. Luckily the agents didn't ask us about the dog either."

Shawn smiled at her. "I know. Major mistake on our part, but we were rescuing Fisher, the man, so it was a tough situation to deal with." He looked at his phone and said, "Well, it's already all over the news about a woman named Kira who had saved Billy's life and a dog and his owner being shot that she had to rescue."

She sighed. "I figured the news would be all over it. I just hope they don't locate Fisher and me to question us." Then she got a call on Bluetooth, and she realized she had cell reception again. The call was from Martin Sullivan, her boss in charge of the USF.

"How are things going so far? I hadn't heard from you, and I thought I'd better call since I saw something about it in the news." Her boss was good about keeping in touch with his agents to ensure no one went missing, and especially probably with her because she was a new agent with the USF, and she didn't have a partner this time.

But hearing about it on the news first? Martin might not like that she hadn't already called him to let him know what had happened. She explained the whole situation and her boss swore. He rarely did, so she wasn't sure if he felt she had done wrong by not catching the three wolf kidnappers or had been concerned about everyone's safety—Fisher's, the boy's, hers, and other potential kidnap victims since the kidnappers were still on the loose. Not to mention the trouble it could cause if regular law enforcement picked the men up before they could.

"Everett and Demetria just finished up a case and they're available. Yours is a priority, given what these men are capable of, so the Andersons will be headed your way pronto," Martin said.

"Great." She loved working with the jaguar couple. "I'm staying at Devlyn and Bella's place and some of his pack members are helping us with this." She had kind of figured Fisher's cousin, Vaughn, would have wanted to be here after Fisher had been shot, but the case he and Jillian were on might be just as dangerous and as important as the one she was on. She hadn't had time to learn about it before she went on this one.

"Do you have any idea where these men have gone or who they are?" Martin asked.

"They never said their names since they leave their kidnapped victims alive. They wouldn't be foolish enough to say their real names in front of their victims," she told her boss.

"Right."

"Fisher's brother is with me, Shawn Greystoke. He's Vaughn's cousin." She figured she should tell her boss that she wasn't alone while speaking with him on Bluetooth in case he said anything that was for USF agents' consumption only.

"Okay, I'll let you go. If you get any leads let me know and Demetria and Everett will join you as soon as they can."

"Thanks, sir."

"Just stay safe."

"I will."

Then they ended the call. She thought she might get more of a lecture from her boss for not catching the kidnappers once she was alone.

"Will your boss and your fellow USF agents still want us to help out if the jaguars are coming to assist you?" Shawn asked.

"Yes, because of the seriousness of the case and we don't have a clue where they've gone to next. Plus, they've shot one of your own, so we know it's a pack territorial situation also now. If they go beyond your territory, it will be up to Devlyn and Bella." She really wanted to take a detour and check on Fisher at the clinic before she went to Devlyn and Bella's house for dinner and to sleep. "As far as we know, these men haven't tried to kill anyone before, so this shows they're getting more dangerous and more out of control."

As if Shawn knew what she was contemplating, or he was considering the same thing, he said, "Devlyn will be stopping at the clinic first so if you want to go there, just follow him. Bella will probably head over there too just to check on Fisher."

"Yes, that's just what I was thinking." Wolf families were often close to each other so she couldn't imagine them not seeing how Fisher was faring after he got out of surgery.

Devlyn called Kira to tell her he was stopping at the clinic first to check on Fisher.

"I want to see Fisher too, if I can." With wolf shifters, their rules were often different than humans. Kira hoped she didn't have to be a family member to see an injured wolf in the wolf clinic.

A half hour later, they arrived at the Greystoke Clinic. They all got out of their cars, and she saw a woman walking straight toward them. She looked like she was about six months pregnant and she practically glowed. Bella? She was a redhead too. And a red wolf. Kira smiled at her, thrilled to see another red wolf among the gray wolves. She didn't see them that often.

"Hi, I'm Bella Wilder Greystoke," Bella said to Kira, giving her a hug. "Devlyn filled me in on everything that has happened. I'm so glad you and the boy weren't hurt also."

"Thank you. Me too. It could have been so much worse. I appreciate all your pack's help. I don't know what I would have done without it."

"Well, we have you covered as long as you need our help," Bella said.

"I so appreciate it," Kira said.

They all went inside the clinic where several people were gathered in the lobby. The clinic was so different than anything Kira had ever seen. Warm oak floors and light stone walls, ceiling fans and oak furniture made it appear like a home instead of a sterile clinic.

Tanner introduced his mate to Kira. "This is Serena, Bella's twin sister."

Kira smiled. She was another red wolf and just as pregnant.

"We're so glad you're here and staying with us. I know Devlyn said we would put all our resources together to help you find these guys," Bella said. "That means even if the kidnapper leaves our territory. As long as you need our help, we'll be there for you."

"I sure appreciate it. Jaguar USF special agents Demetria and Everett are coming to help also," Kira told them.

Bella smiled. "I love the Andersons. They came to visit us for Christmas one year once Vaughn had joined the USF, and they were such a cute couple. Of course all of the wolves wanted to see them wearing their jaguar coats."

Kira smiled. "Yeah. I know the feeling. I wanted to see them in their fur coats too when I first joined the organization."

Then a strawberry blond-haired nurse, a gray wolf, came out to the lobby and introduced herself as Bethany Hollister. "Doc said Fisher is out of surgery and in recovery. But he's asking to see Kira." She looked at Kira. "Is that you?"

"Yes." Kira couldn't believe he would be asking to see her and not one of his close family members. She hoped they wouldn't be miffed about it.

But when she glanced at his brothers and cousins and their mates, they only smiled at her.

"Alright. If everyone's okay with it," she said, not wanting to alienate anyone.

"If it makes him feel better, sure," Tanner said, everyone else agreeing.

Then she went back with the nurse to the recovery room, but Fisher was sound asleep. Kira frowned. She was glad he was resting, but she thought Bethany said he had asked for her.

"Fisher? Fisher?" Bethany said, trying to get him to wake up again.

"Are you sure he asked for me?" Kira reached down and grasped Fisher's hand and caressed it.

He opened his eyes slowly, and he gave her kind of a loopy smile. "Hey, you're alright." He sounded really groggy.

"More importantly, are *you* alright?" Kira was still worried about the fall he'd had and the gunshot wound.

"I'm feeling great."

Kira laughed. "You're feeling great because of the medication they gave you, I bet."

Smiling, Bethany nodded.

Then the doctor walked into the room. "I've told the family how you're doing. Do you want me to tell Kira?"

"Yeah, and me too," Fisher said.

Heath shook his head. "I've already told you. But I'll tell you both. The bullet went clean through the shoulder, missing anything vital, thankfully. You have a couple of bruised ribs that will heal up fairly quickly. You'll need to be on bedrest for a few days for the bullet wound." Heath said to Kira, "You or the others who know his medical history can tell Fisher what I told him if he forgets what I said—again."

Fisher grunted. She smiled. She really liked the brothers. They were funny.

Then Devlyn and Bella walked into the recovery room. "Doc said you can't go with us to have dinner, Fisher. Kira's staying with us at our place. I'm sure she'll be leaving as soon as she learns where the kidnappers might have gone," Devlyn said.

Fisher looked at Kira as if she could intercede on his behalf so that he could have dinner with her, his cousin, and his mate.

"I won't leave Greystoke without seeing you first." Kira leaned over and squeezed his hand. Then she took his phone and added her number to it.

He smiled, looking like she had made his day.

Devlyn and the nurse moved Fisher out of the recovery room into a patient's room and though he appeared to be trying to stay awake, he fell asleep, and they all left. Kira really wanted to stay with him until he woke again, but she needed to eat and get some rest so if she had to run after the kidnappers, she would be ready.

It was really late for dinner, but Kira was hungry, and she enjoyed the pepperoni and cheese pizza Bella and Devlyn had made. After they ate, Bella showed Kira the guest room where she would be staying. The small room was light and airy, large pictures of scenes of forests and lakes hanging on the wall, making her feel like she was staying at a boutique guest retreat. Blue and green bedding gave the room a restful appearance for a sleepy guest. She loved how they had chargers for phones and computers, extra blankets, guest towels, and even fresh pink and white roses in a blue vase as if she truly was a special guest.

"If you need anything at all, just let us know," Bella said.

"Thanks. All I need is a shower and then to get some sleep. I love your home. It's really pretty."

"Thanks! We had fun decorating it. In the morning, we'll have breakfast as soon as you wake."

"That sounds good. Thanks for everything."

"We should be thanking you for saving Fisher's life. If you hadn't been there for him, he would have perished."

"It was my pleasure."

Then she and Bella and Devlyn all said good night and retired to their beds.

After Kira showered, she tucked herself into bed, glad that Billy would be reunited with his family, and that Fisher was going to recover from his injuries, but she still wished that she had taken down the kidnappers too. In the worst way, she wanted to know where they were.

5

Fisher woke later in the morning, realized he was in a room at the clinic and was annoyed—again—that he'd been shot. He knew Devlyn was having some of their men help Kira with her investigation, but Fisher wished he would be able to go with her.

Bethany came in to see him and took his vital signs. "Everything looks good."

"Then I can be released?" Fisher asked, hopeful, but suspecting his brother would say no.

Which, as soon as Heath walked into the room, he said, "Nope. If I released you and you remained on bedrest, you would be fine. But you would try to track down the kidnappers with Kira if she gets a lead and takes off and that's not going to happen."

Fisher released his breath in annoyance. He knew his brothers would be going with her, all but Heath who had to stay here for his patients.

"Maybe you can join her later, when you are in good enough shape to return to work," Heath said.

Not only did Fisher want to be one of the ones helping her to catch the kidnappers, he wanted to do it for personal reasons. He wanted to see the kidnappers dealt with after they had tried to kill both Kira and him.

Then Devlyn, Bella, and Kira walked into his room. Kira looked like a ray of sunshine, her red hair shimmering in the morning light, her blue eyes sparkling. "Hey, how are you doing?"

He smiled brightly, feeling so much better to see her. What was up with that? It wasn't like they were dating or anything, but man, every time he saw her, he wanted to see more of her.

"I'm great, but the doctor won't let me out of here."

"If you developed critical issues from being shot because I released you and you were running around searching for criminals, how do you think I would feel?" Heath asked. "It would be on me."

"How about we keep you informed of what we discover? If you can join us, we'll welcome your help," Kira said to Fisher, her voice bright and cheery. She squeezed his hand. "I'll keep in touch. I promise."

"Thanks," he said. But it wouldn't be like being there.

"Do what you need to do to get well. I hope to see you soon."

"Don't catch them before I can help you." He was serious.

She smiled.

Devlyn folded his arms. "Listen to Heath." To Heath, he said, "If he gives you any trouble at all, just call me."

Heath smiled. "I will."

Bella gave Fisher a light hug. "Listen to your brother. You'll see Kira again, I'm sure." Then she, Devlyn, and Kira left the room.

Not long after they left, Tanner and his mate, Serena, came to see Fisher.

Tanner said, "The FBI agents want to talk to you. We've put them off for as long as we could."

"What do I say?" Fisher wasn't sure how to deal with this since he knew the shifters had to capture the men, not the human law enforcement officials.

"Describe them just like you saw them. Kira and Billy did

already so there's no sense in saying anything differently," Tanner said. "Though if you did describe them differently, I'm sure they would understand because of all the pain and suffering you had gone through."

"Okay."

"About Kira," Tanner said.

"What about Kira?" Fisher hadn't meant to sound so annoyed. He so wanted to be with her on her mission.

"I spoke with Vaughn about her."

"Vaughn?" Fisher's brother totally lost him with the comment.

"Yeah, you know, because he works with her. So he told me that as a young girl, she was kidnapped, so a case like this has to be hard for her. It probably brings back bad memories."

"Oh." Fisher couldn't believe she had been kidnapped herself when she was young. That had to have been traumatic for her.

"Yeah. She's new to the USF and they do a thorough background check to make sure that the person hasn't had issues that would cause them to have trouble on the job. She shared her story with the rest of her USF agents so they knew where she was coming from if she ended up having any problems with it."

"Hell." Fisher was surprised her boss had even given her this assignment then.

"I just thought if you ended up working with her on this case you should know about her past even though she might tell you about it herself. Just keep an eye out if you're working with her and she's battling PTSD over it."

"Sure, thanks, Tanner."

"Yeah, no problem." Then Tanner smiled. "Serena and I went over to Devlyn and Bella's home to have breakfast, and Kira wanted to come here to see you right away."

"Probably because she had to get on the road to find these guys. I guess you're going too." Fisher hated sounding so down about the whole business.

"Nope. Some of the guys are staying here to watch your back."

Fisher was surprised to hear that. "Why? You don't think the kidnappers would try and locate me to eliminate me as a witness, do you? The boy already knows what they look like also."

"Yeah, we do. The boy is being guarded around the clock also. So Devlyn has already set up a schedule for those of us who want to guard you to do so."

"Even when I go home?"

"Especially when you go home."

"What about Kira?"

"Devlyn is making sure she's going to be watched too, just in case the kidnappers learn the two of you survived and go after you to get rid of loose ends. I think they figure the kids they take for ransom are so traumatized, they don't remember what the men look like. Maybe also that adults don't believe their recollections as well either."

Fisher appreciated that his family and the wolf pack were looking out for him.

Then two FBI agents walked into the room to speak with him. Fisher was ready for them, telling them his human version of the events—hiking, hearing the boy in distress wanting to go home to his parents, and then Fisher being seen, running to avoid getting shot, but reaching the edge of the cliff. Since he'd had no time to run anywhere else, he was shot and fell off the cliff. "Purposefully," Fisher added.

Tanner and Serena frowned at him. The agents exchanged glances.

"I couldn't have outrun a bullet at that point and once I was hit, I fell, figuring I might survive. If I'd dropped to the ground at the edge of the cliff, the shooter would have shot me until he was sure I was dead." Fisher knew that for certain.

"But he shot at you when you were down on the ledge also," one of the agents said.

"Yeah, when they realized Kira had arrived to take care of me. It was the black-haired guy that time and he shot at both of us, but she had moved me under a kind of shelf before that and stayed with me there until she felt they had left the area."

Then he gave a description of the three men.

"Did they call each other by name?"

"Not in the short time that I was listening in on their conversation as I was heading to their location."

"Alright. Did they give any indication where they were going?" the one agent asked.

"Just that they were going to the pickup for sure. They didn't say it was for a ransom. I didn't know that they had kidnapped the boy, though I had assumed it might be the case. I didn't realize they planned to leave the boy in the woods by himself while they got the ransom. Oh, they mentioned they were going to abandon the younger kidnapper when he balked about leaving the kid behind in the woods. They said they were going to Florida. But I suspect they said that in front of the kid to throw the FBI off their trail if he mentioned it to the agents."

"They didn't say where they were going to pick up the money?" one of the agents asked Fisher.

"No. If I had known, I would have mentioned it right away."

"If you think of anything else that can help that you haven't recalled because of your own trauma, just contact us." The agent gave him his business card. "Thanks for your help."

"Sure."

Then the agents left, and Tanner said, "Okay, Heath said you can eat whatever you want, so if you have a preference, we'll make it for you."

Fisher smiled, feeling a little better about that. "Steak, eggs, and hash browns."

"Fruit? Greens?" Serena asked.

"Not unless Heath says I have to have them." Not that Fisher

didn't like fruits and vegetables, but he figured after surgery, eating
steak, eggs, and hash browns was going to fill him up.

Serena said, "Okay, I'll make it for you. Tanner's pulling first
guard duty. Do you want the same thing for breakfast, honey?"

Tanner smiled. "I sure do."

"Three orders coming right up." Serena left the clinic and
Tanner pulled up a seat next to the bed.

"I have a solution on how you can see more of Kira if you want
to," Tanner said.

Fisher raised a brow. He admitted he wanted to see more of her.
To thank her for saving his life for one thing. He realized he hadn't
said that once to her when they were on the ledge, though he'd
been in a lot of pain, and he'd been worried about the boy being
alone on top of the cliff. And he hadn't thought of saying it to her
when she was visiting him in his room here either.

"You can join the USF. You're a former Army Ranger and our
cousin works as one, so why not? I'm sure his boss would hire you
in a minute."

"You would miss me too much."

Tanner laughed. "Vaughn would be thrilled. Not only will he
recommend you, so will his mate. Jillian would love to have you on
the team also."

Fisher smiled. "As long as Vaughn stays in Martin's good graces,
that could be a good thing."

"For sure."

Fisher became so drowsy while he waited for Serena to return,
he must have drifted off. Then he heard her voice and smelled their
steak and eggs breakfast. He was amused to see that she also
brought a fruit platter. He was glad they all were having breakfast
together. He didn't feel as isolated from the others then, and he
really appreciated his brother and sister-in-law for being there
for him.

Once they had eaten breakfast, including all the fruit, Tanner said, "I'm letting you get some rest. It's the only way you're going to heal up more quickly."

Fisher didn't want to admit that the fall off the cliff and the bullet had taken a lot out of him. He thanked Serena for making breakfast for them and he thanked both Tanner and Serena for eating with him. Then they left and closed his door. He heard them walk down the hall together, though he knew Tanner would return after he walked his mate to the car, and he would pull guard duty until he was relieved.

Every time Fisher was half awake, he was thinking of joining the USF. He loved the idea of catching shifter criminals. After meeting Kira, he really wanted to join her and the organization. He lifted his phone off the bedside table and called his cousin Vaughn. "Hey, Cuz, can you give me Martin's number?"

"Hey, Fisher. I'm so glad to hear from you. You sound good. We've been getting updates about your condition. I've called you a few times to check on you, but you've always been asleep. How are you doing?" Vaughn hadn't answered Fisher's question.

"I'm stuck"—Fisher almost said stuck at the clinic, but he didn't want his cousin to know he was kind of incapacitated for now if he didn't already know it—"uhm, I'm doing great. I'm going with Kira soon to help her catch these bastards."

Vaughn didn't say anything for a moment. Fisher knew he was surprised to hear the news.

"Devlyn said you would be at the clinic for a while longer," Vaughn finally said.

"Yeah, just maybe through tomorrow morning. No big deal. So can you give me Martin's number?" At least Fisher hoped that he would be released from the clinic tomorrow morning.

"Martin Sutherland? My boss? Why do you..." Vaughn paused, and then he chuckled. "Yeah, sure."

Because the organization was kept under wraps as much as possible, Martin's phone number wasn't available publicly.

"Okay, here it is." Vaughn paused. "Are you thinking of joining us? I mean, the USF?"

"I'm all for good causes and taking down rogue shifters is a good cause," Fisher said.

"I agree. I have to warn you that one of the interview questions for new recruits is—why do you want to join the organization? You can't say that it's because you want to work with Kira."

"Who said that would be the reason for me applying for the job?"

Vaughn laughed. "I know you, Cuz. The part about going after rogues is acceptable. Going after a she-wolf you want to date is not. Martin will also ask you why you would suddenly decide that you want to do this."

"As a USF special agent, I would not only be protecting the kidnapped victim and trying to capture the kidnappers, but also I would be taking care of innocent bystanders if it came to it. It just makes me want to do something more heroic than working at the tannery."

"Sometimes we just do a lot of paperwork, interviewing witnesses, reinterviewing them, going through any evidence against the rogue shifters, and not a whole lot of running from bullets or jumping off cliffs."

Fisher smiled. "I could do without a lot less of that in my life, truly."

"Kira is new to the USF so she has had a more experienced partner to work with in the organization for her last few missions. Though Jillian worked with her on one and both of us worked with her on her first mission."

"Where was the guy who was supposed to be partnered up with her when all this went down?" That really irritated Fisher when he realized she had been there trying to save his and the boy's life on her own. He hadn't even gathered that she had been new to the job right away. She was a natural at problem solving and taking care of multiple, critical tasks at a time.

"He was injured in a car accident and so he's on bedrest. I'm just saying that you can't pick and choose your partners. Now the boss will like that you're a former Army Ranger so you've had a lot of military training, combat, weapon's experience, and you're fit. But Martin makes up the assignments."

"If you're mated, he doesn't make them then, does he?" Fisher thought that Vaughn and Jillian went on all their missions together.

"Whoa, what's this talk about mating?" Vaughn asked, his voice teasing.

"I'm *not* talking about Kira. I'm talking about you and Jillian." Fisher couldn't hide his exasperation with his cousin. He figured it all had to do with being stuck in a bed at the clinic, and that he was feeling some discomfort from the bullet wound in his shoulder, more than he liked to admit.

"Sometimes we're on different missions. She was looking into a crime involving a beauty salon recently. Even though men can go in there to get a haircut, it's mostly women. So she suited the situation better. It wasn't dangerous, so she could handle it on her own. One of the beauticians had stolen another shifter's child and had moved out of state. Jillian found her and took her into custody and returned the child to her parents." Then Vaughn took a breath. "You're really thinking of applying to work with the USF? If you make it through the approval process, and the rigorous mental and physical training, you'll be required to serve a year in the organization. After that, it's up to you. But you have to make a firm commitment. Unless you're dropped for not being a team player or some other unforeseen circumstance. Even a wounded agent will work office duty if he can to keep up on cases. Most of us would rather do anything but. However, we still prefer that to sitting at home, licking our wounds until we can go back to work."

Which gave Fisher an idea. Maybe he would go to work for

them while he was still in recovery. He didn't mind doing paperwork. Of the four brothers, he was the most organized.

"Okay, thanks."

"What is family for? I'll let you get some rest and check in on
you later."

"Thanks, Vaughn."

"Yeah, just get well soon."

Then they ended the call and Fisher fell asleep for a while. He
had planned to call Martin right away, but he had suddenly felt so
tired, he just closed his eyes and was out. When he woke a couple
of hours later, he called Martin. He wasn't sure how this was going
to be received, but he was trying to be as positive as he could be.

As soon as he got a hold of Martin, the director said, "Fisher
Greystoke? Cousin to Vaughn Greystoke? I just got off the phone
with Vaughn. So you want to work with us?"

"Yes, sir."

"I understand you're a victim of the same kidnappers who stole
Billy."

"Uh, yes, sir." Fisher figured Vaughn had told his boss he was
lying in a clinic bed while his brother, Heath, was keeping him
confined until he was well enough to leave. He wanted to groan.
But he was also afraid that Martin would think that he wanted
vengeance for the kidnappers shooting him and shooting at him
and Kira later.

"You want to go after the kidnappers."

"Yes, sir."

"Okay, well, you can fill out an online application that is only
available through a link I will send you. Get it back to me whenever
you're feeling better."

"Thanks, sir. I sure will." Fisher was going to give Martin his
email address, but his cousin had already done so. He smiled. He
guessed Vaughn really did want him to work with them. He felt he
had a new mission in life. Maybe he couldn't help with the kidnap-

pers' case if he didn't get over his injuries quickly enough and they caught the men first, but he really looked forward to working as a special agent with the USF when he could. If he was approved, of course. He knew it wasn't a done deal until Martin actually hired him.

Then he wondered if Kira would even want to work with him, given the mess he had gotten himself into already!

6

Working on her computer in Bella's home office to learn anything she could about the kidnappers, Kira couldn't stop thinking of Fisher, the whole while that she was trying to determine where the kidnappers had gone.

She thought of calling Fisher to check in on him again, but instead she would just run by the clinic in a little while. She really needed to concentrate on the mission right now. Never had a male wolf distracted her this much when she was on a job. She tended to be focused, determined, and serious about it since she usually had grave missions to complete.

Then Vaughn called her. She suspected he was calling her because she had saved Fisher's life and he wanted to learn the details from her. As far as she knew, he and Jillian were still in Oregon on their case.

"Hey, I wanted to touch base with you because Fisher wants to join the USF."

"What? Really?" Kira was both surprised and elated. She really hoped he wanted to. Anyone who was as courageous as he was to try and save the boy as a wolf was worthy in her eyes of being a special agent.

"Yeah. Jillian and I each gave Martin a glowing report on Fisher, since we know him so well. But Martin might think we're a bit biased. So if you could talk to the boss about how you feel about Fisher joining us, you would have more of a neutral recommendation. That's only if you feel he would be a good addition to the force. You might not see him in the same light as we do though."

"I'll recommend him. He was brave and heroic. I'm thrilled he wants to join us." She hoped it wasn't because of the pain medication he was on, and it was making him see this in a foggy and dreamlike way.

"Thanks. I'm talking to Devlyn about recommending him because he's our pack leader. Bella too. And I imagine our other cousins and his brothers will step in to make recommendations. Again, we'll be a little biased, but we all know each other the best."

"Exactly. Okay, well, I'll talk to Martin then, and after that, I'm going to run by the clinic to check on Fisher." Kira was so pleased he would be part of their team.

"Let us know how your case goes. If we get done with ours, we'll join you. We've been trying to catch a wolf who has been scamming people out near Leidolf and Cassie's Portland, Oregon pack."

"I hope you catch him. And I sure will let you know what happens." Though she figured his packmates would be keeping him informed also. Thanks, Vaughn." After they ended the call, she got ahold of Martin.

"Have you located the kidnappers?" Martin asked right away, recognizing her caller ID.

She was almost embarrassed that she wasn't thinking of them at the moment, but about Fisher joining them in the USF. "Nothing yet, sir. I've been monitoring police reports of kids being kidnapped in Colorado, but so far, there haven't been any new kidnappings. Which is good news, in a way."

"Don't tell me. If you're not calling about that, you're calling about Fisher joining our organization."

She laughed. "Yes, sir."

Martin chuckled. "I think he has more recommendations than anyone has ever had for any of our jaguar branches."

She was thrilled. Then she explained why she thought Fisher would be a good fit for their organization. "As a wolf, Fisher had gone to check on Billy, afraid the boy was in danger. It shows how he is an investigator at heart, worried about the boy, and trying to learn what he could before the kidnappers had seen him. If they hadn't been wolves themselves, they might not have been aware that he was observing them. He'd been more concerned for the boy's safety than for his own. He was brave and I would be willing to work with him any day."

"I'm glad to hear that from you since you were there when this had happened. I'm proud of you for rescuing both the boy and Fisher."

After they talked and she promised to give her boss updates on the case, they ended the call, and she took a deep breath and called Fisher.

As soon as he answered the phone and saw it was from her, he said, "Hey, I hope this isn't bad timing, but I wanted to thank you for saving me."

"No, it's not a bad time. And you're welcome. Vaughn told me you want to join the USF."

"Uh, yeah. I hadn't expected my cousin to tell you."

"He had a good reason." Kira thought Fisher sounded better, his voice less groggy, since the last time she'd spoken to him. She was glad. But she realized he must not have remembered that he had told her three times already how thankful he was for her coming to his aid. Not wanting to upset him while he was recovering, if the fact that he had such poor recall due to his injuries bothered him, she didn't mention it.

"So why exactly do you want to join the USF?" she asked.

"After knowing what you do, I like the idea of taking down our shifter kind who are causing grievous problems, who could even get our kind into trouble."

She suspected there was more to it than that. Why hadn't he tried to join them earlier? Why would he want to do so now? "You know Martin won't hire you if he believes you want to do this because one of the kidnappers shot you." Though after so many people had recommended him, she suspected Martin would hire him without any problem.

"Even if he believed that's why I wanted to do it, which isn't my reasoning, he would just put me on a different case, wouldn't he? Vaughn said he wouldn't put me on a mission with you because you're a new USF special agent and so it would have to be someone who has been doing this for a while." Though the organization was still in its infancy. And he really did want to work with her.

"Oh, I hadn't thought of that. We would be like the blind leading the blind."

He laughed. "That's hard to believe when you found the kidnappers and the boy on your own. And you took care of both of us. I think you can handle any situation you encounter without any trouble at all."

She so appreciated Fisher for saying so. Her other partner wouldn't have acknowledged that she had done a great job. It was just something that would be expected of her. But she suspected her other partner didn't believe a woman could do the job as well as a man. Maybe it just seemed that way to her or maybe he just treated her like that, but some other woman? No problem.

"Vaughn said you were a former Army Ranger, so Martin will like that. And of course Vaughn, Jillian, and I put a good word in for you," Kira said. "Others have too. I imagine your brothers and cousins, maybe other pack members also."

"Wow, thanks so much." He sounded truly astounded.

"When are you applying for the job?"

"Right now."

She laughed. Man, when Fisher was ready to do something, he was going full force. She liked that in a person, even when he was injured and still healing up. "Oh, by the way, your pack members grabbed all the casings that were left behind so that the FBI agents wouldn't get them to identify the weapons that were used on you."

"And on you."

"Right. And if they didn't tell you, they found your backpack after much searching."

"Oh, great, I'd forgotten about it, but I had my phone in it." Then he laughed a little. "That I'm actually using right now, and I think you put your phone number into it when I was a little groggy. I guess they didn't mention finding my backpack to me."

"That's good. Everett and Demetria are getting here tomorrow night and we're all going to have dinner. Maybe you'll be able to join us by then." She really hoped he would. Wolves healed faster than humans, but she figured enjoying a meal with his family would lift his spirits and that would help him heal quicker too.

"I should be better by then."

She sure hoped so. Then they ended the call so he could get more rest. Afterward, she called Billy's parents to see if he got home alright.

"Oh, yes," his mother said.

Billy wanted to talk to Kira right away. "Is the dog okay?"

She smiled. "Yes, he's at the vet, but the doctor said he would be good as new soon. How are you feeling?"

"Glad to be home. I was going to put out the trash, but Mom wanted to help me. Between you and me, I don't think she wants me out of her sight for now. I don't mind. I fear every car that passes by the house means danger. Thanks again. Mom wants to talk to you."

"You're welcome, Billy."

Then his mother got on the phone and said, "Thanks so much

for saving my Billy. He's the only child we've got. I...I can't thank you enough. Did you catch the kidnappers yet?"

"No, I'm sorry. We're still working on taking them down and we won't stop until we do."

"Can you let us know when you do? It would make us feel better if we knew for sure."

"Absolutely." For their peace of mind, they would, though they didn't want this information in the press because they would want to learn more about the kidnappers.

After they finished the call, Kira was checking again for any other new cases of kidnappings, just in case the kidnappers grabbed another kid. They sure didn't want that to happen, but it might be the only way they could catch these guys, if they had a clue as to where they were now.

She still didn't find any recent kidnappings, which was good for kids and their families, but it didn't help her find the kidnappers. She glanced at the clock and realized it was lunchtime. Bella came into the office and asked Kira if she wanted to have lunch with her.

"Oh, I would love to, but I was going to check on Fisher and see if I could bring him something he would like to eat."

"He will love it. His favorite is Chicken Delights chicken pot pies if you wanted to drop by there and grab one for him. Heath said he can eat anything he wants."

"Great and thanks. I'll check with him first to make sure that's what he would like, unless he has eaten already." She called Fisher and said, "I hear your favorite lunch is a chicken pot pie from Chicken Delights. Would you like me to bring one to you?"

Fisher whooped. "Yes! And lemonade. If you're going to eat with me. I don't want you just to make a special trip for no reason."

"I'm definitely eating with you. I'm going to get one of their grilled chicken sandwiches. I'll be over in just a few minutes."

"I'm looking forward to it." He sounded so cheerful, she was glad that she had offered.

She thought his family would be over there all the time, sharing meals with him so he wouldn't have needed any more company, but apparently not.

She picked up the chicken pot pie, two lemonades, and a grilled chicken sandwich at the restaurant, then headed over to the clinic. When she arrived, Shawn was guarding his room and he smiled at her.

"Man, he sure is getting special treatment," Shawn said, eyeing the bag from Chicken Delights.

"I'm hoping that helps him to heal faster."

"I'm sure it will. So that he can work with you?"

She smiled.

"You didn't bring me anything from Chicken Delights?" Shawn asked.

"Quit hassling her," Fisher called out from his room. "You're supposed to be guarding me, not eating."

Shawn laughed.

She loved the dynamics between the brothers. Not having any siblings, she wasn't used to that. She walked into the room and set up the table over the bed so that Fisher could eat. But he reached his arms out to give her a hug.

"Thanks so much for making my day."

She gave him a gentle hug back. "I'll bring dinner over for you tonight too if that's how much it brightens your day."

"Absolutely. I'll be out of here in no time then."

She prayed he wasn't getting his hopes up for nothing, but she was glad he was so upbeat and positive.

7

That night while doing some searches for the kidnapper, Kira got a report that a black Suburban had been stopped for speeding near her family's home in Loveland, Colorado. She got excited, but the license didn't match the one the kidnappers' vehicle had. And the driver the highway patrolman pulled over was a woman and she had been alone.

Kira walked out of Bella's office and into the kitchen where Bella was making spaghetti for dinner.

"Are you having dinner with Fisher?" Bella stirred the sauce.

"I am."

"This is one of his favorite dinners that I make. Would you like me to make a couple of containers filled with spaghetti for the two of you?"

"I sure would. Thanks."

Bella and Devlyn were so nice. She felt like she was a member of the family, not an outsider.

"And four slices of garlic toast. I would send wine, but Heath would give me heck for it," Bella said, laughing.

That was funny because even though Bella was a pack leader, the doctor still had the final say when it came to his patients.

Once Bella had packed the food in an insulated container and Kira put it in her car, she drove over to the clinic. The staff greeted her and one of the nurses said, "He's waiting for you. He had offers all day for dinner with pack members, but he declined them and they knew just who he was turning them down for."

Kira smiled. He was so sweet, but she was glad to hear that other pack members had been interested in his welfare too.

When she arrived at his room, Tanner was pulling guard duty again. "Hmm, Bella's delicious spaghetti."

"I can't wait to try some," she said and walked into Fisher's room.

He was sitting up, smiling. "Oh, I smell Bella's spaghetti and garlic toast."

"Yeah. She said it was one of your favorite meals of hers."

"It is."

Before Kira could set up the dishes on his table, he wanted another hug from her. She was so amused, but she loved giving him a hug, though she was careful not to hurt him.

"You know if Martin hires me, we're going to have to work together," Fisher said.

"I think, despite me being fairly new, he might. I told him how great you are. And he might believe we would make a good team. That's really important in the business we do."

"I sure hope so. That would make me the happiest wolf in the world."

She sure hoped so too. "We'll see. We might find we have a completely different way of going about solving a mission and end up just bickering or fighting all the time." She didn't believe it, but they would have to work together to see.

"No way," he said.

She laughed. Then she sat down next to his bed, and they began to eat.

But in the middle of eating their spaghetti, Heath walked into the room, surprising them. "Okay, I have good news. I'll release you tonight if you stay with somebody."

Fisher immediately looked at Kira. "You can stay with me at my house."

"I trust you," Heath said to Kira. "I know he would feel better at home. Of course it's up to you."

"No, that would be fine. I would love to."

Fisher looked like he was in heaven. She smiled.

"Enjoy your dinner. I'll have your marching orders by the time you're done."

"Thanks, Heath," Fisher said.

"I need to free up the bed at the clinic in case I have a real medical emergency." Heath winked at Kira. He left them to have dinner in peace.

"Don't wolf down your meal just so we can leave the clinic quicker," Kira warned Fisher.

Fisher laughed. "I don't mean to be eating it so fast, but I love Bella's spaghetti." Then he crunched on a slice of garlic toast. "And I love her toast."

"Yeah, it's all great."

Once they finished eating, she packed up the dishes. He was having difficulty dressing and she hurried to help him into his boxer briefs first. She was totally impressed by his hot physique.

He sat on the bed, and she put on his socks. Then she began to pull up his blue jeans and was amused to see his arousal, which meant it was harder to get his pants pulled up over it and zipped.

"You'll have to settle down a bit so I can get you zipped up," she teased.

"That's not possible when you're doing all the zipping."

She chuckled and finally secured his pants. "You need to get your mind on something else."

"It's impossible."

Then she picked up his shirt, but he said, "I could go without."

She smiled. "It's too cold out tonight. What if you got hypothermia while I'm supposed to be watching over you? Besides, I know you just want to show off your beautiful chest to me for longer—which, if it was summer, I would totally agree with." She carefully pulled his shirt sleeve up his bad arm. He flinched and she hated that he was still sore, but she figured he would be for a while longer. She slipped his shirt on the rest of the way and buttoned it. Once she was done with it, she affixed his sling and then he sat down on his bed so she could put on his boots.

"You come in handy for sure."

"You would do the same for me," she said.

"In a heartbeat."

Then they left the room and Tanner rose from his chair. "We'll have someone sitting outside your place as additional protection on different shifts."

"Thanks, Tanner," Fisher said.

"Brock is over there already."

"Okay, great."

Then Fisher got into Kira's car. "I can't believe you have the same vehicle as me. The same color too."

"Like minds. I guess someone drove your car home for you," she said, not having thought of that earlier.

"Yeah. Brock did. He said he left it in the garage."

"Good. Oh, I need to drop by Bella and Devlyn's home and get my bag. I'll be just a minute."

"Their place isn't far from mine."

Kira called Bella to let her know she was staying with Fisher for the night.

"We know," Bella said.

"I should have figured that," Kira said, laughing. "I forget you're a wolf pack and everyone knows everything."

"Yeah, we have to work together, plus we're making sure that you both are being guarded in case the kidnappers track you here and want to eliminate you. Not that we really expect it because I'm sure they're trying to keep anyone from catching them. But we just want to make sure."

"Exactly." Then Kira arrived at their place, gave Bella her dishes from dinner, and hugged Bella and Devlyn. "We loved your spaghetti and garlic toast. It was great."

"I'm glad you enjoyed it. If you want any more meals, just let us know. I guess we're still having dinner with you tomorrow night."

"Yes, thanks. We'll just eat breakfast and lunch at Fisher's home. He can rest and I'll be searching every resource I can to try and locate the kidnappers in the meantime." She went into the guest room and packed up her things. Then she hugged them again. "I'll let you know if I find out where the kidnappers are. Otherwise, I'll bring Fisher over here for dinner tomorrow night."

"That sounds good," Devlyn said. "If you need any help with anything, let us know."

"I will, thanks."

"Enjoy your evening," Bella said.

"We will." Though Kira didn't plan to do anything but put Fisher to bed and then continue to work on her case.

She rejoined Fisher in the car and began driving to his home. "So, what do you like in a she-wolf?" She'd never been interested enough in a male wolf to ask the question. But with Fisher, she was fascinated with him and wanted to know all she could about him.

"I've never really had a type. Not until I saw you rappelling down a cliff to save my life. And then I knew I was in love."

She laughed.

"Especially when you weren't afraid of me, and then I smelled you were a wolf too. But, man, a sexy, red wolf who came to take care of me? Not only that, you were so worried about the boy too and risked your life trying to protect him. You have a real heart and a real compassion for others. You're totally selfless."

"Nobody has ever said something so nice to me. Thank you."

She was thinking about her last partner that she'd been teamed up with. "You could have died from your injuries, but you perked up right away when you realized I was a she-wolf."

"That's for sure. For me, it was the best way of all to start the healing process. So what kind of wolf appeals to you?"

"I look for a wolf that's funny, attentive, active, loves trying new things, and enjoys life. A boon is being protective and loyal. You're totally all that and more. I was shocked and worried when you shifted out of your wolf form and were naked. Though you were quite impressive to gaze at, I was afraid you would get hypothermia."

"I got a kick out of you ordering me to shift back." He smiled. "I couldn't control my shifting because I was in so much pain."

She smiled. "I can be bossy at times. But I appreciated that you weren't annoyed with me."

"Believe me, I hadn't wanted to shift into my human form at the time, but I was glad I could talk to you."

"Yeah, me too."

FISHER PLANNED to give Heath an extra special gift for Christmas after releasing him from the clinic so he could go home, but best of all, so he could be with Kira. As far as he was concerned, the situation couldn't be any better than this. Well, if he wasn't wounded and hurting, then it would be. He really wanted to court the she-wolf.

She grabbed her bag and followed him into his house. "Your home is lovely. I love your large fireplace."

"Do you want me to start a fire?"

"No." She set her bag down next to the couch. "You need to go to bed. If you had been at the clinic, you would have been resting."

He sighed. "What are you going to do?"

"I'll go to bed after a while. If you can give me your Wi-Fi access, I'll check and see if I can find any clue as to where the kidnappers have gone."

"I can help you."

She frowned at him. "You...are...going...to bed." Then she took his arm and led him to the hallway.

"Our bedroom is at the end of the hall."

"Our?"

"Yeah, you're going to stay with me, aren't you? I mean you can sleep with me in my bed and then if I get feverish or start groaning in pain, you'll know it right away." Fisher wanted her to stay with him in the worst way. He couldn't help that he had the hots for the she-wolf.

"You are such a charmer. Well, I can't let you suffer alone when I could be there to take care of you. And I did promise Heath."

"Yes!" Fisher said. "Will you be long?"

"Probably not too long." Then she pulled aside his covers so that he would sleep on the left side of the bed so she wouldn't bump his shoulder. "When I join you in bed, there will be no monkey business."

He laughed. Not that he wouldn't like to cuddle with her, but he probably couldn't manage it. "Maybe later, when I'm all healed up."

"Do you need me to help you undress?"

"I can manage." He struggled to remove his boot.

She watched and then said, "I'll help you."

"Yeah, thanks. I can do it, but it would take so long you would probably be done with your searches and be on your way to bed by then."

"Go ahead and sit down on the bed and I'll remove your boots and socks. Just don't get all excited on me so it will be easier to remove your pants."

He loved her sense of humor. But her touching him got him all worked up in a heartbeat so he wasn't promising her he could behave where his other head was concerned, at least as far as her undressing him went.

Sure enough, as soon as she began to unzip his pants, his erection was swelling in anticipation of making an even greater connection with her.

She laughed. "It sure doesn't take much to get you all stirred up."

"You're the reason."

Once he stepped out of his pants, she set them aside and removed his sling. Then she began unbuttoning his shirt, glanced down at the bulge in his boxer briefs, and smiled. "Once you're healed..."

"Yeah?"

"We'll see."

"You're killing me, you know?"

"You should have dodged that bullet."

"We wouldn't be here now," he said, sure of it. As much as he hated being shot and falling off the cliff, if he hadn't done that, she wouldn't be here acting as his caretaker.

Then she removed his shirt and with his good arm, he wrapped her in his embrace. "Thanks for all that you're doing for me."

She gave him a soft hug back. "I don't want to hurt your bruised ribs."

"They're feeling better."

She lifted his face to his, her gaze shifting to his lips, her tongue licking her lips as if getting ready to kiss him, and he pressed his mouth to hers. She felt glorious, warm, wet, and willing. He loved it. He knew with her nurturing him that he would heal in half the time a wolf shifter would take.

Their tongues explored each other, and he was so into her, his hand caressing her back, her eyes closed as she seemed to revel in the kiss as much as he was. They finally ended the kiss and man he wanted her in his bed now. He hadn't ever known a she-wolf he wanted to get this involved with like he did with Kira. She was just everything he could ask for in a girlfriend. Though everything he said about joining the organization was true, his driving need to join the USF was to be with her, to aid her, to protect her, and to deepen their relationship.

"Off to bed with you now. The more rest you get, the faster you'll be back to normal. And we can do more than this." She gave him a brief kiss.

He groaned. He wanted more now. His shoulder was only hurting just a little bit. Then he climbed into bed, hurt his shoulder again, and really groaned, but in pain this time.

"See?" She covered him up. "I'll be in bed in a little while. Don't wait up for me. *Sleep.*"

Then she kissed his mouth again and he knew she was his. At least he sure hoped so.

He gave her his password for his Wi-Fi. She turned out the bedroom light and left the room. He didn't think he could sleep, but before he knew it, he was out.

OHMIGOD, Kira knew it was too early to have feelings like she did for Fisher, but he was such a good kisser. He was the kind of wolf she could envision being with forever. She told herself she really had to slow down, but then again, if he hadn't been injured, she would have been going as far as they could without having out and out sex, since that would amount to a mating for life.

Before she got to work on her computer, she had to look over his house. Interior design had always fascinated her. Not that she wanted to work in the business, but she just loved seeing different floor plans and furnishings. Fisher had done a beautiful job decorating his house. He hadn't expected to have a sleepover guest, yet his place was neat and clean, which really impressed her. She tended to be neat, but if someone just showed up at her place, she wasn't sure it would be this clean!

She ran her hand over the velour couches sitting in a semi-circle, all a robin's egg blue. The floor was tile, but a Turkish rug in blues, beiges, and tan covered part of the floor. Matching blue recliners sat on either side of the sectional and a round oak table rested in the middle. Pictures of the Colorado mountains and fields of flowers hung on the walls. And a large screen TV hung between bookshelves. She glanced at some of his books. Science fiction, fantasy. Some of the same books she liked.

Then she looked over the kitchen—open, airy, white cabinetry, big windows that looked out on several acres of trees. Really beautiful. She looked in some of the cabinets. He even had matching dishes and glassware, enough for twenty people. She figured he probably entertained his family here too. She checked the fridge. Full. Fruit, vegetables, a six-pack of beer, and everything he would need to eat normal meals. The freezer was packed with chicken, beef, and fish. Wow, she didn't have half the food he did. But then with taking trips like this one and feeding only herself, she didn't need as much.

She looked out on his back deck that was equipped for entertaining. A grill, seating for a dozen people, and woods surrounded the backyard too. Okay, she needed to get to work. She loved his large office. It also had large windows with a view that made it feel as though she was in the woods and not stuck in a closed-in space in a walled room.

She set up her computer and started searching police reports again. Still, nothing. She didn't believe the men would think that any wolf shifters were after them. They probably were surprised that other wolf shifters had been in the area. But then she looked back at the earlier kidnappings she figured they had done and saw that they had waited about a week before they did it again. Shoot. So if they followed their old pattern, they would lay low for a few days before they tried to grab another kid. It could be that they took that time to stalk one instead of just grabbing one out of the blue. They seemed to be calculating and smart about it, which was the reason they hadn't gotten caught yet. But they hadn't planned for a bunch of shifters to be on their trail. Well, once she found their trail again.

She finally glanced at the clock and realized it was after midnight. She didn't want to disturb Fisher's sleep, but she was afraid if he woke in the middle of the night, he would come looking for her, so she decided to slip into bed with him as quietly as she could. She took a shower in the guest bathroom, then pulled on her wolf in sheep's clothing pajamas and headed for his bedroom. He had a big king size bed, plenty of room for them to sleep together but they would still be apart so she wouldn't hurt his shoulder. He was sound asleep, looking so sexy, a light stubble covering his peaceful face, his hair all messed up as if they had already had a wild night of sex, his brown comforter tossed aside, showing off his well-muscled torso that she wanted to snuggle against.

She sighed. She wished she could, but in due time if they were still on the same page by then they would, and she believed they would be. She carefully pulled aside the covers on her side of the bed and climbed onto the mattress trying not to disturb him. But as soon as she pulled the covers over herself, he turned, and she was afraid she'd woken him.

"I'm cold," he said.

She smiled at him. "You tossed your covers aside. But I suspect you just want me to snuggle with you."

"You're supposed to be taking care of me."

She chuckled. "Hurting your shoulder is not taking care of you."

"This shoulder doesn't hurt."

"Alright, but if I hurt you, you tell me. Don't suffer through it just so I can cuddle with you. We'll have more time for this when you're all healed up, I'm sure."

She hoped they wouldn't regret it and she moved closer to him, and he wrapped his good arm around her. His heart was beating hard. So was hers. And already their pheromones were saying—go for it!

"This is nice." She rested her head on his chest.

"It sure is."

"You must be a light sleeper." She really thought he would have slept through her climbing onto the bed.

"Only when I'm waiting for you to join me."

She kissed his chest. "I love your bed. It's just the perfect softness." And he was the perfect hardness.

"I'm glad you like it. Did you learn anything about the kidnappers' location?"

"No. I'll try again tomorrow."

And then they snuggled. She figured once he fell asleep, she would move away from him, but when she woke in the morning, he had cocooned her and oh, man, that was nice.

8

After spooning Kira during the night and feeling like a million bucks, Fisher woke to discover she had left the bed already. Then he realized what had awoken him. The aroma of bacon and eggs cooking, and coffee brewing in the kitchen. What a beautiful night, all because Kira had made it so special. He was about to climb out of bed when she came into the bedroom, carrying a tray with his breakfast.

"Wow, thanks so much." He really hadn't expected her to treat him like a king.

"You deserve it. Did you sleep okay?"

"It was my best night ever. I can't believe I didn't wake when you left the bed."

She laughed. "I didn't expect you to be spooning me this morning. I really didn't wake you when I got up to do some searches?"

"No. I must have needed all the extra sleep."

"You do. Your body is healing itself."

"It is. I feel really great this morning. Where's *your* breakfast?" He ate his eggs.

"I ate before I began doing research while you slept a bit longer. No luck yet. This is the tedious part of our jobs."

He drank some of his coffee. "I don't mind it. I'm a good researcher. I can do some of that for you."

"I'll take you up on it. I've got logins for several sites that we can access to view police reports and all kinds of other information to help us find the shifters we're after. I finally realized these guys have a pattern though." She explained to him what she had learned.

"So that gives us a couple of days before they snatch another kid," he said.

"Yes. Unless they change their modus operandi."

"Let's hope not." He ate the two slices of bacon. "Thanks for breakfast. It was great."

"You're welcome. I'm sure you slept better in your own bed than at the clinic."

"With you? Yes." Then he climbed out of bed to get dressed.

She carried the tray of his empty dishes back into the kitchen to clean up.

He hollered out, "I'll get the dishes."

"I've got them. You need to rest your shoulder."

Then he realized just how hard it was to dress one-handed. He struggled to pull down his boxer briefs before he heard Kira running down the carpeted hall to his bedroom.

She quickly joined him. "So sorry. I forgot how hard it was for you to dress with only one good working arm." She eyed his boxer briefs.

"Go for it."

She laughed. "You're cute, you know?" She pulled his boxer briefs off.

"That's my underwear drawer over there." He should have already pulled out a pair.

She fished a pair of black boxer briefs out, then helped him into them. Then she found a pair of jeans and a T-shirt in the closet, then helped him into the jeans. She was being super careful when she pulled his shirt over his injured shoulder.

He really appreciated her help, though he wished he could do this on his own. He could, but it would have taken him a lot longer and been more of a struggle. "I hadn't expected you to dress and undress me. This goes above and beyond the call of duty."

"I'm happy to do it for you."

Once she had helped him finish dressing, she set him up on his computer to do searches for her. He was thrilled to help her and if he did get the job with the USF, this was a great way to learn about one aspect of it.

"I'm going to finish cleaning up the kitchen and I'll join you in a few minutes. Do you want some more coffee?"

"Yeah, sure, that would be great."

A few minutes later, she brought in a couple of cups of coffee, and she sat in a chair next to him while he was searching police reports of arrests, missing persons, and crimes of any kind that might yield the results they needed.

"Okay, nothing is showing up that might be a clue as to where they are." She leaned over and kissed his cheek, then took him to the site of the JAG Headquarters.

There, he saw the organization and their resources to get things done. "So there are four main branches. The Enforcers, who police shifters, ensuring everyone abides by our rules. The Guardians, who protect our people, secrets, and real wild animals."

"Right. Demetria was a Guardian before she joined Everett and became a USF special agent. Before the organization added wolf shifters, the rules said wild jaguars, but now it encompasses other wildlife in danger also."

"Okay, that makes sense. Then the Avengers go after the hard-core criminals that they have no hope of rehabilitating."

"Exactly," Kira said. "Then there's the JAG Special Forces unit that takes care of all kinds of missions like extractions from hostage situations. They're known as the Golden Claw JAG Elite Force. They do a little of everything. That's what Everett was."

"Aww, okay. And the USF falls under that branch."

"Yes, and Martin heads up the Golden Claws and the USF agents."

Then Fisher saw the page for the USF and the special agents' photos, phone numbers, emails, and addresses so they could keep in touch if they were working on missions or for socializing with one another.

"This is a really great site. Does it show the training facility?"

"Yes!" She opened the page that showed pictures for possible new hires in the various training exercises. "This is for any of the jaguar law enforcement agencies. Not just for the USF."

"Rope course, rappelling, hand-to-hand combat, weapon training, water survival. This will be a piece of a cake."

"Uh, turn to the next page."

He did and saw that he would have to also outmaneuver jaguar and wolf shifters in several courses in their fur coats. "Oh, now this will be interesting."

"Yeah, you can prepare yourself for all the rest, but when it comes to dealing with jaguars in their fur coats in their element—climbing, biting, clawing—they're hard to beat. But they're not allowed to bite and have to keep their claws sheathed. So that helps. If you're after rogue jaguar shifters you need to take down, that's another story. They'll come after you with tooth and claw. They can crush a tortoiseshell with their teeth and swipe an opponent, knocking them out for the final kill. What they'll do is show the force they can use, not on live subjects. But Martin decides what training you go through, so it might not be anything like this."

"I'm ready for anything. I've never seen a jaguar in killing mode," Fisher said.

"Same with me until I started working with them."

"Okay, well, I'm ready to sign up for the training."

"After you heal. Did you turn in your application?"

"Right after I told you I would. I filled it out online."

"Good. You already had a few million references so you should be good there. And your military record puts you ahead of other candidates also."

"That's good to hear." Then he returned to the search for missing kids. "Hey, this one is close to us in the same national park where we ran into the kidnappers. They're forming search teams. Tammy Lee is the little lost girl, so it isn't the kidnappers' MO. She was walking the family sheepdog and maybe she just wandered off and we can find her."

"Let's do it. I'll be your German shepherd companion, a search and rescue dog."

"Hell, I would rather be running as a wolf too."

"Yep, but you can't because of your shoulder." She got on the phone and called Heath and put it on the speakerphone. "Hey, Doc, I want to get your approval to allow Fisher to go with me on a missing-child search. I plan to turn wolf and he can be my handler."

Fisher smiled.

"Just for this mission," she said to Fisher.

"As long as he doesn't run as a wolf and if he's in pain, he sits it out," Heath said.

"Thanks, Heath. He will."

Fisher didn't have any plans to sit this one out. If Kira was going to be a wolf, he had to stay with her at all times as her handler. She might be able to run faster and locate the girl more quickly, but he needed to be there to alert the others that they had found her.

"Do you need more volunteers?" Heath asked.

"Sure. I'll call Devlyn and if he has got anyone available, we can all go out and help to find the little girl." Then she ended the call with Heath and called Devlyn and put it on speakerphone.

"Yeah, I'll contact our emergency list and send people out there. Did Heath approve Fisher's going or do we need to have someone stay with him at home?" Devlyn asked.

"I'm going," Fisher said. "Heath okayed it."

"Okay, good luck and I'll get to work on gathering folks at this end," Devlyn said.

Then they ended the call, and Fisher and Kira grabbed a first aid pack, bottles of water, and snacks and headed out to her car.

"Do you have a leash and a collar?" Fisher asked.

She gave him a get-real look.

He laughed. "Okay, I take that as a no." He just hoped the coordinators of the search teams didn't have an issue with her not being on a leash.

When they arrived at the location where people were searching a large area of woods, they parked a distance away from everyone else. She stripped out of her clothes in the back seat of her Kia and then shifted.

She was a beautiful red wolf—her fur was a shiny copper color, her tall, pointed ears twisting back and forth listening to everything that was going on. She had long, slender legs with big feet, like any wolf, and a bushy tail tipped with black like it had been dipped in an ink well, twisting back and forth in happy anticipation of finding the girl. Glad to be doing something important, he led her to the location where they were coordinating the search efforts. The family's sheepdog was waiting with the mother and Fisher and Kira smelled the dog.

"The dog returned to their campsite without the girl," one of the search coordinators told Fisher. "She is seven and had been walking the dog, Shep, until he ran off, the leash still attached to his collar."

Kira and Fisher also smelled the scent of the girl on the dog's leash and then they hurried off.

He hoped they could find the little girl quickly. They hadn't seen anyone else yet from the wolf pack, but he suspected they were on their way. The girl had been missing for six hours and he just hoped that they would find her before she ended up with hypothermia.

EVEN THOUGH SEARCHERS were doing a planned grid search to make sure they didn't miss her, Fisher and Kira followed their noses and tore off in another direction. She had done this a few times with her parents in Loveland, Colorado when she was younger so she knew just what she needed to do.

She was running one way, then another, but at least she wasn't losing Fisher because he could smell the scents as well as she could. She just didn't want his wound to begin to hurt. Loving that he was with her, she had mixed feelings because she wanted him to heal and not feel any pain. And she wanted him to be in good shape to help her find the kidnappers. She really wanted to work with him. If he did, she knew it would be another way to impress Martin.

In the direction she was currently running, she found the girl's scent was stronger this way. Tammy had sure run a long way for being a seven-year-old. But she could understand how come Tammy had gotten so lost. She must not have been taught about hugging a tree so that search teams could find her. Kira didn't smell any sign of the kidnappers or any other people in this area, so that meant the girl was on her own, that no one had grabbed her—as in a kidnapping scenario—and Kira was grateful for that.

Fisher hollered, "Tammy! We found Shep, your sheepdog, and everyone's searching for you. My dog and I are coming for you, and we will get you to your mom and dad, who are waiting to see you."

Well, that was one good thing about having a "dog handler" with Kira! And then she saw the little girl stand up in the brush ahead, her cheeks streaked with tears. Now this was the part that Kira didn't like when she was running as a wolf. She couldn't hug the little girl and wipe away her tears. She woofed and wagged her tail, to show Tammy she was a good dog and loved kids. Tammy reached her hand out and Kira approached her. She licked her hand and her cheek, and the girl laughed. It was music to Kira's ears. Fisher was only a short distance behind her, having lagged behind as a human. She hadn't realized she had left him way back there. But as soon as she saw him, he was smiling.

"Hi, Tammy. I'm Fisher. This is my beautiful search dog, Kira. She loves little kids."

Kira howled to let anyone know she had found the girl. Another howl rent the air, but she knew it was a human howling—most likely someone from Devlyn and Bella's wolf pack.

"That's my brother Tanner, acknowledging that we found her." Fisher brought out water for Tammy and pulled out the emergency blanket and covered her with it.

Tammy was drinking the water, shivering a little. He tried his phone, but he wasn't getting any signal.

When Kira realized Fisher couldn't get through on his phone, she howled again to let everyone know where they were again.

Tanner howled back. He was getting closer, and she knew he was running to where they were.

Before long, Tanner, Shawn, Devlyn, and even Heath were running to catch up to them. Tanner said to Tammy, "I'm so glad Kira and Fisher found you."

"I'm a doctor," Heath said to Tammy, and checked her over. "We're going to take you to the rescue station where your mommy is and get you warmed up further."

Then Fisher said, "Do you want me to carry you?"

She shook her head.

Fisher said, "Here, take my hand. If you get tired of walking, one of the guys will carry you, okay?"

Tammy nodded.

But once they began to walk, they were moving so slowly, Fisher asked, "How about if I give you a piggyback ride?"

Tammy finally agreed.

But Tanner gave Fisher a look as if he couldn't be serious, crouched down, and she climbed onto Tanner's back instead. Then he began to jog, and everyone kept up with him. It didn't take them long at this rate of speed to make it back to where Tammy's mother and the family's dog were. Shep began to bark and raced off to greet Tammy. Her mother was in tears as Tanner crouched down and Tammy released him, then she ran to join her mother, the dog nearly knocking the girl over in his exuberance to greet her.

It was a joyful reunion and Kira howled with elation. Then she licked Tammy, saw a news crew coming to speak with Fisher because he had found the girl, and Kira headed back to the car. She didn't want anyone to take pictures of Fisher because she was thinking if the kidnappers saw him in the news—but no, he had been a wolf. Okay, so no problem there.

"Good job, guys," Tanner said.

Fisher waved goodbye, and he jogged after Kira. Before long, she was standing at the car, and he opened the door for her. "Well, that was a great experience."

She jumped into the back seat of the car and shifted as people, including the girl's father, began to return from searches, and headed out. "It was." Kira began getting dressed while he sat in the front passenger seat. "I just didn't want the news reporters to get a picture of you but then remembered you were a wolf when the kidnappers saw you. And if anyone caught pictures of me, I wasn't a wolf when they saw me, so we're good."

Fisher laughed. "I wondered why you were in such rush to get out of there."

She finished dressing and climbed into the driver's seat. She could have let Fisher drive, but she didn't want him to have to use his shoulder that much. Not when he was supposed to be at home, resting. She couldn't believe that he had offered to give Tammy a ride with his injured shoulder, but then again, she could. He was truly heroic. She was glad when Tanner took over instead.

Heath came up to the passenger door and she rolled down her windows. "How are you doing, Fisher?"

"Great. No pain at all."

"Okay, good. I want you to go home and rest. Kira, make sure that he does. We're all having dinner tonight at Bella and Devlyn's home, so I'll be checking on you again. And no more offering to give lost kids piggyback rides," Heath said, shaking his head.

"He'll rest. He has a mission to go on once I learn where the kidnappers are. If he doesn't rest, he's going to be left behind." Kira was sure that would be an even bigger incentive for Fisher to take all the downtime he could get.

Heath smiled. "She has got your number. See you all tonight."

"See ya," Fisher said.

Then Kira drove off and they headed home. "I guess you and your pack members run as wolves in the park some. I've never been here before, so I figured that I would only think of it as the place where we rescued the kidnapped boy."

Fisher had his phone out and was checking it out. "Now we have a new memory—a little lost girl. Everyone there with a phone, and that was *everyone*, was taking photos of us, by the way. Everyone's sharing them and news sources are sharing them now too. I'm sure that they'll try and track us down to get the whole story."

"You. I was just a dog."

"A beautiful wolf."

They finally reached his home, and she pulled into the garage and parked next to his car. "It's so neat that you have so many wolves to back you on ventures like this," she said.

"It is. We always pull together when people are in need. If we hadn't been searching for kidnapped victims, we might not have come across the news about the missing child. But if anyone else had heard about it on the news, they would have organized the pack to help search for her."

"No one else was in their wolf coat." She had thought that

maybe a couple of his brothers might have been. She'd been glad to see Heath there in case Tammy had been having a medical emergency.

"No. Once they learned you were running as a wolf, they figured there was no need. Now if there hadn't been a ton of searchers out looking for her, because we'd had the jump on learning about the missing girl, more of our pack members would have run as wolves. And of course if it had been a shifter in trouble, some of our members would have been running as wolves, and others carrying first aid packs."

They headed inside and despite what Heath had told Fisher to do, he immediately started up his computer.

"I hope you're starting the computer because you want *me* to do more searches on it, while you go to bed. Though I can use my own computer."

Fisher let out his breath in exasperation.

She smiled. "Go, or I'll have to report you to Heath tonight."

"You are brutal on me."

"Only because I want you to be on the search as soon as we find the kidnappers."

Reluctantly, he rose from his computer chair, but before he retired to his bedroom, he pulled her in for a kiss.

"Hmm," she moaned against his mouth, pulling him closer for a snug fit, smiling when she felt his arousal swelling. Their tongues luxuriated in touching each other's, then she finally pulled away. "Rest."

"Hell, that's going to be hard to do after that."

She laughed and then he went to bed.

9

Fisher was serious about having a hard time, literally, when he tried to fall asleep. All he could think of was being with Kira, snuggling, and kissing her some more. He thought about finding the little girl and feeling so good about that. He felt that he and Kira made a great team, now that he was more able to assist her. He finally fell asleep for a couple of hours, telling himself he was doing great at making the effort. If Kira hadn't been making him lie down, he knew he wouldn't have been resting at all, which Heath had known. Fisher so appreciated Kira for sticking to her guns and making him rest.

When he woke, he left the bed and heard her on her computer typing away and peeked in on her. "Are you having any luck?"

"Nothing yet."

"Would you like some coffee?"

"Decaf, if you have it."

"Coming right up." After he made them both cups, adding cream, and sugar, he carried the coffees into his office. He rubbed her back and pulled up a chair next to her to see what she was doing.

She took a sip of her coffee. "Ooh, this is so good."

"Thanks. I like it for later at night."

"How is your shoulder?"

"Better because you're making me rest even when I wouldn't have if you hadn't been looking after me."

"Good." She sat back on the office chair and sighed. "I just hate that we can't get a clue as to where these guys are right now."

"I know."

"This is really the hard part. Once we know where they are, that's the fun part. Do you want to do this for a little bit? I'm going to take a break."

"Yeah, sure. This is a great way for me to learn how to do this."

"It is. And I appreciate your help with it."

An hour later and when they didn't find anything, Fisher said, "It's time to go to Bella's and Devlyn's home for dinner."

"Okay, let's go."

He was looking forward to having dinner with his family and he felt like he was bringing his date with him. As soon as they arrived, Bella and Devlyn gave them hugs, but carefully with Fisher to make sure they didn't hurt his shoulder or his bruised ribs.

Jaguars Everett and Demetria came out of the living room and gave them hugs. Everett was a blond with smiling green eyes and Demetria was a beautiful brunette, her long hair tucked up in a bun.

"Oh, I'm so glad you're here," Kira said.

"You have a case and a half," Demetria said. "We're glad we were able to wrap up ours so we could join you. This definitely is a case that requires a team."

"I so agree."

Everett said to Fisher, "We're so glad you are with us too, learning the ropes until Martin decides if he's going to hire you or not. But I suspect you'll be hired no matter what."

"I sure hope so," Fisher said, so he could continue to see Kira. Kira squeezed his hand as if she was hoping the same thing.

"How are you doing?" Everett asked.

"I'm doing great. Kira's making me rest and I'll be fully fit in no time."

"Hell, I would have taken off a month for a wound like that," Everett said.

Demetria punched him teasingly in the shoulder. "You would not have. You would have been right up and running around no matter what I said you had to do."

Everett leaned down and kissed her.

Fisher's cousin Aaron and Aaron's mate Angie welcomed them. Fisher's brothers, Heath and Shawn arrived together, followed by Tanner and Serena.

The only ones missing were Vaughn and Jillian who were still out in Oregon on their mission.

Shawn and Devlyn began making steaks for the bunch, while Bella and Demetria made mango margaritas for everyone except Bella and Serena who had mocktails without alcohol.

Kira and Fisher made a salad, though she told him twice, "You should be sitting in the living room resting." She really didn't want him to use his arm until he was sufficiently healed.

"I've been in bed for long enough, and I'll be in bed after dinner anyway."

"Okay." She let him add some grated cheese on top of the lettuce, but she was really watching to see if he was flinching with pain at all. But so far, no. She took deep breaths also, trying to sense if he was smelling of pain. He seemed to be okay. She was glad for that.

Then they all sat down to have dinner. She just loved how friendly the members of Fisher's pack were, how welcoming and how they made both her and the jaguars feel like family.

"Has anyone got any idea of where the kidnappers might have gone?" Devlyn asked, cutting into his steak.

Kira said, "We thought they might head to the location where the ransom money was supposed to be paid, but they never showed up. I think when they realized a couple of wolves had been involved, smelled our scents, knew what we looked like, that might have scared them off. Fisher and I have been searching police records to see if there are any more missing kids that might have been kidnapped, but we haven't come across any. Just the missing girl whose dog ran off and we helped to find her."

"We heard about that," Everett said. "The dog ran after a rabbit when the girl and her parents were camping in the national park. She was just walking the dog, but when it took off, she had to chase after it and then she got lost."

"Oh, we didn't know about the rabbit," Kira said.

"Yeah, they had it on the news and they featured Fisher's picture with a wolf. We recognized that it was you." Demetria smiled.

"It was. Fisher wanted to run as a wolf but between his injured shoulder and the fact I needed a 'master,' I went as a wolf," Kira said.

Everyone laughed.

"Do you think that the kidnappers, having been seen by other shifters and worried they might get caught now, will prevent them from trying to grab any other kids?" Bella asked.

"Maybe," Everett said. "But once they found an easy way to make money and they haven't ever been caught, they might not want to give up their criminal pursuit. Last year, Demetria and I went after a jaguar who was robbing banks. He thought he was invincible. He would have continued robbing banks until the police, or the feds caught him. We couldn't let that happen. His ex-girlfriend, also a jaguar, turned him into us. She couldn't believe he was doing that. She said that he had told her he worked for a company online. When she saw some of the security videos of him on several news stations, she realized it was him, despite his disguise, and knew about our organization and called Martin. So we were assigned the mission of taking him into custody. When we arrested him, he said he'd lost his job and to make ends meet, he found robbing banks was an easy way to make the money. He doesn't have to any longer. He's in prison and will be there for years."

"These kidnappers might be wired that way too. Who knows if they might have been doing crimes throughout the ages," Demetria said. "The kind of crime they were committing might have changed is all. And they just haven't been caught yet."

"The kidnappers hadn't expected to run across a couple of wolves," Fisher said. "That was a shock to them. I'm sure they didn't know if I was a shifter or not, but they would know for sure that Kira was when they smelled her. When she went to my aid, they probably figured I was too then."

"I agree," Kira said.

"Oh, and by the way, Fisher," Everett said. "Demetria and I are thrilled you're going to join us in the organization."

"It's not a done deal," Fisher said, sounding like he didn't want to get his hopes up in the event Martin said no to hiring him.

"Sure it is," Everett said. "When we say we want you to join our team, Martin listens."

"Everett's right about that," Demetria said.

Fisher smiled and glanced at Kira to see her opinion on it.

Kira smiled. "They're right. We have to work in teams most of the time. When several of us say we want to work with you, Martin seriously takes our opinions into consideration. We need more agents. Though he usually hires people he doesn't know well, based on their prior work experience and how well they get along with others in a pack, if they're wolves and belong to a pack, he still doesn't really know what they're like or if they'll be a good fit with the rest of us. Even I was a questionable hire. So yeah, I would say it is pretty much assured."

Devlyn agreed. "You've had so many pack member recommendations also, not just the family's, that I doubt Martin is going to consider not hiring you."

"Vaughn would lead a revolt," Demetria said, "and several of us would be right there with him."

Everyone laughed.

After dinner, they all sat on the back deck and had hot cocoa and whipped cream and watched the sun set. Kira sat next to Fisher, and she really felt like she was on a date with him. She leaned against his good shoulder, and he kissed the top of her head. Of course everyone noticed and smiled.

They finally finished their mugs of cocoa, then everyone said good night and they headed home.

When Kira and Fisher arrived at his house, she told him, "I'll help you get undressed so you can take a shower."

"Can you help me shower?" He looked so hopeful.

She laughed. "Okay, normally, I wouldn't do this with a male wolf I wasn't seriously dating, but..."

"You're taking care of me. And I want to seriously date you."

Smiling, she shook her head. "Be serious."

"I am completely serious."

"Alright then." She could go along with that for now. She helped him out of his clothes and eyed his bandage. "You're not supposed to get it wet."

"You know how fast we heal. It probably will be fine. Doc sent me home with spare bandages."

"You can wash and then I'll replace the bandages."

He went into the bathroom to get the shower started. She quickly stripped off her clothes and joined him in the shower. Man, she never thought she would be doing this with a wolf while she was on this mission! Or dating him? She thought the stars must have aligned for them to meet like they did.

With Fisher, it just felt so natural with him. That was one thing about a wolf finding a mate. They needed to have a certain amount of compatibility, though like with humans, they would also disagree about things.

She began soaping him up and he was immediately aroused. He was soaping her up one handed, which was taking him longer, but she didn't want to rush him because this was super nice.

He soaped between her legs, working a little longer down there than he needed to, which was getting her all worked up. At that point, she didn't want him to stop. Ohmigod, he was going to make her come. Okay, so he was totally serious dating material.

He kissed her mouth with passion, just lips to lips at first but then deepening the kiss. He kept his fingers between her legs, stroking her beautifully. She loved the way his tongue stroked hers, titillating and tantalizing. She swiped at his, matching his passion with long, lingering caresses. He was an amazing kisser.

She felt like she was going to slide to the floor when he slipped a finger inside her feminine lips and swirled it around, sending her flying sky high. The orgasm was amazing, shattering her, and she wanted to do the same thing with him. She touched his full erection and kissed his mouth. "Are you hurting at all?"

"Nothing that your touch won't take care of."

She laughed. "I meant your shoulder."

"That's not what's aching so much," he said.

Smiling, she took hold of his erection and began to skillfully fondle him. He put his arm around her back and kissed her mouth again, their lips meeting and melding, soft, tender kisses, hot, passionate kisses. She barely felt the hot water sluicing down their bodies as she concentrated on his kisses and then he groaned and she thought his shoulder was hurting, but then he was climaxing, and she smiled.

She took the sprayer and washed his body, and he rinsed her off.

She dried him off and then herself. Before she helped him dress, she checked on his bandages.

FISHER LIKED how careful and tender Kira was. He recalled, in his groggy state after being shot and the fall off the cliff, just how gentle she'd been then too, trying to ascertain his injuries, bandaging him to stop the bleeding, but all the while concerned about the boy up above on the cliff.

When she pulled off the wet bandage, she smiled brightly. "Your skin has healed sufficiently now. You don't have to wear this bandage any longer." Then she checked the one on his back. "The same with this one. The wound might still be tender, and your muscle tissues and everything else the bullet went through will still be healing for some days, but it looks good on the surface."

He was so glad for that. No bandages meant he was nearly back to normal. Or at least kind of.

She slipped on a pair of pajamas while he pulled out a pair of pajama shorts for himself and she helped him into them.

Then they climbed into bed and this time she didn't ask if he was hurting. After what they had done in the shower? He figured she assumed he was feeling no pain. No matter what, he was snuggling with her.

"If Martin doesn't hire you, I'm quitting the USF, getting a job in Greystoke, and will officially date you for good," she said.

He couldn't believe she would give up a job she loved to be nearer to him. "That's the nicest thing anyone ever said to me."

She smiled and kissed his bare chest. "I'm serious."

He knew she was. "I'm glad." He just hoped it wouldn't come to that for her sake, but he would do everything to make her feel like she had made the right decision, no matter what happened concerning the job with the USF.

10

The next morning, Kira woke first, but she didn't want to get up. Fisher opened his eyes and smiled at her.

"I hope I didn't wake you." She stretched out in bed.

"No, I felt you stirring, but I was already awake, and I didn't want to end being with you just yet."

She leaned over and kissed him. "Yeah, this sure has been nice. I'll make breakfast, if you want to start looking at the police reports." She climbed out of bed.

He joined her and she helped him to dress first.

"I'll do that." He would love to make her breakfast and he had planned on dressing himself this morning, but she had tackled the job so quickly that he had just let her help him.

Once they were dressed, she headed for the kitchen, and he went into his office. He sat down at his desk and was just getting signed onto his computer when she brought him a cup of coffee and kissed his cheek.

He pulled her in for a deeper kiss. With her, he always wanted more.

"Breakfast will be ready in a few minutes."

"I'm just getting logged in and then we can eat." He was just hoping he would find the kidnappers and prove that he had what it took to be a real partner as a USF special agent.

When she left him to do the searches, he smelled hash browns, eggs, and ham cooking. His stomach grumbled. He never had anyone over fixing meals for him, so it was such a homey experience. He liked the idea of continuing the way they were getting to know each other like this.

He began searching through all the police reports since last night, looking for anything that might give him a clue when he saw one about a car being pulled over for having the wrong license plate. What caught his eye was that it was a black Chevrolet Suburban near Yuma Town, Colorado, like the vehicle Kira had described.

Not that it had to be the same one they were looking for—what would the chances of that be?—but these guys could be driving a car with the wrong plates on purpose in the event anyone saw them taking a child and reported it. The driver's name was Reggie Olson, and he was living in Denver. Two of the earlier kidnappings had been in Denver.

"Hey, Kira, this might be nothing, but—" he hollered.

"I'm coming with our food." She brought in their breakfast and looked at the police report. "Oh, that might be one of the men."

"The traffic report didn't mention anything about the other men."

Kira read the report. "Pull up his driver's license."

Fisher did, and they both eyed the black bearded guy.

"Yeah, he's one of the men. He's the one who ordered the other to cut the rope I was on and was shooting at us when we were on the ledge, the bastard. At least we know his name now, if it really is his name or he didn't change it after this traffic stop," Kira said. "At least we're getting a little further on the case. Let's eat and then I'll tell Demetria we have a possible lead. Good work."

Fisher was thrilled that he really had contributed to the searches. "I just hope it pans out."

"Me too." She finally finished her breakfast and got her phone to call her other USF team members. "Hey, Fisher might have found a lead for us." She explained what he had discovered while he finished his breakfast and carefully carried their plates into the kitchen. "Okay. Talk later."

He began cleaning up the kitchen to prove to her he was fine, and they could go and catch these guys and she wouldn't leave him behind.

"I'm calling the Yuma Town sheriff's department and asking about the vehicle to see if they can tell us if there was anyone else in it when they were pulled over and what they looked like." She frowned at Fisher when she realized he was scouring the frying pan that she had cooked the eggs in. "Are you okay doing that?"

"Yes. I'm being careful and we need to get everything cleaned up before we rush off to nab these guys."

"Okay, well, you'll need to pack a bag and I need to repack mine too."

He smiled. She was taking him with her.

She punched in a number and called the sheriff's department in Yuma Town. "Hi, I'm Kira Westwood. Can I speak with a Deputy Sheriff Stryker Hill?" She put it on speakerphone.

"Yes, let me just transfer this call to him."

"Hi, I'm Deputy Sheriff Stryker Hill. What can I do to help you?"

"I'm Kira Westwood, a special agent with a special unit that's trying to track down a trio of kidnappers. They were driving a black Chevrolet Suburban like the one that you had pulled over near Yuma Town, driving with a license plate that didn't belong to that vehicle. We pulled up his driver's license, a Reggie Olson, and that's one of the men who was involved in a kidnapping that I'm trying to catch up to. Were there two other men in the vehicle when you pulled it over? We don't know their names."

"Yeah, there sure were. I didn't ask for their IDs because, other than having the wrong license plate on the car, Reggie Olson explained that he had two vehicles and swapped them out accidentally. When I checked it out, the other plate was for another vehicle he owned, so it didn't raise any red flags. It happens," Deputy Hill said.

"Can you give me the other men's descriptions?"

The deputy sheriff said, "The guy in the passenger seat was about the same build as Reggie, stocky, lighter brown hair, blue eyes. When I flashed my light at them, they were sweating, so I figured something was up, but there was no smell of alcohol or drugs, so I couldn't really determine why they seemed so nervous. The guy in the backseat was younger, blond haired, blue eyed and he had the same angular face as the front seat passenger. If I had to make a calculated guess, I believe they were related to each other."

"Okay, thanks. I'm going to share my contact information with you, and if you see them again in your area, be sure and get in touch with me right away," Kira asked.

"Can you use our help?" the deputy asked.

Normally law enforcement agencies did help on a case that was in their jurisdiction so they didn't want to tell them no, they couldn't aid them. Besides, if they were able to catch them, that would be the best thing at this point.

"If you catch them, hold onto them and we'll take them off your hands." But she hoped the local police force didn't locate them and the wolf shifters did instead. "Which direction did they go in?"

"Directly east of our town."

"We're on our way. Thanks a lot, Deputy Hill."

"You're welcome. We'll send out patrols and see if we can locate them and give you a call. Where are you coming from?"

"Greystoke. We'll check in with you when we get there." Then she and the deputy ended the call. She said to Fisher, "Go ahead and pack your bag for a few days' trip. I'm calling Demetria back." She followed Fisher into his bedroom and packed up her clothes, while she called Demetria. "Hey, it's a go to Yuma Town. The driver is the same one who shot at Fisher and I when we were down below the cliff. Deputy Sheriff Hill gave us the descriptions of the other two men, and they sound like the other two kidnappers we saw. We're packing and on our way in a few minutes."

Then they ended the call so Demetria could tell Everett they needed to get ready to go.

Fisher was so glad they had a clue. He just hoped they could catch the men before they lost their trail.

"Yuma Town is off the beaten path, which is probably why they would go there," Kira said.

"Right."

"You know, I should call Heath, and get his approval before I take you with me. It'll take us two hours to get there."

"Alright."

She called Heath and put it on speakerphone. "I'm taking Fisher with me on a trip to try and catch the kidnappers. Will you okay it?"

"Yes, but if he's feeling any pain, call me about it and Shawn can return him home. He'll take his own vehicle for that reason."

"Okay, that sounds good."

Fisher smiled and headed into the kitchen. "I'm going to make us a couple of thermoses of coffee."

She joined him and picked up his phone off the dining table. "I'm going to add a tracking app between our phones since you're going with me and I'm responsible for you."

He smiled, so glad he was going with her. He thought what better way to learn how they handled a mission than to be with them when they did it. He was determined to prove he had what it took to be a special agent too.

"If you have trouble and start feeling any pain because of your injuries, Shawn will take you home. He's driving his own vehicle just in case. Everett and Demetria have their own vehicle also," Kira said. "Demetria just texted me that Brock and Aaron are going with Tanner in his pickup truck. They're meeting us at the gas station. I'll be leading the way because I was in charge of the case even though I'm newer at the job than Everett and Demetria who had been two of the first special agents on the force. I just hope we can capture the kidnappers and not have to deal with the local law enforcement in the small Colorado town."

"Yeah, I agree." Then he grabbed their bags, and they headed out to her car. He loaded them in the trunk, while she brought the thermoses of coffee out with her and then he locked up the house.

"So what made you join the USF?" Fisher asked as they got into her car and drove to Yuma Town.

"Well, I was nearly kidnapped as a young girl."

"Vaughn mentioned it to me. He said the men paid the consequences for their actions."

"They did. I...bit the one. It was the only way for me to get away from them."

"So they were human."

"Yes." She explained in more detail how it had happened.

"So the men hanged themselves."

"Yes, and when the police learned of it, they were glad to finally discover that they were the ones who had perpetrated so many child abductions. I...I was the only one who ever managed to escape them."

"Then what you did was the right thing to do. And the men who went after the kidnappers did the right thing. Is that why you joined the USF?"

"I was a homicide detective for years, but when I ran into Demetria and Everett on a job they were doing that had to do with a murder case I was investigating, they told me about the USF.

They convinced me to apply to Martin for a job and I was thrilled to be hired on to help our kind and at the same time take down rogues who could hurt anyone—humans or shifters alike."

"I understand. So if we catch the kidnappers, then what?" Fisher asked.

"We'll take them into custody, and they'll either be terminated or imprisoned. Which is a good thing for the safety of any child they might kidnap. You never know when one of these incidents could result in the death of the child. The JAG headquarters is in Houston, so they'll be transported there where the jaguars will determine their fate."

"Okay good. Thanks for taking me with you."

She smiled at him. "I knew you wanted to work with me to take these guys down. Not because you want revenge, but because you want to be with me. No way did I want to leave you behind, unless you begin to hurt too much. Besides, this way you can learn the ropes, like on-the-job training. And we can get to know each other better."

"That sure works for me. Do you have any siblings?"

"No. But my parents live in Loveland, Colorado, which is north of Denver."

"Are you going to see them for the holidays?"

"If we can capture these guys, then yes, for Thanksgiving. Christmas too, if I don't have another emergency case to handle. If we're still chasing after them, I probably won't have a chance."

"What do your parents think of the job you're doing now?"

"Actually, they're glad. They thought the job I was doing as a homicide detective was more dangerous. I hadn't planned to tell them about the kidnapper shooting at us."

"Or cutting your rope. Any place or any job can be dangerous, no matter what you're doing."

"Exactly."

They had driven for a couple of hours when she said, "Okay,

we're east of Yuma Town. We can check out that motel there—the Cougar Country Motel—to see if they might have a video of the black Chevrolet Suburban driving past there." She pulled into the parking lot.

"That sounds like a good idea." Then he got out of the car with her, and they went inside the spacious western-themed lobby.

"Hi, I'm with a special police unit"—Kira flashed her badge to the lady at the counter—"and needed to see if you might have any video of a black SUV with this license plate driving past here."

But everyone's jaw dropped about the same time. The woman smelled like a cougar and of course she must have smelled that they were wolves.

"Wow, this is a surprise. Three guys checked in here yesterday who are wolves too. I'm Myrtle Dixon and my husband Calvin are the owners."

"Unreal, but this is great news. I'm Kira Westwood and this is Fisher Greystoke. Your husband is a cougar also, I take it."

"Yes! How may I help you?"

"You said you had three wolves staying here. They wouldn't per chance be driving a black Chevrolet Suburban with this plate number would they have? Or maybe your security camera picked up a view of them driving past your motel."

"Oh, no! Yes, the one man was driving that vehicle. Have you contacted our sheriff's department? They're all cougar shifters also."

"We didn't realize that," Kira said.

Fisher figured that changed the rules of the game if they had more shifters they could count on.

"Yes, all of Yuma Town is cougar run."

"Oh, that's perfect. We've been in contact with Deputy Sheriff Stryker Hill. We had learned he had pulled the driver over and gave him a citation for having the wrong license plate on his vehicle. He and his companions are dangerous. The three wolves have kidnapped kids and one of them shot my friend here, Fisher Greystoke." Kira showed Myrtle Reggie Olson's driver's license photo.

"That's definitely the man who rented a room for the week. We need to get a hold of Dan Steinacker, the sheriff, and let him know about it."

"I'll call him," Kira said.

Myrtle gave Kira the phone number and Kira called Dan right away.

"Hello, Sheriff Steinacker? I'm Kira Westwood. I'm with the United Shifter Force and we take down rogue shifters, if you hadn't heard of our organization before. Jaguar shifters set up the organization, and they have a confinement facility for rogue shifters who engage in criminal acts. I talked to your deputy Stryker Hill about a man he'd pulled over and he's the one we're after." She told him about his companions and everything that they had done so far. "We're at the Cougar Country Motel where the men have reserved a room for a week. We have more shifters coming here to help us capture these men."

"Can you meet me at the sheriff's department?" Dan asked.

"Somewhere else that doesn't seem like I'm conducting police business could be better," she said.

"Meet me at Fitz's Bakery and Coffee Shop," Dan said. "I'll bring some of my men."

"Okay, we'll be there as soon as we book a room and have more of our people here to watch the motel. See you in a few minutes." Then Kira got on her phone and called Everett. "Okay, we have an interesting situation. Yuma Town is cougar run. I'm meeting with the sheriff. Can you and Demetria come to the Cougar Country Motel and get a room, and watch for the return of the wolves? They've booked a room for a week."

"That's great news. Yeah, we're on the next street over from around the corner of the motel. We'll be there in a few minutes."

"Okay, they're staying in room seven." They ended the call and she said to Myrtle, "We want a room and we'll be watching for Reggie and his buddies."

"Everyone will be there to help you catch these people. We'll do everything we can also. Would room ten work for you?" Myrtle asked.

"Yes." Kira paid for it.

"What do you want me to do?" Fisher asked Kira as they went outside and got into her car to move it.

"You're coming with me."

He looked relieved. She smiled. "You're my partner in training."

"Maybe they're scoping out a new kid to kidnap," Fisher said. He sure hoped not.

"I wouldn't be surprised." She pulled into the parking spot for their motel room.

The motel was two stories tall in the center, and then on either side, the building was one-story, brick and brown siding, very western appearance with wagon wheels between windows. "This is cute."

"It looks like a nice place to stay. Love the western design." He glanced at the five vehicles parked there.

"None of them are the kidnappers' vehicle. Maybe they are scoping out the area, or off eating lunch somewhere. They don't have a restaurant here," she said. "The others will come and grab places as soon as we're settled in so it doesn't make Reggie and his cohorts suspicious if they see us arrive en mass."

11

Kira was still shocked that Yuma Town was cougar run. She was thrilled because she was sure they would really be able to help them. She called Demetria to tell her where she and Fisher were going.

Demetria said, "Tanner, Brock, Shawn, and Aaron are in two vehicles. We're nearly to the motel. Let Tanner know where we are."

"I'm on it."

Then Kira called Tanner and explained the situation. "If you can just drive around Yuma Town and look for any sign of the men's SUV, that would really help. If you see them, let the rest of us know right away. Reserve a room at the Cougar Country Motel and we'll all take turns watching the room they are staying in."

"We will. Cougars, eh? Well, I'll be damned. But that's great news," Tanner said.

Then Everett and Demetria pulled into the parking lot of the motel, and Kira inclined her head to them. They did the same to her and went inside the lobby to get a room.

Kira drove Fisher to the bakery to meet with Dan and loved how it was decorated for fall—scarecrows and pumpkins, colorful

ornamental stalks of corn, and all kinds of desserts that were fall
festival themed. She didn't see any sheriff's car so figured he would
be there soon. "Let's go in and have a cup of coffee and wait for the
sheriff."

They went inside and found an empty table. Patrons sat at three
other tables, and they smiled at them as they walked inside. She
smelled cougars in the building, and she was sure the cougars realized they were wolves. She breathed in the sweet treats offered for
sale and the fragrance of different varieties of coffees brewing—
maple, pumpkin spice, peppermint mocha, chocolate, salted
caramel, candy cane, all smelling delightful.

"Oh, my, we're so thrilled to have you join us here," an older,
platinum blond-haired woman said, smiling as she came out from
behind a glass counter filled with baked goods—including
pumpkin cream cheese-filled muffins, chocolate chip pumpkin
bread, cranberry orange muffins and other goodies—to greet them.
She wore light blue eye shadow that enhanced her pretty blue eyes.
"I'm Florence Fitzgerald and I own the bakery."

Kira and Fisher introduced themselves as they ordered lattes—
hers a peppermint mocha and his, a pumpkin spice latte.

Florence went off to get their drinks.

A younger woman came out of the back and served up some
bakery treats and hot drinks to the customers at one of the tables,
and glanced at Kira and Fisher. She hurried over with her empty
tray and said, "Oh, I'm Ava Kensington, and...you're the wolves I
envisioned coming here who are in trouble."

Kira raised a brow.

"I'm psychic. Chet, my husband, works for the CSF and he's
going to be helping his fellow agents out with your case. My twin
sister, Nina, is also psychic and she had the same premonition this
morning. She's married to Stryker Hill."

"Stryker, the deputy sheriff?"

"Yes."

"Oh, that's wonderful." Kira had never met anyone who was truly psychic. She wondered how Ava and Nina's abilities worked.

Then three cars pulled up outside and parked. Six men got out of the cars.

"Unless I'm mistaken, that's the cavalry," Kira said.

None of the men were wearing uniforms, but she still suspected the sheriff and some of his men were coming in the door now.

"Sheriff," Ms. Fitzgerald said, sounding a little surprised as she came out of the back with Kira and Fisher's drinks. "Day off?" But then she glanced at the other men. "Oh...something bad is going down. How can I help?" She glanced at Kira and Fisher. "I'm a retired CIA operative."

Kira's jaw dropped.

Mrs. Fitzgerald smiled at her. She probably often got that response when she told someone what she had worked at.

Then Dan Steinacker introduced himself as the sheriff, and his deputies: Chase Buchanan, Hal Haverton, Stryker Hill, and Ricky Jones. "And Stryker's twin brother, Leyton Hill, is a special agent with the CSF, Cougar Special Forces. From the sounds of it, their organization is similar to your United Shifter Force, though we concentrate on cougar issues. But I like the idea of a joint shifter force."

Kira could see the resemblance between Stryker and Leyton—both dark haired, same high cheekbones and strong noses. "We have jaguars and wolves who serve as special agents, but we're definitely open to other shifter types who are qualified to join us." She explained the situation with the kidnappers and how they had to be taken down dead or alive. "Fisher and I know their scent. So do some of the men with us." She told them about the kidnappers' SUV.

"Hell, I'm sure I sighted the Suburban out by Pinyon Pines Resort," Chase said. "Shannon and my resort is closed for the winter so we don't get a lot of traffic out there at this time of year."

"Okay, Kira is in charge of this operation," Dan said, "since this is her case. What do you want us to do?"

"If you and your men can look for that Suburban, maybe we can catch them. Two of our agents are sitting at the motel in case they show up back there."

"You don't think they're planning to try and kidnap one of our kids, do you?" Hal asked.

"Yeah, that's just what we figure. They're looking for somewhere they've never been, but like us, they probably didn't know the town was populated by cougar shifters. I'm sure they wouldn't dare take one of your children, if they realize you're all shifters. That would be way too risky," Kira said.

"Just call on me if you need my help," Mrs. Fitzgerald said.

"Will do. Alright, let's go," Dan said. "During this operation, we'll remain undercover so we don't spook them."

Mrs. Fitzgerald brought them takeout coffee for their mission, knowing what they all wanted to drink.

And then they left the bakery to begin their search.

Fisher coordinated with Dan about where they were traveling so that they could be part of a grid search.

"Hey, just to let you know, everyone in Yuma Town is on high alert, not just those of us in law enforcement. So if anyone sees that SUV or three wolf shifters who don't belong who are acting suspiciously," Dan said, "they'll report back to me."

"That's great," Fisher said.

Kira wished she lived in a town like this where shifters ran everything. Nothing would get past them then.

"It really helps that we have the assistance of people who live here since we don't know the lay of the land," Fisher said.

"Absolutely." She drove down another street and Fisher kept everyone informed of where they were.

They also told Tanner and Everett and Demetria what they were doing and where they were now.

But no one saw anything. No sign of the Suburban. No sign of anyone behaving in a suspicious manner.

That night, several families in Yuma Town offered to have the teams over for dinner, but they had to stay at the motel in case the kidnappers returned.

Tanner and the others were in two rooms, keeping surveillance. Demetria and Everett were in their own room.

"Well, I never expected to be sleeping with you in a hotel room while on a mission," Kira said to Fisher. "But it's a welcome prospect."

"For me too."

They took their bags into the room and Fisher shut the door. They ordered food from the bakery—because Mrs. Fitzgerald insisted on it. She even delivered the sandwiches to all their rooms.

Kira thought she was cute because she wanted to be part of this whole operation.

After she left, Fisher took first watch, careful not to be seen. "We'll take turns sleeping. I sure hope that they didn't already take off."

"I know. I was thinking the same thing. If they were scoping out the area, but realized they were in cougar shifter territory, they might have decided staying here might be too risky. I'm going to lie down for a while. Wake me at two and I'll take over." She took a shower and dressed in pajamas and left the bathroom, glad Fisher was staying with her. "How are you feeling? I should have asked that first."

"Where I was shot, I feel a twinge of pain every once in a while, but otherwise I'm fine."

"You let me know if you feel worse."

"I will."

"You better."

He smiled.

Then she climbed under the covers and closed her eyes, but she kept envisioning Fisher injured on the cliff ledge, bleeding. She opened her eyes and watched him at the window while he was peeking out surreptitiously. Even with the lights turned off, if he moved, the wolves could see him if they showed up and were looking for signs of trouble. She liked how dedicated he was to help her in any way that he could to succeed at this mission.

Then she finally drifted off with thoughts of taking down the kidnappers and dating a hot and sexy gray wolf.

12

Fisher glanced at Kira sleeping soundly in the bed and then looked back out the window. He wondered if the men had left the area. He called the motel owner, and a man answered this time. "Hi, this is Fisher Greystoke working on this case with the other wolves and jaguars to take down the kidnappers who checked into one of your rooms. Several of us have been watching the room to see if they would return, but no one has. Are there any bars here open this late?"

"My wife informed me of everything that's going on. I can't believe I was out fishing and missed all the excitement. As to your question, no, sir. We had maid service clean the room earlier. Once we learned there was some problem with the men, I checked with her to see if she had seen anything unusual in the room. She said that they had slept in the beds, used the shower, but didn't leave any bags in the room," Calvin Dixon said.

"Hell, so they might not be returning," Fisher said.

"Or they're just afraid to have someone possibly go through their bags while they're out and about. They didn't cancel the rest of their stay."

"Okay, I'll let the others know in case the wolves have left here for good." Fisher glanced at Kira, but she was still sound asleep. He called Everett next and relayed the information.

"Aw, hell, so they may have left."

"Right. I'll call Tanner and let him know."

"We'll stay here though, just in case they turn up. We don't have any other leads to check on and if they haven't cancelled their reservation, they may still be in the area," Everett said.

"Alright." Then Fisher called Tanner.

"I wish we'd known that earlier," Tanner said.

"It wouldn't have made any difference. They might just be paranoid about leaving their bags in the room, knowing they're guilty of crimes and don't want to leave anything behind while a maid cleaned the room. Then if they actually return, we would have been gone."

"True."

Then someone pulled into the motel parking lot by a tree.

"Someone just pulled up, but it's not a black Chevrolet Suburban," Tanner said.

"Yeah, it's a black pickup," Fisher said.

"I'll ask Everett if he can check on the license plate to see who the truck belongs to," Fisher said.

"Okay. There are three men exiting the truck. Are they anyone you recognize?" Tanner asked.

"I can't tell. But if they go in the room that we're watching, or even if we go to the vehicle and those are the men, I'll recognize their scents," Fisher said.

"Yeah, me too," Tanner said. "Okay, they're going into the room that was assigned to the kidnappers. I'm rousing everyone."

"Doing the same here." Fisher called Everett, then got off the phone and said to Kira, "Three men are going into the room."

She opened her eyes and said, "What?"

"Three men went into the room we're watching."

"Oh, God, okay." She jumped out of the bed, removing her pajamas, and then pulled on her clothes. Once she had her boots on, she and Fisher headed out of the room.

"I want to check out the scents around that black pickup," he said.

"No black Suburban now?"

"Apparently not."

All of them ended up outside of their rooms, moving quietly, silently. But as soon as Fisher, his brothers and cousin and Kira moved toward the pickup, they could smell that the men were humans, and not the wolves they were seeking. Which explained why they were driving the black pickup. Everett and Demetria were now standing with their guns readied at the door to the kidnappers' room.

"But they went into the motel room that was registered to the kidnappers," Fisher said.

"Could the kidnappers have bribed someone to go to their room?" Kira asked.

"If that's the case, the kidnappers could know we're after them," Fisher said.

"Or they're trying to cover their tracks."

As soon as everyone was in place, Everett banged on the door with his fist. "Police, open up!"

One of the men opened the door. He was a redhead with a bushy beard, and he said, "What the hell."

"Come out of the room. All three of you," Everett said.

"What's this all about?" the redhaired guy asked.

"Hell, I told you those guys were up to something," a dark-haired guy with him said.

"We didn't know," another man said, standing taller than the other two. "They gave us the keys to this room and a hundred dollars each to stay the night here. We were on our way to Denver and met them at a convenience store. We were tired, and Denver was too far to drive, so we thought it was a great opportunity that had fallen in our lap."

"Yeah, and I told you it was too good to be true," the dark-haired guy said.

Everett asked to see their ID. "You're from Panama City, Florida."

"Right. We have relatives in Denver. That's where we're from originally, but we wanted to be near the beaches in Florida, so we all ended up getting jobs there. We're good friends and grew up together."

"Tell us what the men looked like," Fisher said.

They gave the descriptions of Reggie and his friends.

"Do you know what they were driving?" Kira asked.

"A black Chevrolet Suburban," the redhead said. "Who are these guys? What did they do?"

"Which direction did they go in?" Demetria asked.

"West," the redhead said.

"Did they give you a reason why they would give up their room and pay you for sleeping there?" The men weren't wolves, so Fisher didn't believe they were in collusion with the kidnappers, but still, he couldn't believe they wouldn't suspect something was really wrong with the whole scenario.

The redhead shared glances with the other men. Then they nodded, and the redhead rubbed the back of his neck. "The one guy said that his ex-girlfriend was stalking him. He thought if she followed him to his motel room, she would find he would be long gone, and all she would discover was us. They warned us she had been physically abusive toward him."

"Which is what clued me in that something wasn't right. All three men were physically fit and looked like they could handle any trouble that came their way," the dark-haired guy said. "So they were wanted by the police."

"Yeah, but despite being concerned about it, you still took their money and the room." But neither Kira nor any of the others would tell them what they were suspected of.

"I hope we're not under arrest," the redheaded man said.

"No, you didn't do anything wrong," Demetria said.

"Do you mind if I take a look around in your room to see if they had accidentally left anything behind?" Fisher asked.

"No, be my guest, though as far as we saw, they didn't leave anything in the room," the redhead said.

Demetria, Everett, Kira, and Fisher investigated the room, smelling the three kidnappers' scents. Even though Demetria and Everett hadn't smelled their scent before, they could distinguish them from the three men now occupying the room. Once they found nothing, they left the room.

"Do you need the money they gave us?" the redheaded guy asked.

"No. Just be careful the next time you get an offer that sounds too good to be true," Everett said.

"These guys are armed and dangerous," Kira said.

All three men looked a little paler after that. Then Kira went to the lobby of the motel and told Calvin that the kidnappers seemed to have left and given up their motel to another three men who weren't involved in any of this. Normally, something like that wouldn't be allowed, but the men were tired, and the owners went outside and spoke to them.

"This is highly irregular," Calvin said. "And I'm a retired highway patrolman, so I know something about this. We'll let you stay the rest of the night, but if you want to stay longer, you'll have to pay for the room. Even so, we need you to register your vehicle and your names."

"Uh, yeah, sure," the dark-haired guy said.

The three men went with Calvin to the lobby to fill out the paperwork.

"What do you want to do now?" Everett asked Kira.

"Sleep. Unless we have a new lead now, we all need to sleep." Kira swore everyone looked at Fisher to see if he was going to stay with his brothers or cousins or Kira.

Fisher glanced at Kira.

Kira smiled at him. "No sense in changing any of the arrangements now." Then everyone said goodnight and dispersed to their rooms. "I'm really glad I have someone staying with me."

He locked the door. "Just anyone?"

She laughed. "A special someone."

"I'm sorry we didn't get them."

"Yeah, I know. Me too. But I've worked on twelve cases since I was hired, and all are so different from each other. So you never know what will happen. The first was solved in a day. I went with my partner to trail a wolf who had been accused of stalking a woman. We caught him at it right away, but before we could take him into custody, he broke into her home, and we arrested him. He's incarcerated now. In another case, a wolf had been breaking into homes and stealing any valuables he could find. It took two days to track him down and put him in the jaguar facility also."

"But in this case, it might take a while to find and catch them."

"Yes." She climbed into bed, and she patted the mattress. "Let's get some sleep."

"I'LL JUST TAKE a quick shower and then join you." He was thrilled to be able to stay with her for the rest of the night, not only because he loved being with her but also, she needed someone to help watch her back too.

By the time he left the bathroom and went to the bed, he thought Kira might be asleep, but she was waiting up for him.

Then he removed his towel, and she looked down to check out his package. He smiled.

He pulled on his boxers and climbed into bed. They naturally gravitated toward each other. As some point while they were sound asleep, she stole the bed covers. He could have left the bed and turned up the heat, stripped and shifted into his wolf, or done what he did next. He tucked her against his body and warmed them both up—which was the perfect way to sleep.

When the light was beginning to brighten the room-darkening curtains later that morning, Kira opened her eyes and raised her brows at him, looking a little surprised that he was awake. "Were you cold?" she asked him.

"You stole the covers."

She smiled. "Sorry about that. I'm sort of a restless sleeper." But she didn't appear to be in the least bit sorry and he sure wasn't.

He hadn't dated a wolf in a long time and snuggling with her at night had been a real perk to the job. "You weren't restless once we were together. I think you were cold."

"So were you."

"Absolutely. At the time, it seemed like the best option to me."

Then she got a call on her phone. She groaned. "Here I'm in charge of the case and probably everyone's awake and waiting on me to make a decision about what to do next." She pulled away from him, lifted her phone of the bedside table, answered the call, and put it on speaker. "We're just getting up, Demetria."

"We just woke too. We thought we could all have breakfast at Dan and Addie Steinacker's home, since we don't have any further leads on the whereabouts of the kidnappers, and we don't have to be watching the motel any longer," Demetria said.

"Yes, let's do that then."

"Okay, I'll call Dan. He said they would just wait to hear from us if we were going to have breakfast with them," Demetria said.

"I'll let the others know," Fisher said, wanting to be useful. That was the one thing about this case. He wasn't a USF agent, so he felt he didn't have a whole lot of say in things. But since the others were his brothers and cousin, he knew that was something he could certainly do.

"Thanks, go ahead." Then Kira said to Demetria, "We'll meet you outside when we're dressed and ready."

"Okay, we'll see you in a few."

Fisher removed his sleep boxers, pulled on a fresh pair of boxer briefs and his pants, then called Tanner. "Hey, we're all going to have breakfast at the sheriff's home."

"And then decide where to go from there?" Tanner asked.

"Yeah. We're meeting outside as soon as we're all dressed," Fisher said.

"Good show."

Then they ended the call.

Then she hurried to dress, and he finished dressing. They both packed their bags and headed outside.

He figured they wouldn't be staying here in Yuma Town any further because the kidnappers had moved on. But where would they go to next?

13

A t breakfast at the Steinackers' home that morning with Dan and his mate, Addie, and their five-year old twins, Maddie and Mitch, Kira, Fisher, and the others on their team were enjoying a nice hearty breakfast of eggs, ham, toast, fried potatoes, orange juice, and coffee when Dan got a call from Hal Haverton. "Yeah, Hal?"

"Ted said he saw three wolves racing toward the old silver mine. He didn't see any sign of a black Suburban, but when he saw the big gray wolves, all males, he was suspicious and suspected they might be the kidnappers."

"We're on our way," Dan said, everyone quickly thanking both Dan and Addie for a delightful breakfast. He explained that Ted Weekum was Deputy Sheriff Hal Haverton's foreman at his horse ranch.

Since Dan's mate was also a deputy sheriff, Addie and Dan left the kids with their nanny, and she and Dan led them to Hal's ranch.

The Greystoke pack members and Kira and Fisher followed Dan and Addie to Hal's ranch in their respective vehicles. They met up with Ted dressed in jeans, cowboy boots, and a Stetson. Ted told them where he had sighted the wolves.

Kira said, "I'm running as a wolf. What does everyone else want to do?"

Ted said, "I'll ride a horse and see if I can catch sight of their trail."

"I'm running as a wolf," Fisher said.

"You might feel some discomfort with running on your foreleg," Kira said.

"I'm sure I'll be fine," Fisher said.

But Kira wasn't sure of it.

"I'll run as a wolf too," Tanner said.

"How secure is it out here?" Everett asked.

Kira knew he asked because Everett and Demetria were jaguars, and they didn't want to run in their fur coats unless it was pretty safe to do so.

"It's safe here," Hal said, "if you want to run as jaguars."

Dan said, "I've called Chase and the other deputies and they're all meeting us here."

Everyone moved into one of the hay barns and began stripping off their clothes and shifting. Kira loved seeing the jaguars in their coats. They were so exotic, and they were bigger cats than the cougars. It was fascinating to see all the cougars too! And of course, they were interested in the way the wolves looked. Everyone had a distinctive appearance.

Then they all headed out of the barn and raced off in the direction the three male gray wolves had taken.

After a couple of miles, Kira smelled that the kidnappers had separated, and so she ran after one of the scent trails. Fisher, Shawn, Demetria, Dan, and Tanner followed Kira. Everett went with one group of wolves and cougars. Addie was with the other wolves and cougars following another trail, so a mix of shifters were with each team. If these guys had any clue they were being chased down by several kinds of shifters, Kira was sure they would be terrified.

They headed toward a river and then they saw a wet wolf several hundred yards on the other side of the river, running in the direction of an old, abandoned, brick building. Kira knew they wouldn't be able to reach the wolf before he went inside. If he managed to run inside it, he could shift, dress, and arm himself with a gun. That could change everything.

Still, they charged forward, swimming across the river, and then reached the opposite bank. The wolf was the one who had shot Fisher. She hoped he wasn't having flashbacks of being shot. She glanced at him. She hoped his wound wasn't hurting while he was running as a wolf.

When the wolf ran inside the building, everyone stopped.

Kira's heart was beating like crazy, and she could hear the rest of her companions' hearts beating just as fast. She wanted to warn the others of what she feared, but they were all wary and she figured they would assume the worst.

Dan shifted. "He could be shifting. In the event he comes out with a gun ready to shoot, I recommend we scatter and take positions around the building." Then he shifted back into his cougar, and they all spread out.

Shawn, Demetria, and Tanner headed to the left of the building. Kira, Fisher, and Dan ran to the right of the building. A cold wind was blowing, and the structure's shingled roof was shaking.

Even though some of the roof was down on one side, the windows were still framed in, dirty glass broken in places, perfect for the wolf to watch out through and shoot at them. But then she saw him coming out of the building as a human, dressed and wearing a black backpack, looking like he didn't have a care in the world. She realized he didn't know they were coming after him. He wasn't holding a gun. Unless he had one in his jacket pocket, he might not have quick access to one. Which would be good for them. She raced toward him. So did Dan and Fisher.

Having heard them, possibly smelling them, the guy turned, his jaw dropped, and his eyes widened. She was sure he was in shock to observe two wolves and a cougar headed his way as fast as they could run. Wait until he saw Demetria in her jaguar coat. He immediately yanked off his backpack, and she knew he was going for his gun in the bag. She was mistaken. He was freeing himself of his baggage and pulled a gun out of his jacket pocket. The wolves could jump sixteen feet at a run, but they were still about sixty feet from the kidnapper. As a cougar, Dan could jump forty feet horizontally and he did. Even a jaguar could only leap around twenty feet horizontally. But suddenly, Tanner, Shawn, and Demetria came around the building behind the guy, ready to take him down.

The man tried to aim at the wolves and cougar coming at him, his hand shaking. He fired at them, but they scattered, and the rounds hit the dirt all around them. It scared Kira to death that if he'd had better aim, he could have killed any or all of them. But then his gun jammed, and Dan leapt again and pinned the man to the ground—a hundred-and-forty pounds of cougar muscle and bones. They all converged on the kidnapper, but then Kira went into the building and found the other men's backpacks and she smiled. Fisher joined her and licked her jaw.

Even though she wanted to howl, to let the other teams know they had been successful with taking down one of the men, they didn't want to alert the other kidnappers. At least they had the other men's backpacks. She smelled the other men's scents on them. Now if they could just find their vehicle and the other men. If the other kidnappers managed to get away from the other teams but couldn't get to their vehicle, they could be stranded here making them easier to apprehend. But now they had a slight problem with taking this guy into custody.

Dan walked into the barn and shifted. "Demetria's holding our prisoner down." He dumped clothes out of one of the backpacks, then began pulling out some of Reggie's clothes and dressed in them. "I'll call Ted and he'll bring help to incarcerate these guys. At least I hope the others have caught their perps." Then Dan went outside with Fisher and Kira and said, "Okay, where's your cell phone?"

"As if I would give it to you," the man said, lying on his stomach, Demetria's paw pressing hard against the back of his neck. She opened her mouth and showed off her long, wicked canines and growled.

"You don't want to know how much her bite could hurt if she bit you. Since you're already a wolf, we don't have to worry about turning you. And burying you out here?" Dan shrugged. "If you didn't realize it, this whole territory is cougar run. So no one would ever look for you out here. Oh, and by the way, I'm the sheriff."

The man's eyes widened a bit.

"So where is your phone?" Dan asked.

Demetria bit into the guy's jacket. He cried out in fright. She pulled him over on his back. Wolves and cougars had strong bites, but the jaguars even more so.

Dan dumped out the kidnapper's backpack, found his gun, and his phone. He took the phone and said, "What's your pin number?"

The kidnapper wouldn't give it to him. Kira moved toward him, growling. He just looked mutinously at her, and she bit his hand. He yelled out, swore at her, his eyes filling with tears. She growled and made the move to bite him again and he said, "Alright, alright." He gave Dan the pin number and Dan used it to access the phone.

Dan said, "Ted, call Hal and the others. We've caught one of the suspects and we're at the old brick building across the river. We have the other men's clothes. We don't know if they've been caught yet. We need to find their vehicle. Tell Dr. Kate the kidnapper we caught has got a wolf bite to his hand. We'll be bringing him in for questioning, but we'll drop by the medical clinic first." Then Dan ended the call. "Okay, Ted is getting hold of some more of our people and we'll take this one in." Then he searched through the backpack. "No ID. Who are you?"

The youngest of the kidnappers wouldn't give up his name. Since he was the one who had shot Fisher, Kira didn't feel any remorse for biting him. She would have bitten him again if he hadn't given up his pin number for his phone so that Dan could get a hold of the others to take this guy into custody.

She noticed then that Fisher was lying down, his head on his paws, watching the kidnapper. Immediately, Kira was worried that Fisher's shoulder was hurting. She and Tanner were sitting up, wary of the kidnapper's next actions. She went over to Fisher and licked his face. He raised his head, smiled, and licked her back. But she could smell he was in pain. She sighed. He probably shouldn't have gone running with them so soon after he was wounded, despite knowing how much he had wanted to be with her and trying to track these men down.

She wanted him checked out by the doctor here also and if the doctor said he should have more bed rest, Shawn could take Fisher home. But she was also wondering what had happened with the other guys. To her surprise, she heard three All-Terrain-Vehicles headed toward the river.

Dan got a call on the kidnapper's phone, and he answered it. "Okay, we're moving that way." He ended the call and said, "We're going to the river. We need to cross it to reach the ATVs. They'll take anyone back who needs to return."

Kira wanted to question the guy in the worst way, but she also wanted to help get the other kidnappers.

Dan pulled the kidnapper to his feet. He grabbed the backpacks and started hauling the kidnapper toward the river. "I don't know what this is all about. Who do you think I am?" the kidnapper asked, as if he was totally innocent.

"Someone caught trespassing on private property," Dan said.

And an attempted murderer, Kira wanted to say. *And* a kidnapper. But she suspected Dan was keeping that information secret until he was ready to reveal more charges. They surrounded the kidnapper as they moved to the river. Wouldn't the other kidnappers be surprised if they managed to get away from the shifters tracking them, walked to the dilapidated building, and found their backpacks were missing? They would also smell wolves, a jaguar, and a cougar had been there.

When they finally reached the river, a guy Kira hadn't met yet showed up with a Sherp ATV. Yes! It could float on water. And then as soon as the driver saw them, he navigated across the river and parked.

"Thanks, Travis. We all knew that your new vehicle would come in handy. Travis MacKay is with the CSF and likes his vehicles," Dan explained.

Travis got out of his vehicle, and he brought handcuffs with him. "Yeah, I knew this vehicle would be useful. So he's one of the kidnappers, eh?" He cuffed the kidnapper and put him in the back of the vehicle.

Demetria got into the back seat with him, all growly like, amusing Kira. The kidnapper wouldn't even think of trying to flee when a jaguar was acting as his guard.

"Oh, Bridget is at the jailhouse to assist us when we interrogate the prisoner," Travis said, tossing the backpacks into the vehicle. "She has a special talent for learning the truth about people. Though occasionally she has trouble with that."

"Bridget is Travis's mate and also CSF," Dan explained.

Kira was glad they had so many cougars to help them. She nudged at Fisher to go with Travis, but he wasn't going along with it until she got into the ATV. Then he did too. She would have words with him about it later, once she was in her human form. She had to get him to see the doctor.

The other ATVs went in the direction the other teams had gone so they could help out the others. Tanner and Shawn went with them.

Once Travis took them to Hal's ranch, Kira, Fisher, and Demetria went into the barn to shift and dress. Dan joined them in the barn to change out of the kidnapper's clothes and into his own.

"Did you have a chance to search the backpacks for IDs?" Kira asked, putting her boots on.

"I checked them. And I searched this guy's clothes for ID. There was no ID in any of the backpacks. Maybe they left them in their vehicle, or maybe the other two men just don't have any on them," Dan said. "We know Reggie had his driver's license when Stryker pulled him over for a traffic stop. At least we have *this* guy for trespassing. All this land out here is private property. The cougars own it. We might not be a wolf pack, but from what I understand, they do the same thing as we've done when they can. Expand their properties so that our shifters can run free without the issue of hunters and the like coming across us and shooting us," Dan said. "Though it doesn't always mean we're completely safe."

When they left the barn, Fisher, Kira, and Demetria went in Kira's car so that Everett, when he returned from trying to track down the other kidnappers, would have his and Demetria's vehicle. Dan rode with Travis and his prisoner into Yuma Town while Kira followed them in her vehicle.

"You are seeing the doctor also," Kira said to Fisher.

"I'm fine."

"No. You're not. I can smell that you are in pain."

"So could I. The guys are all the same, trying to prove to everyone else they're so tough," Demetria said.

"Not me," Fisher said, smiling. "I mean, if I'm hurting—"

"Which you are," Kira said, not about to be bamboozled by the wolf.

"Okay, so I have to admit swimming across the river was rough on my shoulder."

"And running as a wolf?" Kira asked.

"Maybe. A little bit. I was fine to begin with, but the river was a little much."

"So was the guy we caught the one who shot you?" Demetria asked.

"Yeah," Fisher said.

"Reggie Olson, the black bearded man, was the one who fired at us while we were both on the ledge below the edge of the cliff," Kira said. "The one we caught was the youngest of the three."

"I suspect the younger guy shot me because he thought I was a real wolf and would hurt the boy if he was alone," Fisher said.

"He's still a kidnapper," Demetria said. "He knows what they're doing is wrong. He gets some of the payout of the ransoms. He's in the wrong as much as any of them are. Not to mention shooting wolves, shifter or otherwise, is illegal."

"I agree," Kira said.

Then they finally reached the clinic and both Dr. Kate Parker-Hill and Dr. William Rugal greeted them.

"Welcome to Yuma Town." Kate was a pretty redhead with her hair pulled up into a bun, eager to take care of Fisher.

"Yeah, welcome. Though I'm sure you would rather have a happier encounter with our fair town," William said.

"Capturing one of the three kidnappers is a good thing though," Fisher said.

"Absolutely," Kira said.

"I'm Mandy Jones and I'll take you back to an exam room. My mate is Ricky, one of the deputy sheriffs helping with your case," the nurse said, smiling at the wolves and jaguar.

"Oh, thanks," Fisher said.

The RN led Fisher into a room and took his vital stats. Kira didn't even ask if Fisher minded if she was in the room with him. If he was going to continue working for them, she wanted to know if he was physically able to continue working on the case.

"Your pulse and heart rate are normal. No sign of a fever," Mandy said, as another nurse, Elsie Miller, took the kidnapper to an exam room. Demetria and Dan went in with them. Then Kate came into the exam room to see to Fisher's shoulder.

He winced while he was taking off his shirt and Kira went over to help him out of it.

"Are you sure you're going to be alright?" Kira was genuinely concerned about him.

"Yes. I want to continue to work this case with you."

She knew he did, but she didn't want him to end up having real trouble if he didn't heal well enough. Even though wolves healed in half the time that humans did, they didn't heal instantaneously.

Kate checked his shoulder over. She touched the area around the wound.

Kira saw he was holding his breath.

"Breathe," Kate said. "If you want to keep working with the USF, I don't want you to pass out on me and how would that look to Kira?"

Kira smiled at Kate. She really liked the cougar doctor.

Fisher took a deep breath and let it out.

"You have bruised ribs from the fall. You were shot here, and"– Kate looked at his back—"the bullet exited here. And it's only been four days? You look remarkably good for going through all that. But I would suggest no more running as a wolf for about a week and see how you're feeling by then."

"He said he started hurting when he was swimming in the river as a wolf," Kira offered, to see if maybe the swimming had made it worse.

"Ahh, yes, that could make it worse. But I would say running as a wolf will irritate your wounds and injuries also," Kate said. "I'm sure your doctor back home would agree with me on that you shouldn't be running or swimming as a wolf."

"The doctor is his brother Heath," Kira said. "I'm sure he didn't think you would be doing either, or he might have given you some restrictions."

Then Kira got a call from Everett, and she hoped it meant his team had caught another one of the men and they were headed back in with him. That would be the reason he had shifted back into his human form, she assumed. She put it on speakerphone so that Fisher could hear what Everett had to say. "What happened with all of you?"

"The one we were following ended up at a location where we found tire tracks the size that a Suburban would make. We believe he got into the vehicle and took off. We haven't heard from the other team that was chasing down the third guy, but Demetria called to say you all caught the youngest of the three men."

"Yes. Once the doctor patches him up, we can interrogate him and learn who the others are."

"Demetria said Dan had everyone's backpacks. Did you find anything in them that would tell us who they really are?" Everett asked.

"No. None of them had any ID. The prisoner also had a gun and he tried to shoot us until Dan took him down. Boy, I knew you jaguars could jump further than us wolves, but I didn't realize cougars could leap so far," Kira said.

"I heard you bit him," Everett said.

"Yeah, he deserved it, and I knew I didn't have to worry about turning him because he's already a wolf."

"Royal or more newly turned?" Everett asked.

"I don't know. We really didn't get anything out of him, and he rode with Dan back to Yuma Town. Dr. Rugal is patching him up now," Kira said.

"Demetria told us that Dr. Kate Hill is checking out Fisher." Everett sounded a little concerned.

"I'm fine," Fisher said. "I just overdid it a little on running and swimming as a wolf. Other than that, I'm good. So we haven't heard back from the other team?"

"Not yet. But three ATVs went out in their direction to try and locate them," Everett said.

"Either the one guy left his companions behind, or he eventually picked him up," Kira said.

"Some of the other guys are staying at the building, just in case they show up there to pick up their backpacks."

"Good. Maybe we'll still catch all of them," Kira said.

Then Kate said, "Okay, Fisher. No swimming, no running as a wolf for a week. Do you need anything for the pain?"

"No. I'm good."

Kate glanced at Kira as if she was his keeper. Kira nodded. Kira helped Fisher pull on his shirt as they heard a grumbling kidnapper walking past the exam room, his wrists cuffed, his arm bandaged.

"I told you I was just running as a wolf. I didn't know it was anyone's private property. You're cougars. You should know how it feels to need to run in our wild animal form," the kidnapper groused.

"You were carrying a weapon, shooting at us when we apprehended you," Dan said. "There's only one reason you would pull out a gun."

Kira, Fisher, and Everett quickly joined him.

"Hell, yeah, to protect myself."

"We're going to the jailhouse," Dan said.

When they finally arrived at the jailhouse in three separate cars, a pretty, dark-haired woman named Bridget introduced herself and was waiting for them inside. She smiled at them, her blue-gray eyes warm and welcoming.

Dan took the kidnapper into the interrogation room and then Kira, Bridget, and Demetria went into the room to question him, while the others watched through the viewing window.

"What's your name?" Kira asked, sitting across the table from the kidnapper. Demetria joined her, but Bridget stood on the prisoner's side of the table behind him.

"Royce Barmonger."

Bridget shook her head.

Kira raised her brows. How did Bridget know for sure?

"How come you bit me?" the kidnapper asked.

"To get you to follow the sheriff's instructions. What's your name?"

He sat back in his chair, frowning. "I told you."

"You didn't give us your real name. Who are the other guys you were with?"

He said, "I get a right to an attorney, and I don't have to say anything that might be used in a court of law against me."

Kira looked at Bridget, wondering how they handled situations like this.

"He can have a right to an attorney. Larry Pierce is the only one we have here, and you can call him now." Bridget handed him the landline phone and the phone number.

Kira didn't like this change of plan. She figured the guy wouldn't talk and then they wouldn't get anywhere with this.

The kidnapper said, "This is Royce Bergermon and I need a lawyer to represent me. Yes, I'm in the Yuma Town jail. I need him now. Alright." Then he handed the phone back to Bridget. "His law clerk, Stella Weekum, said Mr. Pierce would be here in half an hour."

Kira raised her brows. First, he said he was Barmonger and now Bergermon?

"Good." Bridget said to Kira and Demetria, "We'll move him to the cell and then I'll talk with you for a moment."

Dan walked into the interrogation room and took the kidnapper back to a jail cell and closed the door.

Then they all met in the lounge.

"Our lawyer is a cougar. So is the judge," Bridget said. "Larry's law clerk, Stella, is a rare white cougar and married to Ted Weekum, Hal's foreman at the horse ranch."

"Oh, wow, that is the coolest," Kira said. "As to Royce, how do you know that he was lying about his name? Though he gave two different last names."

Dan made a fresh pot of coffee.

"I can read people's minds. I know when they're telling the truth. Though occasionally, I run into someone that I can't read, like my mate Travis. But in this case, I could."

"Ava, working at the bakery, said she had psychic abilities also. Her twin sister too. It's incredible."

"It is," Bridget said. "So Royce Farmington is the kidnapper's real name. Oscar is one of the men's names that he was running with, though he didn't think of his last name. Reggie Olson is the other."

"Wow, your ability really comes in handy. We need you to join us in the USF," Kira said.

"That's why I'm with the CSF," Bridget said.

Travis walked into the room and gave her a hug. "For a lot more than that. So what did you all learn?"

"We learned his full name, one of the men's first names and a confirmation on the name you already knew," Bridget said.

"He asked for a lawyer," Kira said, sounding disappointed.

"When's Larry Pierce getting here?" Travis asked.

"Two hours," Bridget said.

"Royce said he was coming in half an hour," Kira said.

Bridget smiled. "When we have a criminal in custody, Larry takes his time. It rattles the prisoner and sometimes they end up coming clean. It's his code. Half an hour means two hours."

14

In the staff lounge at the sheriff's office, Dan poured everyone cups of coffee. Then he got a call. "Yeah, Hal?" He put it on speakerphone.

"The two men must have driven off in their SUV. None of us can find any sign of them. Do you want us to leave some men to watch the building in case the kidnappers attempt to retrieve their backpacks?" Hal asked.

"Yes." A phone rang in Dan's pocket, and he pulled it out. "That's the phone we took off Royce Farmington, the younger kidnapper. The call is from an Oscar Farmington."

"Oscar was the other name Royce was thinking of with regard to his fellow cohorts in the crimes," Bridget said.

"He must have shifted, gotten to his phone, and is trying to locate where Royce is." Kira eyed the phone, wishing they could answer it.

"Absolutely. But maybe we can locate Oscar and his co-conspirator," Dan said, leaving the staff lounge and heading into his office.

They all followed him in there.

"We have a state-of-the-art system here for tracking cell numbers. And car GPS systems," Dan said. "I just need to look up

Oscar Farmington from the Colorado area, get his driver's license and learn what vehicle he owns, where he lives and do the same with Royce's information."

"We will recognize him if his driver's license picture is the same as one of the kidnappers involved in the crimes," Fisher said.

Chase Buchanan came into the office then. "I heard you have one of the suspects. Oh, you got a couple of names finally." Chase sat down at another computer and Dan gave him Royce's name.

"We're working on getting confirmation that Oscar Farmington is one of the kidnappers. He's from Denver and owns a white Chevrolet van," Dan said.

"Royce Farmington is also from Denver, and he owns a blue Chevrolet Traverse," Chase said.

Kira was looking over Chase's shoulder, then glanced at Dan's computer. "They have different addresses."

As soon as they saw Oscar's driver's license photo, both Kira and Fisher said, "That's the other kidnapper."

"Yeah, we need to learn if they have other family in the Denver area," Dan said.

Just then, Leyton walked into the office. "I'll get a hold of Jack. He, Chet, Travis, and I can go to Denver and check it out. I know Bridget is needed here to learn if your suspect is telling the truth or not."

"Good show," Dan said.

"Can you learn what they're thinking then, even if they're not talking, Bridget?" Kira thought that was a remarkable ability.

"Yes. I'll probably grab a chair and sit outside of Royce's cell and pretend to be guarding him. Maybe I'll take a book with me and 'listen' in on his thoughts," Bridget said.

"That is the coolest gift. Are you sure you don't want to work with our agency?" Kira asked.

Travis smiled and shook his head. "She's invaluable to me, to us. You'll have to find your own agent to work with who has special talents." Travis carried a chair to the cell for Bridget while she grabbed a book and headed back there with him.

When Travis returned to the office, he and Leyton told them good luck and headed out.

"Leyton is mated to Kate, the doctor who checked you out, Fisher," Dan said.

"You have a really tightknit community here." Fisher sounded impressed. "We've been buying land and trying to spread out our pack a bit, but what we wouldn't give to have a setup like this."

"Yeah, we know of a wolf pack that runs Silver Town," Kira said, "and they have a similar situation. But they have wolf pack leaders and subleaders running the pack."

"We are set up differently, since we don't operate as a pack," Dan said.

"It's interesting that the cougars are self-sufficient and so is the wolf pack run town, but Demetria and I were working a case in Houston where a snow leopard shifter was trying to rescue his buddy incarcerated in the zoo. William Wright was the snow leopard and he told me later he was from White Bear, Alaska, where the polar bear shifters have their own council, but also many other kinds of shifters are friends there and they work together. Wolves, snow leopards, brown bears, polar bears, even Arctic foxes," Everett said.

"We would welcome other shifters into our pack territory, as long as they followed our rules," Fisher said.

"We would feel the same way," Dan said. "We've made some shifter friends—some bears and caracals that came into the area, and we do actually have a snow leopard living among us."

"Now, I've never seen a snow leopard shifter before. I would love to see him or her sometime," Kira said.

"That was what we thought too," Demetria said, "when we met up with William Wright."

"You know what? I'm going to join Bridget for a moment." Kira had to ask Royce if Oscar was his brother or a cousin. Oscar was middle-aged, but too young to be his dad.

Dan opened the door to the cells and Kira headed down the long hall to the only cell that was occupied. Bridget was sitting near the cell and smiled at her.

"Okay, Royce, so we know Oscar Farmington is one of your accomplices," Kira said, looking into the cell at Royce sitting on the bed, chewing on his lip, appearing glum.

"That's not true," Royce said, sounding a little panicked.

Bridget nodded. "You're right. Oscar is an older cousin."

"I never said that." Then his eyes widened. "You caught him?"

Kira smiled as if they had. She sure wished they had! Then she patted Bridget's shoulder. "Thanks for all your help with this." She walked back to the locked door to the cells and Dan let her out.

"Oscar is his older cousin," she said.

Then Royce's phone rang again in Dan's pocket. "It's Oscar calling again."

Kira thought Oscar was probably worried about what had happened to Royce. Had Oscar reunited with Reggie? Or was he on his own, trying to find a way back to civilization? Still, how did he get his phone if he hadn't had one possibly in their vehicle? She wondered if they had more bags in their car and therefore clothes to wear. Probably.

It would take Leyton Hill and his team three hours to get to Denver. She hoped they would get some good intel from there. She realized that though they were from different organizations that dealt with shifter issues, in the future, they could now work together when it was mutually beneficial. No longer was the USF organization alone in their efforts to right shifter wrongs.

Fisher was checking his phone and looked up at them. "We have a full moon phase right now."

Everyone waited to learn why he had even mentioned it. The cougars probably never paid any attention to it. Royal wolves who had been shifters for generations might not think about it, but more newly turned wolf shifters couldn't shift during the new moon and had to shift during the full moon. Was that why the three men had been running as wolves? It made more sense that way.

"They're more newly turned," Kira said.

"Yeah, that's just what I was thinking," Fisher said.

"Oh, I hadn't thought of that." Demetria finished the rest of her coffee. "And that makes it even worse. I mean, if they went to a human prison for kidnapping, they wouldn't be able to stop from shifting during the height of the full moon phase."

"Asses," Fisher said. "They make it more dangerous for all of us."

"I agree," Demetria said. "I'm just glad jaguars don't have that issue, but even so, if they got picked up and imprisoned, and someone tried to beat on them or shank them, they most likely would strip off their clothes and shift. Self-preservation in a case like that would be all that would come to mind. Forget about how it would affect the rest of our kind. Though I would probably feel the same way if that happened to me."

Kira nodded. She was certain all shifters would feel that way as a defensive mechanism, just like when she had bitten the guy who had tried to kidnap her when she was a young girl. If she could have turned wolf, she would have. She was certain Fisher had wanted to tear into the guy who had shot him, if he could have. Since the kidnapper was also a wolf, Fisher could have lawfully done it, according to the wolf shifters' rules of engagement. But since the kidnapper had been holding a gun on him, Fisher would never have reached him in time.

Then Kira and Fisher sat down to look at the one computer and see what they could learn about Royce.

Dan set the phone down on the desk.

"Can I look at it?"

Dan said, "Sure."

Kira picked up the phone and started looking at the text messages. "Reggie was giving the time and place information of when they were going to go hunting. He didn't say anything about kidnapping children."

"So if anyone saw the messages, they wouldn't be privy as to what they were really up to," Demetria said.

"Exactly. It's all in kind of a code. But he texted Royce a number of times about this. And looking back in his messages, Royce and Oscar were also talking about hunting. They don't mention grabbing anyone or being successful at it. But they do mention the time and place for meetups," Kira said. "I'll make a list of the times and places."

"I'll begin investigating those for possible kidnappings in those areas," Demetria said.

"I'll help you with it," Everett said.

Kira began making a list, and Demetria took the first time and location to investigate. Everett took the second one.

Demetria said, "I found a case. A little boy was taken when he got off the school bus and he was left at a clinic two days later. He'd been fed, but he was still traumatized."

"Of course." Kira handed her another possible case.

Everett said, "Okay, in this situation, a boy was grabbed who was skateboarding later at night, no one else around, so in that case, it took a while for anyone to realize he had been picked up. Then the parents paid the ransom, and the boy was left at a library."

"This is the case that was near where I was at when I heard about the kidnapping of a boy—Billy Forsythe. He had been walking home from his friend's house. The guys pulled up in a big black FBI agent car, is how some described it. But that's when I smelled the wolf who had grabbed him and secured him in the Suburban. And that's how I got the case," Kira said.

"That's a good thing too," Fisher said, "or these guys would still be out there doing this. I suspect with one of their co-conspirators caught, they're not going to be out kidnapping for a while." Fisher scrolled through a screen on the monitor. "A ton of black Chevrolet Suburbans are registered to Denver homeowners."

"We have five cougar citizens who have black Suburbans in Yuma Town also, which adds to the confusion," Dan said.

Then a distinguished-looking, dark-haired man wearing an expensive dark gray suit and a burnt orange tie featuring a cougar walked into the sheriff's office and introduced himself to the jaguars and wolves. "I'm Larry Pierce. It's an honor to meet all of you." Introductions were made all around, then Larry said to Dan, "I'm ready to see the suspect...uh, client."

Kira immediately wondered if Royce would realize that since the lawyer was a cougar, he might not truly be on the kidnapper's side. Then Royce might not reveal anything about his involvement in the kidnappings or his partners in crime.

"Bridget let us know that Royce Farmington is the name of the guy we're holding in the kidnapping cases. And Oscar Farmington is his older cousin who was another member of the team. I'll go get Royce from his cell and take him to the interrogation room," Dan said.

Kira was dying to know how their office handled a situation like this. Fisher glanced at her, and she reached over and squeezed his hand, assuming he was thinking the same thing.

Dan escorted Royce to the interrogation room and Larry went in there to speak with him.

Once Larry closed the door, Kira asked Dan, "So can we listen in?"

"It's all being recorded. We need to find all three of the men and take them into custody no matter what," Dan said. "But we can watch in the viewing room also."

Kira and Fisher headed that way, and Demetria and Everett

quickly joined them. Dan entered the room right after them. Bridget hurried to join them too. Kira was glad Bridget would be listening in also.

Then they watched from behind the one-way mirror and listened to the dialogue between Larry and Royce.

"Okay, so first, if I'm going to represent you—" Larry said.

"I don't want a cougar lawyer. From Yuma Town? No way in hell," Royce said.

"Let me tell you how this goes. You're a wolf. A shifter. You're not a human. We don't abide by human laws. Tell me, why were you running as a wolf on private property?"

"I told the sheriff we didn't know it was private property and we just wanted to run."

"It's the phase of the full moon. How many generations back do you have wolf roots?" Larry asked.

ROYCE SHOOK HIS HEAD. Fisher wanted to shake the truth out of Royce. The guy was just not going to cooperate with them—he believed—about anything. Which made him wonder if he and Oscar had been turned at the same time, like recently. That they didn't have a few generations of wolf roots even in their DNA.

"And your name?"

Royce folded his arms over his chest.

"How about Royce Farmington? I understand you're related to Oscar Farmington, an older cousin, and he is involved."

Royce frowned. "You're supposed to be my lawyer. Yet you sound more like a police officer interrogating me."

"I need to know how to represent you. When they catch the others, I need to know how they're related to you and the role you played in the kidnappings."

"Wait, I never said that I was involved in any kidnappings. I thought this was about running as a wolf on private property."

"I need to know how to defend you. If you haven't been in charge of the kidnappings, I can use that in your defense. But if you were all in on the kidnappings, you're equally guilty, right?"

"How are you getting me off? Wait, you work for them. You're a cougar. You're not on my side. You believe I'm guilty without any proof at all."

"Two eyewitnesses? Not to mention shooting at other shifters? And shooting a wolf shifter."

"I didn't know he was a wolf shifter. I thought he was a wolf."

"It's illegal to kill a wolf."

"I was trying to protect the boy."

Larry shook his head. "So they have you one way or another. Now you can either help me with your defense, or you can just go with the USF, and they'll have their jaguars deal with you."

Royce's jaw dropped.

What did he think? That they were just going to release him to rejoin his buddies in the kidnapping business?

Larry rose from his seat. Royce was still staring at him, slack jawed.

"Good luck with your defense. I'm sure you'll get a great jaguar lawyer to represent you next. If you think you'll be judged in a human court of law, think again." Larry started to walk out of the interrogation room.

"Wait!"

Larry glanced back at him.

"Alright. I'll talk."

Larry sat back down. "Talk then."

"I didn't plan any of these."

"How many kidnappings were you involved in?"

"I didn't plan them."

"If you were with the other two men who planned them and you took part in them, you are partially responsible," Larry said.

Royce let out his breath and ran his hands through his hair. "Okay, I was only with them on this last case, and I didn't grab the kid, plan any of it, or anything. I was just supposed to drive and hell, I didn't know that they were going to do it."

Bridget shook her head. "Twelve kidnappings occurred and though he didn't actually plan them—Oscar and Reggie did that—Royce was there and an active participant in *all* of them."

Kira shook her head. "He's good at lying, that's for sure. And here I had believed he was telling the truth."

"Yeah, I agree," Fisher said.

"So what kind of a deal can I get, if I tell all?" Royce asked.

Larry leaned back in his chair. "You'll tell me where Reggie and Oscar are? You'll testify against them?"

"What will I get for it?"

"No promises."

"But you said you would represent me."

"I'll talk to Dan to see what he has to say." Larry got up from his chair. "I'll be right back." Then he left the interrogation room, and everyone went with Larry to the office to discuss the matter.

"Okay, so you heard what was discussed," Larry said. "I told him I would talk to Dan, but I know this is something the USF agents will decide."

Everett sat down on one of the chairs. "The way we do this is that whoever is involved the most in the crime gets a longer sentence. But they'll all go down for the roles they played. We don't make deals. If he wants to give us details, it might help him some, but we can't guarantee he won't be punished for his crimes. He's a more newly turned shifter. He's a danger to our kind if he's released out in the public with his willingness to commit crimes against others."

"I agree," Fisher said.

Bridget said, "He's not trustworthy. I don't believe anything he says. He was involved in everything but the planning, from what I could tell from what he was thinking."

Smiling, Larry shook his head. "I wish I had your gift, Bridget. Criminals are such con-artists and it's hard to see through their BS. Does anyone else have anything more to say before I go back in and talk to my client?"

"Who doesn't want you as a lawyer," Kira said.

"Right, but he'll get a jaguar then and he or she won't treat him any better," Demetria said. "All I've got to say is he'll have an easier time of it if he tells us what he knows. We'll get the truth out of these guys, one way or another."

"Yeah, but if we, or Larry, talks to him about certain things—we'll learn the truth because Bridget can 'listen' in on his thoughts, right?" Kira asked.

"Right," Larry said. "So give me some details and I'll go ask him some more questions. Whether he wants to answer me or not, Bridget might get some more information."

Dan printed out some sheets of information about where he and Oscar lived in Denver, about his relatives, and details about the other kidnappings in Denver and Boulder that had the same signature as the crimes they were sure they were connected with.

Larry took the pages and shook them at everyone. "Now this is what I'm talking about." Then he left the office and returned to the interrogation room while the others headed back into the viewing room to watch more of the interview with the suspect.

"Okay, the deal is"—Larry laid the papers out on the table—"it depends on how involved you are. Here's the information they have on you. So if you believe they don't know anything about you, you can forget that."

"You already know that Oscar is my cousin. The rest of my relatives don't figure into this," Royce said, which Kira thought showed a bit of empathy for his family.

"Yeah. But we need to know the details of the crimes," Larry said.

Royce didn't say anything.

"Where are your co-conspirators?"

"I don't know. We were to meet back at the broken-down building, but I figure you know that since the sheriff found all our backpacks in there."

"Where did you leave the vehicle?" Larry asked.

"About two miles on an old dirt road from the old building. The guys would have gone to it if they thought someone was after us and they would have left. I'm sure they would have tried to call me and when I never answered them, they would have left the area and not gone back for the backpacks. You have men there, right?"

"I'm not with law enforcement, but it's a good bet that they would go there. So what's the deal about the Suburban?" Larry asked.

He sounded calm, but Fisher wanted to put the fear of God into Royce. He glanced at Bridget. She whispered, "The vehicle for sure belongs to Reggie Olson of Denver. It's not stolen. He's Oscar's best friend."

"Man, are you handy to have around," Fisher said.

Dan said, "I'm on it. I'll get a BOLO out for the vehicle, just with our office." He left the viewing room to get on his computer to verify information about Reggie.

"Hey, don't prisoners get lunch around here?" Royce asked.

Larry said, "I'll see what I can do."

Deputy Sheriff Ricky Jones walked into the interview room. "I'll escort you to your cell and we'll get you something to eat."

Bridget got off her phone in the viewing room. "Several families are providing meals for all of you for lunch. Tanner, Shawn, Brock, and Aaron are going to Hal and Tracey's horse ranch because they're in that area right now. Chase and Shannon Buchanan want Kira and Fisher to go out to their house at the cabin and lodge resort. Demetria and Everett will have lunch at Dan and Addie's place."

"What about Royce?" Fisher asked.

"Normally, we would feed the prisoner what they wanted, but since he has been so uncooperative, he'll get standard prisoner food," Dan said.

"Good," Fisher said.

Then Dan gave Kira and Fisher directions to Chase and Shannon's place.

"We'll see you both in a bit," Demetria said to them.

"See you," Kira said, then she and Fisher got into her vehicle, and they headed out to the Buchanan's resort.

"What do you think of the case?" Fisher asked.

"Either the other two men left the area to get as far away as possible from all of us who are searching for them, or they're still in the area, trying to find Royce," Kira said. "It probably depends on whether they're loyal to him, or they're afraid he isn't trustworthy and will tell us everything about the kidnappings."

They finally reached a beautiful two-story, log ranch-style house and eight cabins situated in the woods situated on a pristine lake. Also a lodge that appeared to have five units upstairs and down, based on the location of the windows, was near the home.

They parked the car in front of the house that had a big deck out front. They knocked on the front door. A beautiful, dark-haired woman answered the door, wearing a pumpkin sweater and orange jeans, all smiles. "Hi, I'm Shannon, and you must be Kira and Fisher, our wolf guests."

"Yes, thanks so much for having us over for lunch," Kira said.

"Yeah. We really love Yuma Town. Everyone's so friendly," Fisher said.

"We love being here and enjoy the company of other shifters coming through the area, as long as they're the good guys." Shannon ushered them inside and closed the door.

Two little girls came out to see the guests. They were adorable, wearing pigtails and were dressed in orange jeans and pumpkin sweaters, matching their momma. They hugged their mother, ducking behind her a little. "This is Sadie and Zoey." Shannon patted their heads. A black Newfoundland bounded in, and she said, "That's Muddy. And the two ginger and white cats sitting in the window are Sassy, she has more gold fur, and Shadow. So you've met the rest of the family. Chase will be here in a—"

They heard a car pull up.

"Now," Shannon said.

15

S hannon had made ravioli for lunch and while she was serving it, Chase was making garlic toast. The girls set the table and Kira and Fisher placed glasses of water out for everyone.

"So," Chase said, "we couldn't find anything out our way while we were searching for the kidnappers."

"I sure wish we had all of them in custody," Kira said.

"We've alerted everyone in the area to be on the lookout for the men and to keep a close eye on everyone's kids and vehicles to make sure they don't grab someone's vehicle either," Chase said.

"You sound like us as far as our pack alert system goes," Fisher said.

"Yeah, we have emergency call lists," Shannon said.

They all took seats at the table. Then Kira got a call. "It's my boss." She answered the call. "Hello, Martin. Fisher and I are having lunch with Deputy Chase Buchanan and his lovely family."

"I'm glad that the townspeople have all been so instrumental in helping you with this case. Everett called me and said that Royce wasn't forthcoming on information about the other men."

"Did Everett tell you that a CSF special agent, Bridget, can read minds? She has listened in on the conversations and told us when he's not telling the truth," Kira said.

"We need her to work for us," Martin said.

"Yes. We suggested it but her mate also works for CSF and they're not giving her up."

Martin chuckled. "I don't blame them. I talked to Everett about bringing Royce to Houston. If his cousin and his friend think they can free him, they won't be able to while he's incarcerated down here."

"Who's going with him?"

"Demetria and Everett. You're still on the case to locate the other two men. As long as Fisher and his brothers and cousins can help out, you'll be in good hands."

"Alright. I agree. Unless we use Royce as bait to try and get one or both the men to come for him, then I think he should stay here, and we'll try to capture the other guys," Kira said.

Martin didn't say anything for a moment. "But it could cause problems for the townspeople."

"Who are all cougars. So they are not exactly just plain human citizens and they're all for helping us with the case. It impacts on them also."

"Okay, we'll try it for two days. If the kidnappers don't show up, Demetria and Everett will take him to the confinement facility in Houston," Martin said.

"Yes, sir."

"How's Fisher doing?"

She smiled at Fisher. "He's doing great."

"I knew he would be. Enjoy your lunch and we'll talk later."

"Thanks, Martin." Then they ended the call, and she began to eat some of her ravioli. "This is delicious, Shannon."

"It's made with special spices. Even the kids love it," Shannon said.

"Well, it's great," Kira said.

"I agree," Fisher said.

"I made a chocolate cake also, but you kids need to eat your ravioli first," Shannon said to her girls.

"So what is the plan now?" Chase asked, then bit into his garlic toast.

"We'll keep Royce at the jailhouse for a couple of days, waiting to see if the other men will come to get him. If they don't, then Demetria and Everett will deliver him to the jaguar confinement facility in the Houston area," Kira said.

"Okay, that works for me." Chase got on the phone and called Dan. "We're going to keep Royce for a couple of days and use him as bait." He chuckled. "Yep. Maybe we'll get lucky."

"Bait like fishing bait, daddy?" Zoey asked.

"To catch big, bad fish, right," Chase said.

Muddy suddenly started barking, and they wondered if he heard someone coming to the front door. Though Kira hadn't heard anything, and her hearing was better than a dog's.

Chase hurried to check it out. Fisher went with him, just in case he needed backup. But there was no one at the door.

"Maybe it was just a case of the wind blowing something out here."

"The windchimes or something else alerted them that had nothing to do with any people?" Fisher asked.

"Yeah, it could be. I don't smell any scents except for ours." Then Chase and Fisher went back to the dining room to eat the rest of their lunch.

"Nothing?" Shannon asked.

"Nah, just the wind or something," Chase said. "You know how the dog is. One little sound and he's all jumpy."

"That's for sure," Shannon said. "We can bump the table with our knee and send him into a barking fit. Though sometimes it's a bear smelling our good home cooking."

"A real bear?" Kira asked. "We were told you have bear shifters around here."

"Yeah, the bear shifters don't live here permanently, but sometimes they come through. But we do get real bears, wolves, and cougars too."

Then they heard a car drive up and Shannon rolled her eyes. "That's Carl Nelson's car. Hal's mom and dad run the newspaper and he's one of their reporters. You know Deputy Sheriff Ricky Jones? He and his brother Kolby bit Carl—long story. So he's one of us now. But he's always looking for a story. Knowing him, he went to Dan already and he said no to giving him the scoop about the kidnapper since he's a wolf."

"So what do we do?" Kira asked. "If it's just in the local paper... but then I guess if someone picked it up and ran with it, the FBI would be here."

"Exactly," Chase said.

Kira realized Muddy didn't bark this time, she guessed because they knew who he was.

Chase got up from the table again and went to greet Carl.

"If he wants a story, he has uncanny timing, always showing up when we're eating," Shannon said. "Does anyone want any more ravioli or garlic toast?"

"Cake," the girls both said.

"Okay, you ate all your food." Shannon cleared their dishes away. She cut a couple of slices of chocolate cake for them.

"Hey, I hope I'm not interrupting anything." Carl smelled at the air and smiled. "Ravioli."

"Have you eaten?" Chase asked, bringing Carl into the dining room.

"I haven't, but I don't want to bother you none," Carl said, eyeing Kira and Fisher. "I heard that some wolves and a couple of jaguars arrived in Yuma Town. I also heard that it was about three wolves who are kidnappers."

The word had to have gotten around because Dan had told everyone to be on the lookout for the three men and their SUV.

"Would you like some lunch?" Shannon asked Carl.

"Yeah, thanks. You make the best ravioli."

"You say that about all my meals." Smiling, Shannon returned to the kitchen.

"So what's going on with these guys?" Carl asked, sitting next to Kira.

"Did you ask Dan?" Chase asked.

"Yeah, but you know he's always closed mouth about these cases, except that everyone is supposed to report if they see the men or their vehicle," Carl said.

Shannon set a plate full of ravioli and a slice of garlic toast at Carl's place setting.

"Thanks, Shannon." Carl turned to Kira. "You're in charge of the investigation." He said it in a way that meant it was up to her, not Dan, as to what she wanted to reveal, if anything, about the mission. But they were in cougar country and Dan knew more about Carl than she did so it was his call.

"I am, but I'll have to defer to Dan on the topic," Kira said.

Carl smiled. "What about you?" He raised his fork to point it at Fisher.

"I'm just here to help the USF special agents in any way that I can," Fisher said.

"Yeah, but from what I learned, one of the kidnappers shot you. Was it the one who is in jail?" Carl asked.

"Is that why Ricky and Kolby bit you?" Fisher drank some of his water. "Because you asked too many questions?"

Carl smiled and lifted his garlic toast off his plate. "It was just all a big misunderstanding. How was I to know that they were cougar shifters and not real cougars?" Carl took a bite out of his toast and then ate some more of his ravioli.

"So how does this work for you now that you're a cougar too?

Do you report on fun happenings? But stay away from anything that might lead human law enforcement here?" Kira finished her meal.

The girls finished their cake and were dismissed to watch animated features in the den. The dog ran off to join the girls.

"Yeah, sure. Social events, births, deaths, weddings, awards, and commendations—the usual stuff. But I also report on any human trouble we have here. Like a couple of cars filled with humans racing down our highway, who eventually wrecked with each other, or human hunters targeting animals on our land. I say ours because the land is for all the cougars in Yuma Town. When it comes to shifter news—I mean in the real sense of the word—I have to be careful. Now, if a human tried to kidnap a cougar, that's frontline news because they are turned over to the human police, based on that and any other crimes he or she has committed.

"One of the worst cases we had was a human woman who tried to steal one of three triplets from the clinic after a cougar shifter passing through here had birthed them. It was a brazen act on the kidnapper's part, but she didn't stand a chance to even grab one. Not when she smelled like a human and Dan, Chase, and Stryker were called in to arrest her. She swore up and down that one of the babies was hers and that the mother had stolen the one from her," Carl said. "Of course, Dr. Kate had delivered them so she knew differently. Not to mention the woman was human and the babies were all cougars, in their human form at the time."

"Oh, wow," Kira said. "How did the woman even know about the triplets being born?"

"She was at Mrs. Fitz's shop when the lady went into labor there and then the would-be baby-napper followed the ambulance to the clinic. The woman hung around the waiting room since there was such a hustle and bustle of nurses and both doctors working together with the cougar mother in delivery. No one even noticed the baby-napper until she came down the hall, looking for the babies. That's when a nurse asked what she was doing in the clinic —because she was human and didn't belong—though she didn't tell her that. If someone has an emergency, they'll take care of a human, then send them to another city, usually Colorado City, to take care of the patient."

Kira couldn't imagine anything more horrible than one of the mother's babies going missing just after she'd had them. And what a shock it would be to the kidnapper when she discovered the baby was a cougar, not totally human.

"Anyway, FBI agents were following her case, looking for her after she had tried the same thing at three other clinics in Colorado. She'd told her husband she was having his child, and that was the only reason he was staying with her. She'd never been pregnant. Dan and Chase arrested her and then turned her over to the FBI. She went to prison, and her husband divorced her," Carl said.

"That's good," Kira said.

"Right. So those kinds of stories I'm able to report on. The cougar mother and her triplets went back to Denver where her husband was working and she was reunited with him," Carl said.

"So what's *your* story?" Fisher asked Carl.

"I'm an investigative reporter. I've dug up dirt on cases where no one wants to go. Of course, once I became a cougar, my focus had to change because the cougars work together to take care of each other. We don't have crime and corruption among the cougar residents of Yuma Town. Which was a real shock to me in the beginning. I was used to every town, big and small, having dirty little secrets. Like one small town where they had high stakes gambling, and the Mafia was involved. You would never believe it because they operated out of a shoddy, no-name, square, concrete-block building. They brought diamonds in, drugs, money. It was a real snake pit."

"Did you uncover it?"

"Are you kidding? Government corruption is more my style. And murder cases. When you get into dealings with the Mafia, you go missing, end of story. I'm all for getting to the nitty gritty of a situation, but not with the Mafia. In another case that I was investigating, this guy stole all kinds of money from investors—"

"Boy, that happens a lot," Kira said.

"Yep. But he also had murdered his wife and told investigators that she flew away to somewhere else to get away from it all. They could never prove it, but when the Securities and Exchange Commission went after him, he committed suicide. So he might have gotten off with murdering his wife, but miffed investors—who had lost lots of money while investing in his scam—finally got him. They were offered so much money as a return on their investments. They should have realized it was a shady deal. Lawyers, judges, doctors, anyone who had money were in on it."

"And you reported on it," Fisher said.

"I sure did. His son and daughter knew he'd murdered his wife. He had a mistress, even though he was still married. He just didn't want to have to give up half his money and estates to his wife if he had divorced her," Carl said.

"The woman he was with didn't know the risk she was taking by staying with a murderer." Shannon began clearing away dishes and Kira helped her.

"So true. I reported on a case where a husband had killed three of his wives before the police got wise to what he was doing." Carl glanced at Chase. "No offense. If you were in charge of the investigation, you would have checked into his background and realized three accidental deaths were a bit much, especially when they had huge insurance payouts. And two of the deaths were identical—falls in bathtubs and subsequent accidental drownings. He figured he got away with it that many times, he might as well keep going with the same scheme. Easy money and lots of it. Most of the criminals like him believe they are smarter than everyone else."

"Exactly," Chase said.

Kira came back with slices of cake for Chase and Fisher. Carl was still eating his lunch. Then she went back to the kitchen to get some cake for herself and for Shannon. Shannon was making a pot of coffee and brewing tea for whoever wanted it.

Then Carl finished his toast and ravioli and took his plates into the kitchen. "Is this slice of cake for me?"

"Yep," Kira said, having cut him a piece in case he wanted some. She figured he would.

Then Shannon brought in coffee for Chase and Carl. Kira, Shannon, and Fisher had tea. Carl brought in his cake and sat back down at the table.

"Have you ever reported on something because everyone was saying the same thing, like for instance, a spouse had murdered his wife, and it turned out the neighbor did it, but the spouse has to live with the accusation for the rest of his life?" Fisher asked.

"No. I want the truth. That's why I'm considered an investigative reporter. I don't repeat something that half of the town, and sometimes even the prosecutor's office, is saying. It's easy to get caught up in the sensationalism of a case, but if you have it wrong?" Carl shook his head. "I don't want to be issuing a statement of apology for getting it wrong. By then? The damage is already done."

"I agree." Kira had a lot more respect for the news reporter then. Her phone jingled and she pulled it out to see that the call was from her boss again. "Yes, sir?"

"Tell Fisher that he is officially a special agent working with us with full pay and benefits now. He'll still have to go through rigorous training with us in Houston once he has fully recovered from his injuries," Martin said.

She smiled broadly at Fisher. "He will be thrilled to learn of it. Would you like to speak to him?"

"Yeah. I tried to call him on his phone, but it's going to voicemail."

"Okay. Martin wants to talk to you, Fisher." She handed the phone to him, beaming.

16

Fisher took the phone from Kira and hoped that Martin truly had good news for him. "I'll speak with you outside, sir. We have a cougar reporter at the house."

"I wouldn't whisper a word about anything you wouldn't want the world to know about." Carl licked his fork clean.

Still, Fisher didn't want to speak in front of Carl in case it was for his ears only. Feeling like he was walking on air, Fisher went out on the back deck and looked at the beauty of Lake Buchanan. Trees wearing coats of yellow, red, green, and purple reflected in the water that rippled with the breeze while white clouds floated across the blue sky.

"Yes, sir?"

"Your phone is off." Martin sounded annoyed with him.

Here Fisher thought from the way Kira had been smiling at him that Martin had good news for him.

"Sorry, sir." He fished his phone out of his pocket and switched it on. "We were listening to the kidnapper being interrogated and I didn't want it to ring in the viewing room. I completely forgot to turn it back on." Talk about making a big mistake.

"Do you want to work for us?"

"Hell, yeah." Fisher did a little dance on the back deck, then looked back at the windows to make sure no one was watching him. Both the twin girls were. He smiled and waved at them. They giggled and ran off, their dog chasing after them.

"Okay, I'll send the paperwork to you, and you need to fill it out and send it back to me. You go on the payroll today. You still have to go through our rigorous training program and if you don't pass it, you're out."

"Yes, sir."

"You and Kira keep each other safe," Martin said.

"Absolutely, sir."

"Turn your phone's ringer on."

"Already done, sir."

"I'll see you when you come to Houston."

"Thank you, sir, for this opportunity to serve our kind."

"You'll earn it. Talk later."

Then they ended the call and Fisher glanced back at the windows, but the girls hadn't returned. He walked into the house and handed Kira's phone to her. And smiled. "So maybe we can team up together on more missions."

Kira quickly rose from her seat and gave him a warm embrace. "I sure hope so. We'll have to celebrate the good news. Oh, but what about your pack leaders?"

"They put in a good word for me too. They will be happy for me. But I do need to tell them and my brothers and the rest of my cousins that I got the job."

Carl sighed. "Nothing noteworthy to report on."

They all laughed.

"I'm going to call the family. Be right back." Then Fisher went back out on the deck and began to call his pack leaders first. "Hey, Bella, I got the job."

"With the USF? Oh, wow! Devlyn, Fisher got the job."

"With the USF?" Devlyn asked, coming to the phone. "Hey, Cuz, great news."

"Yeah, I still have to go through the training, but Martin said I'm hired."

"Well, that's certainly good news. Oh, I need to tell you that Aaron is returning home. He has to take care of the horse ranch. He thought capturing these guys wouldn't take too long, but things have come up at the ranch and he needs to return home."

"That's certainly understandable. I've got to call Heath and then get hold of the others to let them know I'm working for the USF. They're at a cougar's horse ranch for lunch."

"Are you any closer to finding the other kidnappers?"

"Not yet, but we're hoping maybe they'll come for the one guy's cousin and then we'll nab them," Fisher said.

"I hope that works out for you. And congratulations," Devlyn said.

"Yes, congratulations," Bella said.

Then Fisher thanked them and called Heath, who immediately worried that he was calling because of a health issue. "No, I'm fine. I ended up getting the job with the USF."

"I heard you were swimming and running as a wolf."

Always the doctor. "Yeah. It was a little too soon for that."

"Are you sure you're okay?"

"Yeah. I am."

"Well, hell, I can't believe you decided to join the USF, but I guess you have a pretty great incentive."

Fisher smiled. "Yeah." He sure did.

"Congratulations. I'm so happy for you, but we'll miss you."

"I'll be living in Greystoke still."

"Oh, well, that's damn good news. What about Thanksgiving?" Heath asked.

"I guess it depends if I'm still on this case. Then I might not have time to come home for it. Or I could possibly be seeing Kira's parents."

"Sure. Well, if you and Kira aren't busy with the case or seeing her family, we would all love to have you join us. If you forgot, it's next week."

"Okay, sure." He hadn't even realized it was getting that close to Thanksgiving.

"I understand your new doctor, Kate, told you no running as a wolf or swimming for a week or so. I want to reiterate that medical advice. I didn't realize I needed to tell you that beforehand."

Fisher smiled. He loved his brother. Then they said goodbye and he called his other brothers and his cousin Brock. "Hey, Tanner, you can put this call on speakerphone. I know we take turns running the leather goods factory, but the USF just hired me."

Tanner laughed. "Here I thought you were just trying to get to know Kira better. Now I know the truth. You just wanted to do something else with your life other than helping out with the factory."

"That means it's just you and me," Shawn said to Tanner.

"Yep. I can't believe our brother is actually abandoning us," Tanner said.

"Sure you did. That's why all of us put in recommendations with USF to hire him," Brock said.

"You guys are the greatest," Fisher said.

"I hope you get to come and visit us for Thanksgiving, or Christmas," Tanner said.

"Or both," Shawn said.

"We'll see how this case goes." Then they all congratulated Fisher, and he called Aaron to tell him the news. Aaron was thrilled to hear the news, but he was disappointed that he couldn't have stayed longer to help catch the other kidnappers.

Fisher called Vaughn and Jillian after that, hoping he wasn't interrupting their mission. "Here I was trying to talk Brock into joining us when I should have been talking to you," Vaughn said.

"We can't wait to work on a case with you," Jillian said. "Vaughn is always telling me how organized you are and very analytical. Welcome to the team."

"That means a lot to me," Fisher said, pleased to no end to be working with Kira and them.

Then they finally ended the call and Fisher called Demetria and Everett to give them the news. He realized they would be just as eager to hear about it. They were thrilled.

"Okay, now you just need to go through your training so we can put you through your paces," Demetria said, laughing.

He laughed.

Everett agreed and welcomed him as a new member of the team.

After ending the call, Fisher returned to the dining room. Carl had left and Chase was about to head out. "I've got some deputy sheriff duties to do. Congratulations," Chase said.

"Thanks, I'm thrilled and everyone else is too."

Chase left the house. Kira was helping Shannon clean up the kitchen after lunch. Fisher stepped in to assist.

"So what are we going to do now?" Fisher asked.

"We ought to talk to Royce further. I still want to know how he was turned. Was it recently? I hope it doesn't mean we have a rogue wolf turning people too."

"Yeah, let's do that."

They thanked Shannon for a lovely meal, then said goodbye and headed for the jailhouse. "We need to call Bridget too so she can listen in and let us know if he's telling the truth or not," Kira said.

"Good call."

Kira got a hold of Dan since she didn't have Bridget's number, "Hey, Dan, Fisher and I are going to see Royce and speak with him about being turned, if he was or not. Can Bridget drop by and see if he is telling us the truth?"

"Yes, I'll call her right away. Deputy Sheriff Ricky Jones is on duty there right now."

"Okay, we're on our way."

When they arrived, Ricky greeted them. "We're going to get the truth out of him this time. Bridget is on her way here."

Before they could proceed, Kira got a call from Leyton. "Did you find anything out from the relatives in Denver that could help the case?" She put the call on speakerphone.

"The Farmington's relatives are all human."

Which meant someone had turned both Royce and Oscar more recently. "Are they worried about where the two cousins have gotten off to?" Kira asked.

"They told their family that they were going up to Alaska to hunt and fish. They didn't know when they would return home. Royce still lived at home. Oscar had an apartment, but he gave notice and vacated it. The family is upset with them because both quit their decent jobs to just run off and have fun," Leyton said.

"Because they're wolves and they can't hold their shape during the full moon, betcha," Fisher said.

"Yeah, that's what we suspect," Leyton said.

"And couldn't hold down their jobs either," Fisher added. "Which is maybe why they took up kidnapping as a way to make an income."

"I agree. What about Reggie? Were you able to speak to any of his relatives, if he has any, up there?" Kira asked Leyton.

"His family is human also. His house is up for sale by a realtor. No one is living there right now," Leyton said. "We suspect he knew he would have to sell out—if he's newly turned also. Which makes us wonder if someone else did this to the three men."

"Possibly, or maybe Reggie bit the cousins. But if someone actually turned the men and left them to fend for themselves, then he's a rogue every bit as much as they are for kidnapping kids. Then we'll have to go after him or her also," Kira said.

"It sounds like they've been on the run all this time then," Fisher said, "if they've told their family they're off to Alaska and not returning to Denver. I wonder though if they really are planning on moving to Alaska. They would be able to run as wolves more freely up there."

"That could be," Leyton said.

"Did they mention anything that had happened that they believe might have made them uproot their lives like that?" Kira asked.

"Jack asked that of the Farmington families. The only thing they said was that Reggie, who is Oscar's good friend, and Oscar's younger cousin Royce, who seemed to always tag along with his cousin, had all gone to a bar the night before everything changed. The families were afraid something might have happened at the bar because a few days after that, they started making plans to move to Alaska. Maybe it was coincidence. Maybe they had discussed it at the bar and decided to do something new with their lives," Leyton said.

"Or maybe somebody had bitten them around the full moon phase and the men turned into wolves and knew they needed to get out of Denver," Fisher said.

"Right. Travis asked Reggie's parents what they thought about the sudden change of plans. They are friends of the Farmingtons and believed something similarly. That something happened that night at the bar. They wanted to just say it was because they were drinking and came up with this wild plan. But it was something more than that. They were avoiding seeing any of their families as if they were ashamed of something they had done when they normally weren't like that. After we go to that bar tonight and talk about any issue that might have occurred for that timeframe, we will have done all we can here. I don't believe the families are hiding anything about the whereabouts of their kin," Leyton said. "They're in the dark about all the rest of this stuff."

"Did they wonder what all this is about? Your questioning them?" Fisher asked.

"We told them that they were persons of interest in a case," Leyton said. "The families didn't seem happy about that prospect. They might have assumed something more was going on with the three men than they had let on. But they also cast glances in each other's direction, and we figure they had suspected something was wrong. In a case like this where their families are human, we really can't tell them what had happened to them. And they have too many family members to turn them. After the visit to the bar tonight to see if we can learn anything else, we're heading back to Yuma Town for the holidays and to help you with your case if you need anything further. Our boss said your case has priority for now."

"Okay, thanks, Leyton." Kira was glad they had learned something about the men at least through family members.

"I'll call you if we learn anything more," Leyton said.

Then they ended the call.

"Well, at least we know they were turned—not that they have just a few generations of wolf roots. So now let's ask Royce who turned them," Fisher said.

"That was just what I was thinking," Kira said. "We need to call Larry in case Royce feels he needs to have his lawyer present."

"I'll call him." Ricky got on his phone. "Hey, we're going to interrogate Royce about his wolf roots. All three men have families that are human, so they were turned about six months ago, when all the kidnappings began taking place. Alright, see you in a few."

"Will he really be here in a few minutes?" Kira asked.

"Yes, if we ask him to be here," Ricky said.

Then Bridget arrived and Ricky went back to get Royce so he could be interrogated again.

"Haven't you people already questioned me enough?" Royce asked. "And you said you got my cousin. Where is he?"

Ricky glanced at Kira.

"We can't reveal that information. We want to question you about when you were bitten and by whom," Kira said. "We shouldn't need a lawyer for that, though Mr. Pierce said he would be right over."

"Like the last time?" Royce sounded annoyed that his lawyer had taken so long to show up the first time here.

Ricky took Royce into the interrogation room. "Do you want me to stay with you?"

"No. I don't think he does anything bad but kidnap little boys. I'm really not his type." Kira patted Fisher's hand. "And I have an Army Ranger wolf to keep me safe."

Bridget went into the interrogation room with them, and she stood behind Royce against the wall. Like before, she would indicate to Kira whether or not he was telling the truth.

Shortly after that, Larry joined them in the interrogation room. "Okay, so you really don't need me here if all we're going to talk about is how and when you were turned and by whom. Unless you feel the need to have me here for you."

"Yeah, you can stay. I don't know why you have so much interest in my being turned though," Royce said to Kira.

Larry sat down next to Royce.

Ricky was probably in the viewing room.

"If a wolf turned you and your other kidnapper friends and left you to cope on your own, he would be in trouble himself," Kira said. "That's why we need to know which wolf turned you."

"I don't know."

"You were at a bar in Denver—" Fisher said.

"How did you know about that?" Royce ran his hands through his hair. "How were *you* turned?"

"Generations ago. We were all born as wolf shifters," Fisher said.

Royce's eyes grew big.

"We don't have the issue of shifting during the full moon phase like newly turned wolves do. The one who turned you should have had a good reason for doing so. Like he was protecting himself from you and bit you in self-defense." Kira straightened on her chair. "Or you caught him shifting and he had to make you one of us or kill you."

Royce's jaw dropped. "You're kidding."

"No," Kira said.

"We didn't see her shifting," Royce said.

"Her?" Kira asked.

"Yeah, she was at the bar."

"Alone?" Fisher asked.

"Uh, I don't know. Maybe she was with others." Royce shrugged.

"Okay, so if she was at the bar when you were, she wouldn't have been shifting into her wolf to bite you. The three of you were there? You, your cousin, and Reggie?" Fisher asked.

"Yes."

"So how did it happen?" Kira asked.

"She was a beautiful blond, and she had the most entrancing blue eyes. Reggie wanted to talk to her and of course we went with him. She wasn't interested in him, or us. Probably because we'd had too much to drink."

"You badgered her," Kira guessed. "She would have been dressed. To shift and bite you, she would have had to have removed her clothes."

Royce ground his teeth.

"Tell the truth. You know we can smell deception on you," Kira said. Though Bridget was the key to learning the truth beyond a reasonable doubt.

Royce began tapping his foot on the floor under the table. And he sat back away from the table as if wanting to distance himself from the discussion.

"You pushed yourselves on the she-wolf and she had no other choice but to protect herself." Just like Kira had to do when she was young when the kidnapper grabbed her. At least that's what she suspected had happened to the she-wolf.

"Reggie tore her dress," Bridget said. "The she-wolf was both angered and afraid."

Royce swung around to look at her. "You don't know that."

"I can guess that's why she was out of her clothes so quickly. The next step was for her to shift," Bridget said. "If she was mostly undressed, she would have been able to shift more easily."

"When you saw her shift—" Kira said.

"I didn't! I mean, after we started shifting, we realized that all we had time for was to blink our eyes and the person was a dog. Besides, I was a little inebriated. All of us were. All I remember is that a vicious dog was suddenly standing there, growling. Reggie brandished a knife and I thought he was going to protect us."

"You were going to kill a dog?" Fisher asked.

"No. I mean, Reggie was just protecting us. He ran at the dog, but she was backed in a corner. She couldn't get out of the situation without reacting. She bit him on the arm, and he cried out and dropped the knife. My cousin grabbed the knife to keep the wild dog away from Reggie before she bit him again. The dog attacked him next, and bit him on the wrist, but he cut her, and she yelped."

Kira shook her head. These guys needed to be incarcerated.

"What? She was vicious."

"How did you get bitten?" Kira asked.

Royce rubbed the back of his neck, looking down at the table. "Oscar turned me. The dog leapt at Oscar and knocked him down on the pavement, knocking him out. Reggie ran for the car, leaving us behind. I shook Oscar, trying to get him to wake up and then he came to, and the dog took off. I got Oscar into the car and Reggie drove to the clinic. At the clinic, we had to wait for a couple of hours, and then Oscar and Reggie had stitches and we left. Once we were in Reggie's SUV, he suddenly said, 'I'm burning up.' I asked if he thought he had an infection, but I figured that was too soon for it to appear. But he was frantic and yanked the vehicle off the road and parked. Then, I thought maybe it was because he was drunk. He began to yank off his clothes. Which was too bizarre to consider."

Kira didn't believe so, knowing just the reason for Reggie's frantic actions that night.

17

W hile still questioning Royce at the Yuma Town sheriff's office, Fisher could understand why a she-wolf—who had been alone and threatened by three drunk men—had to react in any way that she could to save herself. He reached over and took hold of Kira's hand on her lap and squeezed, hoping that she wasn't feeling bad about her own experience as a child.

She smiled at him and squeezed his hand in response.

He wondered what had happened to the she-wolf who had bitten the kidnappers. Was she a lone wolf? Maybe that's why she hadn't done anything about the men she had turned. He could see why she would have had difficulty dealing with them further if she didn't have a pack to back her up. Though they still couldn't allow the men to be on the loose. They had to resolve the situation.

"Reggie yanked off his clothes and then?" Fisher asked Royce.

"I thought maybe the dog that had bitten my cousin and Reggie was rabid. But Reggie wasn't foaming at the mouth. Then he turned into a dog. Or a wolf, we later realized. So that gave us a whole different perspective on the situation. I was in the front passenger seat when all this was happening. I jerked off my seatbelt and grabbed the door handle. But the door was locked. Then I heard a low growl coming from the backseat. My heart was beating so hard that I felt it was going to jump right out of my chest and I was sweating up a storm. I glanced at the back seat. I couldn't believe what I was seeing. Oscar's clothes were on the back seat, a dog was sitting on top of them, and Oscar was gone. The only explanation was that he was now the dog, just like what had happened to Reggie."

"Then Oscar bit you?" Kira asked.

"He was still growling at me. I mean, I was drunk so I wondered if I might be hallucinating. Maybe someone had even slipped something into my drink at the bar. I was in a panic to leave the vehicle, hallucinations or not. Then the dog in the backseat climbed over the console and bit my arm as if to tell me to stay in the vehicle. I cried out. Hell, that hurt, and he broke the skin. I was bleeding and I was angry and terrified. I fumbled with the door again, but I swear my brain was all mush. I did have the thought that we couldn't return to the same clinic so that I could get patched up this time. I mean, how could I explain that this time I was bitten by a new dog if the same medical staff that saw to Reggie and Oscar took care of my bite? But then it began healing on its own."

"When did you figure out that you were wolves?" Fisher asked.

"About an hour later, I felt the change and I had to take off my clothes and turn into a wolf. I kept thinking that we couldn't turn into dogs. Then I thought of werewolves and that we really were bigger, like the one who had bitten my cousin and Reggie. I couldn't see what I looked like, except my legs and feet, and my bushy tail. Then Oscar howled. Reggie joined him. It took me a minute before I was willing to give it a try. I howled and realized how easy it was. It made me think about every werewolf movie I had ever seen. That's when I saw the full moon on the clear black night. Once Reggie was able to turn back into a human, he dressed and drove us to his home. At least he was pretty much sober by then. I was sitting there as a wolf and couldn't change back. My cousin was human again and was stretched out on the back seat, naked, snoring loudly."

"Then you realized you couldn't deal with the issue of being wolf shifters," Kira said. "And left Denver."

"Hell, we couldn't control the shifting. One minute, we were eating breakfast at Reggie's house, and the next, he was shifting, growling, mad over his loss of control. But also what was worrisome was we thought someone had been prowling around the outside of his house."

"The she-wolf?" Fisher asked, thinking she had some unfinished business and maybe she had planned to do something about the men after all.

"Yeah. I mean, we didn't believe one female wolf could take on all three of us, but we knew we couldn't go back to our jobs or even see our families. We finally left the area because we knew we couldn't be around our families when we couldn't control the shifting. We thought it would only happen during the full moon, but it happens any time except during the new moon. We never paid any attention to the moon phases until this happened. We can only plan to do any work when it's the time of the new moon now."

"Well, truthfully, I'm sorry this happened to you and that no one was there to teach you how to be one of us," Fisher said.

Kira glanced at Fisher, her jaw dropping.

"That said, the reason you are wolves was because you threatened the she-wolf, and she had no other recourse but to protect herself. But if she was trying to undo her mistake, that was also the only way she could take care of the mess that *you* had forced on her." Fisher could tell Kira finally got the point that he wasn't excusing the men one bit. If they hadn't cornered the she-wolf, none of this would have happened.

"Who had the stupid idea of kidnapping kids to get easy payouts as your new choice of job?" Kira asked.

"Reggie. Oscar is his best friend, and he always goes along with Reggie's schemes. The plan was to gather enough money and then we would go to Alaska and figure out something from there," Royce said.

"You never thought of the kids you traumatized? Their families?" Fisher knew the truth of it. At least with Reggie and Oscar, they hadn't given a damn. But he thought Royce had more empathy for the kids they'd kidnapped, at least for Billy as far as Fisher had witnessed. "Or that one of the kids, like Billy, whom you had left in the woods by himself, might not have even survived?"

Royce put his elbows on the table and held his forehead. "I didn't want to leave Billy in the woods. We always took the kids to somewhere safe like the library or a clinic, hotel, or a church even once. Leaving him in the woods hadn't been a safe bet. It was supposed to be our last job and Reggie was getting nervous about getting caught."

"So he planned to just leave Billy out in the wild." Fisher shook his head. "If we hadn't been there to protect him, he could have died."

Royce rubbed his face. "I didn't want to do it."

"But you didn't stop it either," Fisher said.

Kira let out her breath. "Do you think your cousin and Reggie will try to come here and rescue you?"

"They would be making a mistake in trying to—especially since you are all shifters too. I'm sure they don't know anything about how you're born shifters though and you would have the upper hand on how to deal with them," Royce said.

"You better believe it," Fisher said.

"I don't believe they will. I'm not sure they realized I've been arrested, for one thing," Royce said.

Ricky suddenly opened the door to the interrogation room. "Can I speak with you, Kira, Fisher, Bridget?"

"Yeah, sure," Fisher said.

They left the interrogation room while Royce and the lawyer remained behind.

"What's up?" Fisher asked Ricky.

"A guy came to see if Royce is here," Ricky said.

"Who did he say he was?" Fisher asked.

"Bertrand Johnstone. He's human. I asked him how he is related to Royce, and he said he's his brother-in-law."

"Does he know where Oscar or Reggie are?" Kira asked.

"No, he didn't."

"How did he know Royce is here?" Fisher asked.

"I suspect that Oscar or Reggie told him to see if Royce is here so they could maybe break him out."

"What did you tell him?" Kira asked.

"That I needed to let him speak to the people in charge," Ricky said and smiled.

"Okay, for anyone's information, if they ask, Royce isn't here," Kira said. "Let's go talk to Bertrand."

Then they went into the office and found Dan had returned to watch over things in case they suddenly had trouble. He inclined his head to the others in greeting.

Kira offered her hand to shake Bertrand's. "I'm Kira Westwood. This is my colleague, Fisher Greystoke. We don't have Royce Farmington here. What made you think he is?"

"My brother-in-law called me and said he believed Royce might have trespassed on private property and was arrested. Though I can't believe he would be in jail for just trespassing, unless he did something graver and Oscar didn't want to tell me about it," Bertrand said.

"Why wouldn't Oscar come himself to check to see if Royce was here?" Kira asked.

"I don't know where Oscar is. He just called me to ask me to bail out his cousin. He said he would pay me back," Bertrand said.

"So Royce is missing." Kira glanced at Bridget, so did Fisher, to see if Bertrand was telling the truth.

Bridget gave her an almost imperceptible nod.

Bertrand shook his head. "Hell. I don't know. I live in Colorado City so that's why I came. It is closer than Denver where our other relatives live."

"Maybe you could call Oscar and ask him why he believed Royce was in jail here," Fisher said.

Bertrand stuck his hands in his pockets. "I'll just tell Oscar that Royce wasn't here. I don't know why he thought Royce would be."

"Because Reggie and Oscar had been with Royce and the family knew that," Bridget said. "And because they were *all* trespassing on private property."

Bertrand frowned. "How do you know that if Royce isn't here?"

Whoops.

"They've done more than just trespass on private property," Kira said.

"What?"

"It's all under investigation," Fisher said. "It's nothing we can really discuss."

"Do you want to file a missing person's report for Royce?" Kira asked.

"You know what, the three of them have dropped the whole family and have lied to us about going to Alaska. If they're involved in criminal acts, that's on them. They're not involving us in any of this. We don't have any idea what they've been up to. I just want to make that clear," Bertrand said.

"Thanks. We appreciate you talking with us," Kira said.

Nobody had anything further to ask of him and so he shook everyone's hands and left the building.

"I feel bad for him," Bridget said. "From what I could read, his wife is Royce's older sister, and she just had a baby. So that's why Bertrand made the effort to see if her brother was here. When you were speaking to him, he immediately thought about Oscar saying that he, Reggie, and Royce had been trespassing on private property. Oscar didn't know for sure, but he thought Royce might have been picked up and was in the jail here because he wasn't answering his phone. Bertrand suspected that was the reason neither Oscar nor Reggie wanted to check with us because they were afraid that they would be incarcerated also for trespassing."

"Bertrand thought he could bail him out," Fisher said.

"Yeah, because the charge against Royce, Bertrand thought, couldn't have been that bad," Bridget said. "But when Kira said it was more than that, Bertrand realized he didn't want any part of what the three men had been up to."

"So do you think Oscar and Reggie are still in the area?" Kira asked.

"I do. I think once Bertrand had paid for Royce's release, they would have picked Royce up from Bertrand and then might have decided it *was* time to go to Alaska," Bridget said.

"Do you believe Oscar and Reggie will think we don't have Royce?" Dan asked.

"They couldn't find him. They would have smelled all our scents out there by the broken-down building," Kira said. "I would say that when Bertrand tells Oscar that we don't have Royce, he won't believe we're telling the truth. I believe we need to send Royce with Everett and Demetria to Houston. And then we'll go back to searching for the other two."

Then she got a call from Leyton and put it on speaker. "Hey, we learned at the bar that a woman who had left it had encountered trouble with three men. You could see them on the security video stalking her until she was at a point where no one could see anything," Leyton said.

"Which is good because she shifted into her wolf," Fisher said.

"Exactly. The woman's name is Judi Jacobson. We tracked her down and she gave us the whole story—how they accosted her, tore at her clothes. She'd only had one drink, but the three of them were drunk. She tossed the rest of her clothes, which suited the three men fine, figuring they were going to get some willing action. And they did. Except not the kind they were expecting. She wasn't from the area, didn't know any wolves, was at a hotel, and just wanted to go out for a drink. What a mistake that had been. She bit two of the men who had come at her with a knife. Once they were in their car, they drove off, but she got their license plate number, and eventually caught up to them at a clinic where *she* had to receive treatment for a knife wound also. She followed them to Reggie's house, she later learned. She knew she either had to take the two men under her wing and turn the other, or she had to kill them. Since they had tried to rape her, and then attempted to kill her, she knew her only real choice was to take them down— permanently."

"But she didn't kill them," Kira said.

"She was planning to, but she wanted to make sure no would ever discover who had done it. Then the men all left, and she didn't know where they had gone. So she prayed they wouldn't cause problems for our kind. She's a lone wolf, so she's used to having to take care of herself, though she knows better than to leave men like that turned and not do something about it. She just didn't have the resources to locate them," Leyton said. "She is grateful that we're on the case and she said if you wanted her to join you and eliminate these guys since it's her mistake, she would gladly do it."

"No. We'll handle it. She has been through enough already," Kira said.

Fisher was feeling the same way.

"Okay, we'll let her know that and then we're headed home."

Kira told him about the relative coming to try and bail Royce out. "So we feel the other two men are still in the area."

"We need to be there then if you need us."

Then Leyton and Kira ended the call and Kira called Everett.

"We're ready for you to take Royce to Houston." She told him about Bertrand. "We don't want any family members—human types—to learn he truly is here and want to know what the real charges are for. We just need to get him out of here before word gets back to the rest of the family in Denver and they want to know what's going on."

"We're on our way over. Demetria and I have been combing the area in search of Reggie's vehicle. We couldn't find any sign of it though. Tell Dan we'll be there in a few minutes to take the wolf off his hands."

"I will. Thanks, Everett." Then they finished the call and Kira said, "Everett and Demetria are coming to pick up Royce. Fisher and I are going to ride as backup for a while."

"My brothers and cousin can also, watching to see if anyone is coming for him," Fisher said.

"Some of our people will head out that way for an hour or two also," Dan said. "So if anyone tries to grab him, they'll pay for it."

"Great," Kira said. "I'm going to tell Royce the good news."

Fisher went with her, and they both walked into the interview room.

"That took you long enough," Royce said, sounding arrogant and highly annoyed.

"We're releasing you," Kira said.

Royce smiled and rose from the table. "I knew you couldn't hold me on those flimsy charges."

Frowning, Larry stood. "Seriously?" He appeared a little pale, like he was afraid he'd done or said the wrong thing and Royce was going to get away with his criminal pursuits.

"It's a good thing that I retained you as my lawyer after all." Royce slapped Larry on the back, thinking he had one over on them.

"You'll get a new one where you're going," Kira said.

"What?" This time Royce paled.

Then they heard newcomers at the sheriff's office and footfalls headed in their direction.

"USF Special Agents Demetria and Everett Anderson will be escorting you to your new facilities in Houston," Kira said.

Ricky came in and handcuffed Royce. "Bon Voyage."

Royce looked frantically at Larry as if the lawyer could change their mind. "What about my lawyer?"

"Oh, you'll have a new one appointed to you in Houston, most likely a highly experienced jaguar attorney," Demetria said, pulling Royce through the hall to the outer office.

"Several of us are following you," Kira said, "to help with an escort."

"We've called ahead. We have some other jaguars coming to meet up with us also," Everett said. "They're flying into Amarillo and then renting a vehicle and heading our way."

"Oh, great," Fisher said.

Royce glanced back at Larry. "You're supposed to be my lawyer. You can't let them take me from here. Don't they have to file paperwork to extradite me? And if it isn't approved, then I get to stay here?"

Larry smiled. "You are part of the world of shifters now. It's not the same as the laws of the strictly human world."

"We'll probably stay in Houston for Thanksgiving since it will be so close to the holiday, and then when that's over, we'll catch back up with you on the case," Demetria said.

"Okay, sure, thanks," Kira said.

Fisher figured they would have Thanksgiving with family too, unless they ended up getting more of a lead on where Royce's buddies were.

Then the groups who were headed out, left the station and started the long drive to Houston. It was a sixteen hour drive all the way there, so Fisher was glad they weren't going all that way.

18

"So now that you're a special agent with the USF also, I was thinking I need to move back to Colorado," Kira said, turning her car down another street, following Demetria and Everett's car as they started the drive to Houston with Royce in their custody.

"Oh?"

"Yeah. That's the great thing about this job. Martin said we can live anywhere in the States because we have assignments all over. He has established a group up around Ely, Minnesota. Vaughn and Jillian live with your wolf pack. We could have our own group there. Then it's not that far for me to go to see my family in Loveland," Kira said.

Fisher smiled. "I love that idea. Though I would have gone anywhere to be with you. Being with a pack that has your back is really important. And enjoying family get-togethers is too."

"Exactly."

"The town of Greystoke has national forests, lakes, rivers, lots of places to run as wolves and raise a family. I mean, it's a nice place to live," he said.

She smiled.

He'd gotten a little ahead of himself on that one. "And you're still only about two hours from your family in Loveland."

"True. I've been giving it a lot of thought. At first, I had moved to Houston because I believed it was important to be closer to the headquarters, but we do conference calls when we need to, I'm usually somewhere else on missions, and I just really don't need to live in that area."

"Well, Bella and Devlyn, and the rest of our pack would love it if you joined us. Me especially."

"My parents will be ecstatic also. They loved that I found a job that I really enjoy, but returning to Colorado and only being a couple of hours away from home? Yeah, they would be all for it."

"You let me know when you want to get packed up and move."

"I am renting a furnished apartment, making sure I was okay with the arrangements before I did anything that was more permanent in Houston. I only really need to give notice and pack my personal items and find a place to move to in Greystoke. I spend a lot of time with the jaguars in the organization, like Demetria and Everett, but there's something to be said about being with your own wolf kind, running as a wolf with a pack, howling for joy."

"I agree. As to where you'll stay—I hope you continue to live at my place."

"I'll take you up on it."

"I have to say seeing the jaguars running was amazing though."

"They're great for situations where we have a mix of shifters we need to apprehend. Fighting jaguars is a deadly proposition for us wolves. When you do the training, they could have you fighting jaguars, just to get a feel for it. They'll be careful not to injure you, but you'll realize just how powerful they are. We're more in a reserve role when we are tasked to take down a jaguar."

"I had never considered that."

"We've never had to fight snow leopards or bears, so I don't know how we would come out on top with either. Tigers, though

I've never heard of any shifters who are, could be a deadly advisory also." Then Kira frowned. "Demetria is pulling off the highway to get gas." She drove in behind Demetria and Everett at the pumps and she and Fisher got out.

Demetria said, "We realized we needed some gas. And we're going to have a bathroom break and get some snacks. We should be meeting up with the special agents from Houston in another hour."

"Does Royce need to use the restroom?" Fisher asked, getting gas for Kira's car.

"He said no, but if you don't mind taking him, we would appreciate it," Demetria said.

Everett was pumping the gas. "I'll go with you and make sure he doesn't give us any trouble."

"Yes," Kira said. "Everyone needs to make a pitstop when we're on a trip, at least try, my dad always said."

Then they saw Tanner and the others pull into another pump and Shawn started filling the car with gas.

"I'll be right out," Kira said, and headed into the service station.

Demetria joined her.

"So how are things going between you and Kira?" Everett asked Fisher.

"She's joining our pack."

"Alright!" Shawn said.

Fisher smiled at his cousin. He had every intention of being the one for Kira, not his cousin.

"Wow, she didn't tell us she was going to make that move. But we understand. She has felt homesick about not being able to visit her parents from time to time since she has been living so far away. And she misses being with wolves," Everett said.

"We'll make her feel right at home," Shawn said.

"Me especially," Fisher said, just in case his cousin didn't get that he was seeing the she-wolf, exclusively.

"So does that mean she'll spend Thanksgiving with the rest of the family?" Shawn asked.

"She might be going home to see her parents."

"Aww."

Tanner and Brock were smiling, shaking their heads, and then walked toward the convenience store.

Everett and Fisher took Royce with them to the men's room.

"You could at least remove the handcuffs. It's embarrassing to wear them into the convenience store," Royce complained, while patrons coming out of the restaurant caught sight of the cuffs and the men escorting him into the store.

"You're a prisoner because you've done some awful crimes, so get used to it," Everett said.

"Yeah, you've earned the right to wear the cuffs." Fisher got the door for them. He glanced around at the pizza shop and the mini market but didn't see Kira or Demetria. They might be in line, waiting on a stall in the women's restroom.

Then he and Everett took Royce into the men's room. Royce wanted to use one of the stalls.

When everyone was finished with their business, Royce gave them issues, spending forever in the stall before Everett threatened him with dragging him out bodily. They finally left the restroom and Fisher said, "I never thought I would be working with you and Demetria in the USF."

"I know. Vaughn tried so hard to get his brother to join, and then here you are. Though I suspect he would have had a hard time convincing you until you met the right agent in the USF," Everett said.

Fisher laughed. "You have that right. Though if I had gone on a mission with him, I might have felt differently and wanted to join right there and then."

"Well, we'll miss having Kira around, but we'll get together with you guys on missions."

"As long as they allow us to go on missions together in the future." Fisher remembered the business of her being new and he was too.

"If the two of you pull this off together, Martin will be assured that you can work together." Everett grabbed a couple of sodas. "What do you want, Royce?"

"A pizza."

"You can have a premade sandwich."

"But the pizza place is right here."

Everett gave him a steely-eyed glower. "You are a prisoner. You can have a premade sandwich."

Royce glowered back at him. "Fine." He walked over to the case that had sandwiches and pointed to a ham and cheese sandwich. "I want that one. And two bags of potato chips. And a Coke. And a large bag of chocolates. Those."

"Okay, one sandwich, one bag of chips, and a drink." Everett grabbed the items while Fisher kept Royce in line.

Then Fisher saw Demetria and his brothers and cousin. Everyone had sacks of food. But he didn't see Kira.

"Hey, I'll take care of him," Tanner said, handing his bag of snacks to Shawn.

Brock did the same and the two of them walked Royce back out to Everett and Demetria's car. But Shawn went out too.

"Where's Kira?" Fisher asked Demetria as Everett went to the cashier to buy his snacks.

"I don't know. We went into the ladies' room together, but I figured she was either still in there or had already left the restroom." Demetria glanced around the mini mart. "Maybe she went out to her car."

Everett was checking out at the register so he didn't hear their conversation.

"Hold on. I'll check the restroom and make sure she isn't sick or something." Demetria handed Fisher her bag of snacks and then she headed to the women's restroom.

Fisher pulled out his cell phone and called Kira, but it finally went to voicemail. Now he was getting really worried.

Demetria quickly left the restroom, shaking her head. "She's not in there."

"I gave her a call, but she's not answering."

"Okay, let's check with Everett." Demetria took her bag from Fisher and when they reached Everett, she said, "We're not sure where Kira is."

Immediately, Everett shoved his credit card in his wallet and pocketed it.

"Fisher only got voicemail when he called her." Demetria sounded a little panicked.

"I'll let the others know," Fisher said, and texted his brothers and cousin. "I'm going to run out to the car and make sure she's not there." Though he couldn't understand why she wouldn't answer her phone if she was.

"We'll look over the pizza place and the mini mart further," Demetria said, and she and Everett began searching for Kira.

Fisher hurried outside but when he reached Kira's car, his heart sank. She wasn't there. Which made him think of Oscar and Reggie. What if they had followed them here, but in a new vehicle and took Kira hostage to do an exchange for Royce?

"As long as someone is here to watch Royce, I'm going to search around the building," Brock said.

"I'll stay with the prisoner. If those bastards took Kira, they could come here and try and take Royce if we're not sufficiently monitoring him," Shawn said.

"I'll stay too," Tanner said. "I thought some of Dan's people were coming."

"He said they would. It probably took them a bit of time to get organized. I'll contact Dan and see if they're on their way and tell him that we may have an issue," Fisher said.

"I'll head out," Brock said.

"Thanks, cousin," Fisher said, then he called Dan. "Hey, this is Fisher. Did you send anyone to help back us up?"

"Yeah. Leyton, Bridget, Chet, Jack, and Travis from the CSF. They should be catching up to you."

"We're having an issue. Kira seems to be missing. We're at a service station mini mart."

"Okay, relaying the message to them." Dan waited for a moment. "They said they went past the service station. They're headed back your way. If you need more help, we'll send it. Just let me know."

"Thanks." Then Fisher ended the call. "They missed us when we stopped at the service station."

"Then we've got more help coming," Shawn said.

"From the CSF. Five special agents. I'm going to check the security video and see if it shows anything." Fisher hurried off to the mini mart and went inside. As soon as he saw Demetria, he joined her and said, "We need to see the security video for the store. I don't have a badge."

"I do, but we need to get you one pronto also." Demetria waved at Everett to join them. "Time to see their security video."

When they went to the manager, he hurried to show them the security video, and in horror, the USF agents watched as two men accosted Kira as she came out of the restroom and one of them threw her over his shoulder and took her outside through a side door. That was Reggie, Fisher believed. He was angry that the bastards had gotten hold of her.

"That's Oscar leading the way and that's Reggie." Fisher asked the manager, "Do you have a security video of the parking lot?"

"Yeah, here you go for the one on that side of the store."

Fisher, Demetria, and Everett watched the video closely and

then saw the men put Kira in the back seat of a maroon Volvo. "Hell," Fisher said.

"I'll see if I can read the license plate," Demetria said.

Everett and Fisher ran out of the office and were out the side door to the parking lot in an instant. In that direction, they smelled both Oscar and Reggie—Kira also. But they didn't see the car parked where it had been. Fisher felt the worst kind of dread.

Even so, they looked all over the parking lot in case the vehicle was still there, just parked somewhere else. But he didn't expect it to be. They would have been foolish to sit there once Fisher and the others realized Kira was missing.

19

Kira wasn't sure what was going on. She'd woken up and was groggy, sitting in an unfamiliar car and she smelled Oscar and Reggie's scents, plus human scents. What the hell? Her heart was pounding, she felt confused and angry at the same time.

A rope tied her wrists together. Then she remembered coming out of the women's restroom at the mini mart...and having a...a cloth covering her mouth. She had felt her knees give out, her head swimming, and then nothing. Damn it! This was her case and she just screwed it up by getting kidnapped!

Her phone rang, and her heart skipped a beat, but she couldn't reach her cell in her back pocket.

Then she heard footfalls running toward the car door, and Oscar jerked it open. Reggie and Oscar stared down at her. Reggie yanked her onto her hip and grabbed her phone from her pocket.

He glanced at the caller ID. "It's from some clown called Fisher Greystoke." He answered it and put it on speakerphone. "We need to make a swap."

"Who am I speaking to?" Fisher sounded like he was ready to fight him wolf to wolf.

She wanted to shift herself and tear into both men, but she loved hearing Fisher's gruff voice.

"The guy who has got your girl, I guess. She looks pretty perturbed, but the only way this is going down is you bringing Royce to the place where we had the kid in the national park," Reggie said.

"You mean where you shot at us? I'm speaking with Reggie, the guy in charge of the kidnapping spree," Fisher said.

"Yeah. You're quick. But you can't have anyone follow you or go with you. You alone will bring Royce to the exchange site."

"No," Fisher said.

Kira wanted to clap her hands, but she couldn't with them being tied and she needed to be calm and just listen. Fisher hadn't had his training, but he was doing good on his own during this hostage negotiation. If he had said he would go along with Reggie's plan, she would have shouted, "No, don't do it!" They would both be dead, she was sure, and Reggie and Oscar would have Royce back.

"You don't have any say in this," Reggie finally said, sounding shocked.

"This isn't the offer of money for someone. We both have a lot to lose. All you would need to do is carjack us and grab Royce and then you would kill both Kira and me like you had tried to before," Fisher said.

"Okay, so what do you propose?" Reggie asked.

Kira was surprised Reggie would back down so quickly and give up control of the situation as if he was unsure of himself.

"We meet here and exchange Kira for Royce," Fisher said.

"Nah, you wouldn't let us take him. You would stop us. We wouldn't have any leverage then to guarantee our safety."

Reggie was right. The kidnapper was smarter than Kira thought he might be.

Then she heard Fisher snap his fingers and she hoped that meant he had a plan.

~

FISHER WAS SO RILED and worried, he was having a difficult time keeping his cool. Then Reggie ended the call.

Fisher said to Demetria, her mate, and his brothers and cousin, "Kira and I were tracking each other's phones in case we ran into trouble. I forgot about it because I've never done that with anyone before." He checked to see where her phone was located. It was about ten miles from where they were. "If Reggie thinks of it and checks her phone, he can tell where I am. I want to go there now, but—"

"We'll go," Tanner said.

Shawn agreed.

"I'll go with you also," Everett said. "In case they separate and one of them comes here, trying to grab Royce, we need to be sure we have enough people watching him."

Then Leyton and the other CSF agents arrived.

Great! Fisher quickly told them what had happened. He was so ready to turn wolf and take these men down permanently. They better not have hurt Kira.

Jack, one of the CSF agents, got on his phone to tell Dan the news.

Fisher wanted to go with the guys who were going after Kira, but Reggie might have seen where Fisher was through her phone apps. Then the kidnappers would end the tracking and Fisher would lose their location.

Tanner, Shawn, Everett, Leyton, Chet, and Jack took off in two different vehicles so they could split up and surround them.

With a new plan initiated, Fisher called Kira's phone and Reggie answered it. "Okay, we'll meet at the mini market where there are lots of customers around who would keep us both honest."

"Who are you exactly?" Reggie asked.

"Her boyfriend. We were on a hike when the two of you came into our lives and tried to kill us."

"She was in her human form," Reggie said.

"That's how we take hikes often. Are you a newbie, or what? One person needs to stay in their human form and pretend the wolf is their pet dog." Fisher made up the story, figuring the newly turned wolf wouldn't know the truth. Fisher wanted in the worst way to reach Kira and rescue her. "We met on a hike once and recognized we were both wolf shifters and really hit it off." He hoped he was giving the other guys time to reach her while he kept Reggie occupied on the phone.

But then Reggie suddenly ended the call again.

"Crap," Fisher said.

"Are you guys close to where Kira is yet?" Brock asked Tanner on speakerphone.

"We're nearly there. We're practically flying," Tanner said.

Then Fisher got a call and he frowned. "The phone isn't Kira's. It's an unknown name."

"Hell, he might have realized we're tracking her phone and we have sent others to go after him and Oscar," Brock said.

Demetria called Everett and relayed what they were worried about.

Bridget called Leyton to let the CSF agents riding together know what was going on. "Leyton says they're at the location. Has her phone moved?"

Fisher looked at the tracking. "No. When Reggie switched phones, I'm afraid he knew we were tracking Kira's phone." His heart sank. "Is her phone around anywhere there?"

"Call it," Leyton said.

Fisher called her phone and Leyton answered it, "Crap, it's here. We've got it."

But that meant the kidnappers had moved her.

"Do you see anyone who looks like they could be watching you?" Fisher asked, his heart sinking.

"We're checking now. The phone was lying in the grass at the edge of the parking lot at another mini mart/service station," Leyton said.

Jack said, "Dan is sending a dozen men. We need to end this, incarcerate all of them, and get Kira back safely."

"I'm getting hold of the group from our jaguar headquarters in Houston who are supposed to meet up with us and help take Royce back also," Demetria said.

Then Fisher got another call. "It's Reggie."

Everyone got quiet.

"We need to make this exchange now," Reggie said.

Fisher was surprised Reggie wasn't just dictating the way this would all go any longer. He had to figure he was in way over his head while he was dealing with a bunch of shifters, if he realized several were working together to take him and Oscar down.

"So how do you want to work this?" Fisher knew they couldn't let these three get away.

He could hear arguing in the background and he assumed Oscar and Reggie didn't agree on what they were going to do. Finally, he heard Reggie say, "He's caught. Okay? There's nothing we can do about it now. And if we try to get him, *we're* going to get caught too."

Fisher agreed with that. Oscar was silent.

"You know, this could have happened to any one of us," Reggie said in the background. "And if we keep on with this, it will."

Oscar said, "He's my cousin and I got him into this. All of this."

Jack came over to speak to Fisher and pointed to his phone. Fisher put his on mute since the kidnappers weren't talking to him at the moment, still arguing with each other in the background. "Dan has triangulated the call from Reggie to you and has their location. We're going to grab them."

That was really the best situation.

"I'm going." Fisher was elated to hopefully free Kira.

"What if they notice where your phone is located through Kira's phone?" Demetria asked.

"They ditched her phone and Leyton's got it."

"Oh, good," Demetria said.

Then Fisher and the others got into their cars and headed for the location of Reggie's vehicle. He couldn't believe the kidnappers were still so close by—about ten minutes away if they drove the speed limit, which they weren't.

Hopefully, this time they could catch them.

They were driving as fast as they could to get there, multiple cars enroute, when Fisher saw two men gesticulating wildly at each other in a vacant parking lot, the clothing store there having been closed down and boarded up. Fisher drove Kira's car straight at Oscar and Reggie. He had to keep them from going after Kira if she was in the vehicle.

Reggie turned to look to see who was barreling down on him in the vacant parking lot. He quickly took off running as the others with Fisher raced their vehicles into the parking lot and cut their engines. Oscar looked so shocked that they had been discovered that he didn't react right away, but then ran off in the opposite direction from Reggie.

Fisher would have chased down the bastards, but he had to see to Kira's safety. He ran over to the car and saw her sitting in the backseat, her hands secured behind her back with rope. He tried the doors, but all of them were locked.

Jack rushed over with a tool to break into the car, then broke the lock. Fisher yanked the back door open and pulled Kira into his arms. Kira's left eye had been blackened and Fisher couldn't have been more furious. "Who did this to you?"

"Reggie," Kira said.

Fisher carefully cut the rope off Kira's wrists. Once she was free, she threw her arms around him and gave him a quick hug and kiss and he kissed her and hugged her back.

"I looked up the license plate on the car and it was stolen," Demetria said.

"That figures. Come on. We have to catch these guys. I'm turning into my wolf. *You* are not," Kira said to Fisher, then climbed back into the car and began stripping off her clothes.

Fisher knew it was because she worried about his shoulder after the last time he had run and swum as a wolf. But he wasn't losing her a second time and started stripping off his clothes.

"You aren't supposed to run as a wolf, doctor's orders," she reminded him.

"I'll heal up again. But I'm staying with you." He threw his clothes in the car and looked her over, making sure they hadn't hurt her anywhere else.

"We go after Reggie because he's the leader of the pack." Then she shifted, nipping his bare butt before she took off.

He smiled and knew she loved him. He shifted and tore after her.

"Come on," Demetria told Jack. "Let's disable the stolen car if Reggie or Oscar tries to return here to grab it. Then we go after them too."

Then Fisher and Kira were out of hearing of Demetria and Jack. They raced to catch up to Reggie and hoped the others would catch Oscar. At least with their wolf speed versus human speed, they were soon passing the men who were trying to locate Reggie who had run into the wooded area where the undergrowth was formidable. Which meant he would have just as difficult a time as the other humans navigating through it. But at least they could all smell his scent filled with fear. He was no longer in charge, dictating terms, but running for his life, scared witless. And he probably didn't know this area all that well.

Not that most of the people hunting him did either.

Kira was still ahead of Fisher, and he didn't like that at all. If the bastard starting shooting at them, Fisher didn't want Kira to get hit.

He tracked Reggie going off to his right and Fisher darted that way. He hoped *he* didn't get shot also! His shoulder was beginning to ache, and he figured his brother would give him grief about it if he learned he had run again as a wolf. Kira was still off to Fisher's left and then the scent stopped, and Fisher saw Reggie standing still, aiming his gun right at him. Talk about déjà vu. Only this time there wasn't a cliff to fall off, though there was something better. A tree to dart behind. Which he did in the nick of time. Several rounds were fired off in Fisher's direction, which would only make everyone who was after the kidnappers more determined to take the wolf down, permanently. Several of the rounds hit the trunk of the tree.

But then Fisher's heart took a dive. What if Reggie had caught sight of Kira and was shooting at her? Fisher came out from around the other side of the tree and saw Reggie reloading. Okay, so this could be a big mistake, but he had to take Reggie down now before his bullets hit anyone who was after him.

Fisher charged Reggie while he was busy reloading his gun. Fisher was nearly close enough that he could leap onto him, but not quite. If he got too close to Reggie without being able to take him down, Reggie would be able to take a direct shot and kill Fisher this time without have any shooting skill at all.

Fisher wasn't going to make it, damn it, but he had to give it his best attempt. Reggie raised his gun in a panic when he realized Fisher was practically on top of him. One shot, and Fisher would be dead. Until out of the corner of his eye, Fisher saw the wolf of his dreams, Kira, running as fast as she could to tackle Reggie. Which meant he could turn his gun on her and kill her instead.

Reggie suddenly heard her coming. He turned, forgetting about the male wolf threat in front of him, and aimed his weapon at Kira. Fisher leapt as far as he could go to jump on the man, to stop him from shooting Kira, and knocked him down with his powerful wolf's body. Reggie wasn't giving up that easily though and raised his gun to shoot Fisher, who was on top of him. Kira wasn't going to give Reggie the chance and bit into his gun hand, crushing all the bones. Fisher knew because he heard it when they snapped, and Reggie cried out in pain. Fisher flinched a little. Not that Reggie didn't deserve it and much worse, but Fisher knew how much that had to have hurt.

Fisher was still standing on top of Reggie's chest, growling, letting the man know if he moved, he would bite him. Then he lifted his chin and howled to let the others know that they had him pinned down and he wasn't going to be shooting anyone.

That's when they heard the others who had been following him quickly join them. Jack had turned into his cougar. Demetria was her jaguar. Everyone else was in their human forms, Leyton with a pair of cuffs, the others with guns drawn.

"We'll take it from here," Everett said, smiling at Fisher.

But Fisher wasn't done with being angry with Reggie. Not after he'd tried to kill them before, then taken Kira hostage, and even hit her, giving her a black eye, then tried to kill them again. He bared his teeth at Reggie in the most menacing look he possessed. He swore the guy peed his pants.

Then Fisher moved off him reluctantly. He hoped that Kira didn't believe he *wasn't* special agent material because he kind of held a grudge.

She nuzzled his face with her cheek and then laid down.

Bridget showed up with everyone's clothes that had shifted. "In case you want to shift back in the woods."

Everett and Leyton got Reggie to his feet, though he was crying out in pain from Kira's debilitating bite. If he expected sympathy from anyone, he wasn't getting it. But Fisher wanted to know what had happened to Oscar. He was sure he had been caught too. Hopefully, he hadn't shot anyone like Reggie had tried to do.

Everyone else escorted Reggie back to one of the vehicles while Jack, Demetria, Kira, and Fisher shifted and dressed. Frowning, Kira was eyeing Fisher. He didn't think it was because she thought he was looking hot, but because she was concerned about his shoulder. Yeah, it was aching again, but he wasn't going to say a word about it.

He didn't figure he was going to be doing any more shifting for a while anyway and then in another week or so, he would be good as new. But now he was eyeing her in a very much interested way, and when she caught his eye, she smiled. He liked seeing her smiling at him a lot better than when she was frowning at him.

Once they all finished dressing, they hurried after the others. "Tanner, Shawn, and Brock went after Oscar," Fisher said.

"Five of Dan's men stayed with Royce," Demetria said. "I think the others went after Oscar. I'll call Everett and see if he has had any word from them."

"I need to get a new phone," Kira said. "I'm lost without it. By the way, good work using the tracking app on it from your phone, Fisher. When Reggie realized that was on there, he nearly had a heart attack. He couldn't get rid of it fast enough, got pissed off at me, struck me in the face, and we had to move again. I had so hoped you would catch up to him before that."

"They nearly did, only missing you by minutes. Leyton has your phone," Fisher said.

"Oh, good," Kira said. "I've lost three on the last three missions. Martin would have a fit if he had to replace another."

Fisher smiled at her and took her hand, leaned down and kissed her, then they continued to follow the others. He figured Martin would have been concerned more about Kira being hurt.

Demetria said to Everett on her phone, "What do you mean the others lost Oscar?"

K ira couldn't believe that the others had missed catching Oscar. She had so hoped they had gotten all the bad guys. After transporting them to Houston, their mission would be done. She always felt such a sense of satisfaction when that happened.

All of them headed back to where they'd parked their vehicles.

Demetria said, "Everett told me that the others lost Oscar's scent. He had to have gotten into another vehicle and torn off. Now the question is will he still try and free Royce, or will he decide this is just too hot for him and he needs to leave before *he* gets caught?"

"I don't know, but from the conversation he and Reggie were having," Fisher said, "I got the impression Oscar still wanted to free his cousin. Without Reggie's help though, he might be rethinking his plans."

"Are you and Everett going to continue to take Royce and now Reggie to Houston?" Kira asked.

"Yes. We'll have Reggie in another car. Dr. Kate is coming here to bandage Reggie's hand, but she's not taking him into surgery. Then we'll have two cars take the men separately, but we'll drive as a convoy," Demetria said as they joined the others in the parking area.

Everett gave Demetria a hug and kiss. "Okay, we've got Chase, Chet, Jack, Leyton, Hal, and Ricky going with us to take the men to Houston. Or at least in that direction. The jaguars will be meeting up with us and take over guard duty while Stryker, Bridget, Travis, and your kin, Fisher, stay on this business with trying to hunt down Oscar," Everett said.

Leyton said, "Oh, I've got your phone, Kira." He handed her phone to her.

"Thanks so much." Kira immediately got on her phone and then started the tracking app again so she would know where Fisher was at all times.

Fisher smiled at her, and she figured it was because he had used it to find out where *she* had been.

"Do you think Oscar will follow the convoy like they must have been doing initially when we were escorting Royce to Houston before they grabbed Kira?" Leyton asked.

"Unless he just decides to leave and go to Alaska or someplace else. I don't know how he would be able to manage freeing his cousin on his own now. He might not bother trying to help Reggie, even though they're best friends. After the argument the two of them had about leaving Royce to his fate, Oscar not wanting to do that, I suspect Oscar will just try and free his cousin if he even makes the effort," Everett said.

"If he does," Kira said, "he's not going to be able to grab anyone this time to take as a hostage. Sorry about putting everything through that with me."

"Are you kidding? We were able to catch Reggie because of it," Everett said, smiling. "It was a great, covert plan on your part."

Kira laughed.

"Okay, since everyone knows which group we're going with, let's get on the road," Demetria said.

Kira knew she wanted to get this done pronto. Not only because once they had the two men incarcerated, they wouldn't have to worry about them, but it wouldn't give Oscar that option to try and free them either, which could result in another shootout and someone on one of the teams could be severely injured or die this time.

She was sure everyone was interested in getting together with their families for Thanksgiving too. Then Kira wondered if Oscar would give up kidnapping victims once he wasn't being influenced by Reggie, and since he wouldn't have co-conspirators to work with.

Still, he could end up doing other kinds of crime so he would have money. He had proven he was too dangerous, so they couldn't allow him to live on his own without someone taking responsibility for him to make sure he didn't cause problems, and that would have only been if he hadn't been involved in dangerous criminal activities. It was way too late for him to just get a slap on the wrist for all that he had already done.

Kira glanced at Fisher as they got into her car. She saw him flinch when he fastened his seat belt, and she knew he had been hurting again after running as a wolf. She hadn't wanted him to turn wolf no matter what. Though she understood why he had wanted to—his need to take down Reggie, but also his promise to keep her safe. She had been glad he'd been there when Reggie had taken aim at her, and Fisher had distracted him. And when Reggie had tried to shoot Fisher, she had stopped him from doing so. They really worked well together as if they could read each other's minds and had known just what to do. In this business, it could be a matter of life and death.

"Thanks for stopping Reggie from shooting me," she said.

"Yeah, I owe you thanks for the same thing."

"You're hurting. Do you want to take something for the pain?"

He reached back to get the first aid kit and pulled out a pain pill, then took it with some water. "Just don't tell my brother."

"Heath?" She smiled. "You were lucky Dr. Kate was too busy patching Reggie up to check on you. And I saw the way you were avoiding her."

Fisher chuckled. "So what's the plan?"

"Well, everyone else had time to grab some snacks but me," Kira said.

"Me either. As soon as I noticed you weren't in the store or at the car, I knew you were in trouble."

"I'm so glad you were paying attention. With so many of us involved in this, it would be hard to keep track of everybody," Kira said.

"Are you kidding? You're my priority. Martin gave me a direct order to watch out for you. So we go back to that mini mart and get some food and drinks and then what?"

She headed in that direction. "We need to coordinate with the others on our team about what everyone wants to do." She got on Bluetooth and started a conference call. "We're headed back to the mini mart where I was grabbed so we can get some food and drinks."

Tanner said, "Brock, Shawn, and I are way behind the caravan, watching to see if anyone seems to be watching them from businesses on the side of the road. The good thing is Oscar and Reggie have no idea where we were taking Royce, so except for following them—if Oscar's doing so—he's not going to be able to be way ahead of them to ambush them along the way. If they stop for bathroom breaks, that may be the first time he can try something."

Travis said, "Stryker, Bridget, and I are going to drive along parallel roads to the one the convoy is on so we can look for anyone suspicious."

"Do you want any of us to go with Fisher and you?" Tanner asked.

"I doubt he would return to the mini mart where they took me hostage," Kira said.

"Okay, we'll continue on our path then," Tanner said.

They finished the call, everyone going in the direction that they planned to.

"We work together well," Kira said to Fisher, believing they really were in step.

"I feel the same way. What about the other agent you had been working with? How did that work out?" Fisher asked.

"He's good. Justin Barrymore has been with the USF for a year. He's great at investigating, anticipating a situation, and problem solving, just like you are. But he tends to take charge and it's his way, period. Part of it is an ego thing. He's an alpha male wolf who is used to being in charge and he's that way with women especially. Now Martin likes his work and I needed someone to work with who had been with the organization for a little while, but truthfully, he drives me crazy. He's a nice person, until I have to work with him."

"Is he mated?" Fisher asked.

She laughed. "He isn't. Believe me, I'm not interested in him in the least bit. Anyway, he stymies me when I'm trying to figure out what to do on the mission. I was relieved when I didn't have to work with him on this case, though I soon realized I needed more support. Even if I had been on the mission with him, we couldn't have done it alone."

"Well, you've done a great job of being in charge on this mission."

"Oh, I loved it when you said no to Reggie when he dictated to you what would happen as far as a hostage/prisoner exchange in the national park went. I was ready to shout no, if you hadn't said it. You're brand new, no training at all, and you naturally have taken on the role of a special agent in the best way possible."

"I knew if they got their way, you could be expendable. Me too. So no, I wasn't going with that option. I was just glad Dan had been able to triangulate your position using my phone and Reggie's once

Reggie realized you and I were tracking each other on our phones and used another phone."

"Man, I thought you were going to run him over." She was so proud of the way he had handled the situation.

"I was if he had pulled his gun on me or headed for the car where you were being held hostage. I wasn't going to let him get to you no matter what."

"That would have worked if he hadn't run off."

"Then he wouldn't have had a chance to shoot at us again."

"For sure." She pulled into the parking lot of the mini mart. "Hey, it's actually lunchtime. Why don't we get some snacks to go but grab a slice of pizza each also."

"I was just going to say the same thing."

They headed inside the convenience store, and she felt like she was reliving the nightmare that she'd been in for the last two hours once she'd come out of the restroom. If she hadn't gone to look at the merchandise near the other side door, someone on her team might have seen Reggie and Oscar grab her.

Fisher ran his hand down her arm and took hold of her hand and squeezed. "Are you okay?"

"You know, that's what I love about you. My other partner wouldn't have asked. He figured as a USF agent, you have to tough it out. But you are so sweet and are always concerned about me."

"Just like you are with me."

She tilted her chin down when she glanced at him. "Yeah, but you're supposed to listen to me." Though she was so glad he'd been there for her as a wolf. The other team members hadn't been able to catch up to them until Demetria and Jack had also shifted.

They went into the pizza place, and both got slices of cheese pizza and bottled water. After what they had been through, they were both feeling the adrenaline pumping through their blood. Taking a breather was worth it before they got back into the chase.

Of course, if they had known where Oscar was, they would have pursued him until they caught him.

"I need to call my parents and tell them that if we catch Oscar, or we have no leads by the time Thanksgiving is here that I'm bringing a special guest home for the holiday."

"Me?"

"Absolutely." She called her mom and said, "Hey, I'm in Colorado and I have some news." She put the call on speaker.

"Hey, Kira, I hope you're calling to say you're coming home for Thanksgiving."

"We are, if we aren't in the middle of trying to catch one last perp. But I want to give you early warning that I'm bringing my partner if we can get there."

"Oh, *him*. We didn't think you cared for him all that much. Isn't he the one who is bossy and controlling? Always telling you how things are going to go?" her mom said.

"Not him. I have a new partner this time and he's a dream."

Her mother was silent.

"You'll love him."

Her mother didn't say anything.

"Anyway, we'll be there if we aren't in the middle of finalizing this case."

"Wow, okay, well, we'll be glad to see you if you can get home for Thanksgiving for sure. And we'll be looking forward to meeting your new partner."

"Thanks, Mom! We're about to go on another search for the perp, so I just wanted to take a moment to check in. We caught two of the men already with a team of helpers or we wouldn't have been able to manage. Talk to you later! Love you."

"Love you too, dear. Oh, what's your new partner's name?"

"Oh, sorry. Fisher Greystoke."

"I thought he was mated to a girl named Jillian."

"That's Vaughn Greystoke. He's Fisher's cousin."

"Ohhh," her mother said in an elongated fashion like she was finally intrigued. "I like Vaughn and Jillian."

"They're really nice. And Fisher is made of the same wolf material."

"Then we're really looking forward to seeing your new partner."

Kira was sure her parents would like Fisher, especially since she did. She smiled at Fisher. "So are you ready to meet my parents?

21

"I'm looking forward to meeting your parents," Fisher said to Kira, "though they might be a little shocked to learn that we're dating."

"They'll be thrilled and love you like I do." Kira and Fisher sat down at a table and began eating their slices of pizza at the convenience store.

"Oh, shoot, Demetria or Everett probably called Martin, but I need to check in with him now that we caught one more of the guys. The head honcho, actually." Kira got on her phone and called Martin, putting it on speakerphone. "One of the Andersons probably already let you know that we captured Reggie, the leader of the kidnappers."

"Yeah, Demetria told me what had happened with you and Fisher protecting each other when Reggie was shooting at you. I couldn't be gladder that I hired Fisher. He seems to be your perfect partner," Martin said.

"I so agree. He and I work well together." Kira was so glad her boss felt that way because she would have a greater chance of being paired up with Fisher on future missions.

"I want everyone to keep on their toes with the last guy. Unless he just decides to take off to Alaska or somewhere else that no one knows him, he may still go after his cousin, and I don't want anyone to get hurt. These guys have proven just how dangerous they can be. Keep me posted."

"We will."

"You're both doing a great job. Keep it up," Martin said.

"Thanks," they both said.

Then they ended the call.

"I was afraid Martin might give me grief about allowing myself to be taken hostage," Kira told Fisher.

"It could have happened to any of us."

They finished eating their slices of pizza, then picked up some chips and sodas, paid for them, and then walked out to the car. "I'm glad we came back here so that I could have a better experience— this time with you," she said.

"I agree. We'll have to return to the national park and run as wolves together, just enjoying ourselves, not worrying about kidnappers, protecting a hostage, and getting shot, or searching for a little lost girl or boy," Fisher said.

"Let's make it a date."

"I'm all for it."

They got into the car and decided to just crisscross the area, looking for any sign of the other vehicle that had taken off. She hoped that they would get lucky. She knew that if the others saw any sign of the vehicle, they would let them know, and she and Fisher would join them.

Twenty minutes later, Fisher spied a vehicle that fit the description of the Ford Escape that Oscar had taken off in. "Do you think that's the car Oscar drove off in that the others had described?" Fisher pointed out the car at a service station/convenience store.

"They didn't know the license plate number, but it's the same color, make, and model. Let's check it out."

They pulled in next to the vehicle, got out of their car, and looked inside the Escape. Food wrappers were scattered all over the floor. They smelled Oscar's scent outside of the vehicle. Fisher ran the license plate. "Stolen."

"That's what I figured," Kira said.

But then Oscar raced out of the woods behind the store, dragging a little boy with him.

No, no, no, no!

He tossed a couple of pairs of handcuffs to Kira and Fisher, and they landed on the asphalt parking lot in front of them. "Put them on and come with me. Then I'll let the kid go."

Ohmigod, she couldn't believe she was going to be one of the kidnappers' hostages again. Yet she couldn't think of any way out of it. But what if he didn't let the boy go, once they had the handcuffs on?

"You don't have any choice," Oscar said, sounding angry at the delay. "Put your phones on the ground."

Reluctantly, they both did.

"You, Red, put the cuffs on your boyfriend first. Not in the front, but in the back."

"I can't twist my shoulder back that way," Fisher said. "Your cousin shot me in the shoulder."

"Do it," Oscar said.

"Just shoot me. Go ahead and get it over with. I can't pull my injured shoulder behind me."

"Do it in front then," Oscar growled.

She hoped Fisher wasn't hurting as much as he was acting like he was and instead had a plan. She went ahead and cuffed him. He groaned as if he was in serious pain even though she cuffed his hands in front of his body.

"Now, Boyfriend, do the same to your girlfriend."

Fisher began cuffing her hands in front and Oscar said, "No, wiseass. Was she shot too?"

They could have pretended his friend had hit her when he was shooting down on them when they were on the ledge below the cliff, or even before they took him into custody, but it was a little late for pretenses.

She felt just like she had the other time this had happened, except she wasn't knocked out with chloroform and she was glad for that.

"Get in the back seat of your car," he said.

"What about the boy?" Kira didn't trust Oscar to do what was right.

"Get in the car," Oscar ordered. He was in charge, and he didn't like them questioning everything he was doing.

She knew Oscar had a gun on him, though it appeared he had it in his jacket pocket.

"Come on, let's do it." Fisher and she climbed into the back seat of the car.

She eyed the boy and wished she could give him a hug like she had done with Billy and tell him everything was going to be alright, even though she didn't know that it was going to be.

Then Oscar pushed the boy in through the driver's seat and once he was in the front passenger seat, Oscar got behind the wheel and drove off. "Okay, who the hell are you two?"

They couldn't say that they were with the USF, not in front of the boy, though he wouldn't know what it was.

"We're law enforcement special agents," Kira said. "You, your cousin, and your friend are wanted for the kidnapping of several boys. We handle cases like yours."

"So you didn't just run into us accidentally in the national park?" Oscar asked, sounding surprised.

"No. We were following you."

"You're like us."

"Yep. But we can't discuss it in front of the boy," Kira said.

Silence.

"Where are you taking us?" Fisher asked.

"Where are they taking my cousin?" Oscar asked, not answering Fisher.

"To Houston," Kira said.

"Why?"

"Reggie and he will be incarcerated. What did you think would happen once we caught you? You could just continue to do this and get away with it?" Kira was irate. These men had no conscience. They were destroying lives, impacting on them in a way that could never be undone.

Oscar didn't say anything for a long time, just kept driving. They weren't going to Houston, but someplace way out in the country. Then they finally arrived at a desolate cabin. "You're going to call whoever has got my cousin and tell them that they have to drop him off with bus money to a place I designate."

Then he parked Kira's car and got out. He opened the door for Kira and told the boy to get out. "Kid, you're not going anywhere. We're too far out for anyone to ever find you. So you will stay here until they release my cousin and then you can go home to your parents."

Then he opened the door for Fisher to exit the vehicle. "All of us are going inside."

Once they were inside the dusty cabin, Oscar made Fisher sit on a chair, then he moved another one with its back to Fisher's and made Kira sit there.

He brought out some rope and began to wrap it around the two of them.

Kira sure hoped they could get themselves out of this mess without anyone having to rescue them. Two times on one mission? Martin might want to fire her this time!

After Oscar had tied them up sufficiently, he made the boy sit on another chair. Then he got Kira's phone and said, "Unlock it."

"Hold it up to my face." If she could just get a cryptic message to Demetria, maybe she would realize that they had been taken hostage.

Oscar did, and then he searched her contacts. "Who has my cousin?"

"Demetria Anderson," she said.

"You tell her to put Royce on a bus at Trinidad and take it to Colorado City."

"Alright."

"You tell her I have you and your boyfriend and another kid, so don't try any funny business."

"Alright."

He called the number and held the phone up to her face.

"Hello?" Demetria said.

"Hi, Oscar took Fisher and me and another boy hostage." At least Kira didn't have to be cryptic about it.

There was dead silence on the other end.

"Hello?" Kira knew Demetria was on Bluetooth and that Everett had heard what was going on. Royce too. He was probably grinning his fool head off. "He wants Royce put on a bus in Trinidad and sent to Colorado City."

"How do we have any guarantee that the three of you will be alright?" Demetria asked.

"You don't. If any of you meet at the bus station or follow him, I'll end the three of them. Desperate men take desperate measures. You've probably heard of that before, right?" Oscar said.

"How will you know we've put Royce on a bus at the location you indicated?" Demetria asked.

"You give him a burner phone and he can call me when he leaves and when he reaches his destination."

"And our people and the boy?" Demetria asked.

"Once I know my cousin is free and not in your custody again, I'll tell you where your friends and the boy are, and you can come and get them. No one rides on the bus with Royce. I can smell you like you can smell me. And you know I'm armed with a couple of guns."

"Alright. I've got to check the bus schedule for times of departure," Demetria said.

"Call back when you have the information. And I want Royce to call me on the burner phone when you get him one."

"Alright. Call you back as soon as we have the information." Demetria sounded calm and Kira loved that about her.

It helped to keep a situation like this less emotional and keep the rogue shifter from getting more riled up. Then Oscar ended the call.

"What's your name?" Kira asked the boy.

"Tommy Jones."

"Hi, Tommy. I'm Kira and he's Fisher."

The boy was a redhead, freckles smattered across his cheeks and nose, and his green eyes were red with crying.

"Okay, you and I are going for a trip," Oscar said to Tommy.

"You were supposed to leave the boy with us," Fisher said.

"You're not in charge here, if you didn't realize it," Oscar said. "Come on, kid."

The boy looked at Fisher and Kira as if he had hoped they were going to save him, but all tied up, they couldn't do a thing. Not at the moment. They just hoped Oscar would be honorable enough to leave the boy somewhere safe. She suspected Demetria would make sure everyone was watching for Oscar to pick up Royce. But he might get off at another stop. They would have to have all the places covered.

In the meantime, Kira and Fisher needed to get themselves out of the bind they were in.

As soon as they heard car doors shut—her car, which so irritated her—they began to try and get loose. Then the car engine revved up and Oscar drove off.

"Can you make any headway with the ropes?" Kira asked Fisher.

"I'm trying. What about you?"

"A little, but he tied them tight."

"I'm going to try and shift."

"Can you?"

"I think so. You can't with your wrists cuffed behind your back, but I should be able to."

Then the ropes began loosening and she heard his cuffs drop on the floor.

"Yes! Omigod, we're mating," she said, loving him for being so resourceful and quick thinking.

He woofed, but he was still trying to get out of the ropes. But they were looser, and she was wriggling and wiggling, trying to get free of them. She was still pulling against them, which meant that they were tightening against the fully dressed wolf behind her, though Fisher had lost his shoes.

No one ever liked to shift while they were wearing clothes, but in an emergency, they would do whatever they had to. If they had to, she thought it was like when a dog was dressed up for a human's entertainment.

"Oh, oh, I'm nearly out." Well, not quite, but she'd managed to get one loop of rope over her head. With all the wiggling and jiggling, they ended up knocking over the chairs.

Unlike in the movies where they likely used breakaway furniture, these chairs were solid and didn't break. Darn it.

Okay, so being on their side on the floor wasn't easier.

Then she heard chewing and glanced back at Fisher and saw he was chewing through the rope coiled around them, snarling and growling. She loved him.

With a snap, he was through one coil of the rope and that was enough to loosen it further and she fought to get out of the remaining rope. Her hands cuffed behind her back was what was giving her fits.

Then Fisher shifted and pulled the rest of the rope off himself. She was freer now, and he hurried to remove the rest of the rope tied around her and helped her up. He hugged and kissed her, and she loved him so much.

His mouth lingered on hers and he was still holding close. "We get into the worst binds."

"It's all in the job description," she said, then he released her. "But I'm serious. You're mine."

He laughed and began rummaging through drawers in the kitchen. "I love you and I am thrilled about mating you. I'm looking for something that can open your handcuffs."

"I've got a Swiss army knife in my pocket that he didn't take." She was so glad she had that on her and Oscar hadn't searched her for anything.

Fisher slid his hand in her pocket, but it was the wrong one.

"Other one."

Then he pulled out the knife and smiled. "You're prepared for most anything."

"Your teeth sure came in handy on that rope."

"At 1200 pounds per square inch while biting down, our wolf teeth sure can help when we're in a tight spot." He quickly removed her handcuffs, and she rubbed her wrists.

"Were you in a lot of pain when I put on your handcuffs?" She was worried about him still when it came to his injured shoulder. She gave him a warm hug and kissed him.

He hugged her back and kissed her willing mouth. "No. I knew I would have a better chance getting out of the situation we were in if I was handcuffed in front and not in the back. I was doing a lot of playacting to get my way."

"Not a little bit?"

"Oh, if you had pulled my arms back and handcuffed me, sure I would have been in some pain, but I was doing all the groaning for effect. Are you okay?"

"Yeah, I'm good. Let's go. We have no phones or a car and we're miles from civilization, but we need to head in the direction we heard him go and hope we'll soon find someone that will help us out," she said, heading out of the house.

"I guess we'll jog and maybe we can see a vehicle and flag it down. Do you ever commandeer a vehicle in the name of the law?"

"No. We have to make sure we don't break any laws since we're truly not a human law enforcement agency."

"You know, I could run as a wolf and sprint ahead to see if I can locate anyone," he said, holding her hand as if he was on a date, or maybe because he was so happy she wanted to mate him.

"You're not running as a wolf. Not with your injured shoulder. But it's a great idea." She pulled her hand away from his, gave him a hug, stripped off her clothes, and saw his appreciative smile as he watched her. She laughed at him. "Quit drooling."

He smiled. "I can't help it. And I can't wait for us to become mated wolves."

"Me either." She wished they didn't have to delay it, but of course this business took priority over anything. They needed to capture Oscar and get the boy home to his family.

Fisher bundled up her clothes and then she shifted and took off running. At least both could hear if anyone was in the vicinity with their enhanced hearing. She hoped that the other members of the teams wouldn't worry about them because for now, they were fine. They just needed to find someone who might be able to help them out.

She ran about a mile in one direction, but not hearing any cars or people or seeing any homes, she ran off in another direction. Still, she couldn't find anything and ran the opposite way. This was going to be harder than she thought. They were just miles away from anything. She raced back to where Fisher was walking, and he shook his head.

"You look defeated. No luck?"

She shifted. "Nothing. I thought if I could at least find a house, store, gas station, or something, I would run back to you, and we would head in that direction. But there's nothing out here." She took her clothes from him and dressed. "Maybe we'll get lucky, and someone will come our way."

They started walking again. "I smell my car engine had traveled this way, and I recognize the woods we passed through. See that dead tree over there with one branch sticking out? I was watching for anything that would give us a clue as to how we had gotten here. I was glad he hadn't blindfolded us."

"I was doing the same thing. That fir tree with the yellow top? That's the one I saw on the way here."

"Good. Then we're in sync with doing what we need to do. I guesstimated we are about fifteen miles from where he took us at that service station."

"Me too. And along the way, businesses were situated on either side of the road for the first two miles. After that, traffic and businesses were few and far between. Then farms sprouted up here and there, the farmhouses way off the main road. I saw some silos, and then we turned off on this road and were soon into forested land. No cabins that I saw, just the one he drove us to."

"I didn't go far enough to reach any of the farmhouses. No one's harvesting anything now. But maybe we can find someone out feeding cows or something."

"The first farmhouse was about ten miles back," Fisher said. "It'll take us about four hours to reach it."

"Unless one of us runs as a wolf. Then it'll only be an hour."

"Yeah, but it won't help us because we can't talk to a farmer as a wolf. And with me walking as a human, I still wouldn't be there for another three hours."

Then they heard a van headed their way and she immediately worried it was the kidnapper.

"He was driving your car, and no one will know it, so I'm sure he wouldn't ditch it to grab a van and come back for us," Fisher said.

"I think you're right. At least I sure hope so."

s soon as the blue van drew closer, they saw the cargo carrier on top and that the driver was a man and the passenger a woman.

Fisher and Kira waved them down, though she figured they wouldn't want to risk stopping to talk to strangers on the road out in the woods. Kira wouldn't have wanted to. It could be a dangerous world out there and though it looked as though Fisher and she were boyfriend and girlfriend and not trouble, whoever knew? Lots of couples were criminals.

The van slowed, and the man rolled down his window. "Are you in trouble?"

Kira brought out her badge and flashed it at him. "We're trying to track down a kidnapper and ended up being taken hostage." She hated how foolish that sounded but she had to admit the truth to get some help and she showed where her wrists had been rubbed raw from the handcuffs. "He has kidnapped another boy to use as a hostage so he can try and have his cousin released by other members of our team that have him in custody. He stole my car, and we need to report in so our fellow special agents know we've escaped but that the kidnapper still has the boy. If we could borrow your phone, we would be grateful."

"Yeah, sure." The driver handed his phone down to Kira.

She called Demetria. "Hey, listen, Fisher and I have escaped. We're on..." She glanced at the driver of the van. "Do you know what road this is?"

"Pinebrook."

"Pinebrook Road. We're on foot and need a pick up. We're about fifteen miles from the service station where Oscar stole the boy and my car and took us hostage."

Demetria said, "I'm sending someone now to pick you up. What about the boy?"

"The boy's name is Tommy Jones. I wasn't able to ask him much else before Oscar took off with him and he's driving my car." She gave Demetria her license plate number.

"But you've got someone else's phone."

"A nice couple loaned it to me to make this call to you. But I have to give it back."

"Alright. Tanner's on his way to get you," Demetria said.

"Okay, thanks. I'll let Fisher know. We'll just stay here then. What are you going to do about the kidnapper?"

"We'll have to be careful, but we're having someone posted at all the places where the bus will stop so that if Royce gets off earlier than Colorado City, we'll catch him. If his cousin comes for him at any of the locations, we'll catch both of them. Tanner will pick you up and take you to the bus stop in Colorado City," Demetria said.

"Okay, great. We'll see you soon, one way or another, I'm sure." Then they ended the call, and Kira thanked the driver and handed his phone back to him.

"Do you need us to drop you off anywhere?" The man and woman looked shocked to hear of all that was going on out here.

"No, thanks we're going to get picked up by some of our law

enforcement agents." Not really, if Tanner was coming to pick them up.

"Get them some bottles of water," his wife said to someone in the back of the van.

Then a couple of kids about twelve and fourteen brought some bottles of water to the dad and he handed them out the window.

"Thanks so much," Kira said, glad they had run into them.

"Yeah, thanks," Fisher said.

Then the people wished them luck and drove off.

"I SURE WISH we could go to the third bus stop right now," Fisher said as they sat down on the side of the road. They each drank from one of the bottles of water. "I wasn't sure if the USF policy allowed us to release someone who is in custody for serious crimes and give into a kidnapper's demands."

"As far as Demetria and the others were concerned, three of us were being held as hostages at the time. They couldn't risk losing all of us. But even so, they can't risk losing the boy. So they'll do their best to keep track of Royce while they try and apprehend Oscar too."

"Good. Do you hear a siren off in the distance?" Fisher asked.

"Yeah, and it's headed this way."

They stood and watched for the police car. "Tanner wouldn't be driving one. Someone must be in trouble," Fisher said.

Kira frowned. "It's still on its way here."

The siren grew louder, and they finally saw it off in the distance.

"Maybe Tanner isn't coming for us. Maybe one of the deputies from Yuma Town is," Fisher said, hopeful. It would really help to be in a more official vehicle with the sirens running.

The car approached and flashed its headlights.

"Woohoo!" Kira shouted, waving at the car.

Fisher laughed at her and loved that he was mating the she-wolf.

As soon as it stopped on the shoulder in front of them, they saw it was Deputy Sheriff Chase Buchanan.

"Need a lift?" Chase smiled at them. "Tanner is farther away from here so I came for you instead."

They hurried to get in his car. "Thanks for coming for us. Where to next?" Fisher asked.

"We're going to the bus stop in Colorado City. I'm not in uniform so I shouldn't spook them, if we see them. The two of you will have to hold back because they know what you look like," Chase said.

"Has Royce already gone through Aguilar?" Kira asked.

"No. We're all going to separate bus stops along the route to cover them, just in case he gets off at any of them," Chase said. "We know what both men look like. We pulled up Oscar's driver's license. And we'll be watching for the little boy too."

"He's a redhead, wearing a blue shirt and has red freckles all over his face," Kira said. "He was wearing khaki pants."

Chase called it in to the other teams. "I've got Kira and Fisher. They're in good shape."

Demetria said over the Bluetooth, "We're glad to hear it." Her voice really relayed his relief. "We put Royce on the bus at Trinidad. We're at Aguilar, waiting for it to arrive. The other team of jaguars picked up Reggie and have taken him to Houston."

"Okay, we're headed to the stop in Colorado City," Chase said. "Is Walsenberg already covered?"

"Yes, Leyton, Jack, and Bridget are going there," Demetria said. "We'll let you know if we see Oscar and Royce join each other in Aguilar," Demetria said.

"Roger that." Then Chase asked Fisher and Kira, "So what happened to you guys?"

"We found the car Oscar had escaped in, only he was in the

woods hiding, waiting for the unsuspecting to find it. It was like setting out a dog bone, and we took the bait," Kira said. "I couldn't believe he was taking me hostage again. Only this time without his friend's help."

"And me with her," Fisher said. "I suspect he was just waiting to steal someone else's vehicle because we all knew what his looked like. I don't know how that will go over with my new boss."

Chase laughed. "These things happen. All that matters is that you're both fine. We just have to get the boy. Well, and capture the kidnappers."

"We sure appreciate all your help from Yuma Town," Fisher said, then thought how nice it would be to stay at the Buchanan's lake resort. "Kira, we need to rent a cabin at Chase's resort."

"Oh, I so agree. That would be so much fun. Next year, in the summer? Perfect."

"We'll give you one of the best cabins."

"That would be terrific," Kira said.

Fisher loved that they had made friends with the cougars of Yuma Town.

Then Demetria called them back. "Royce didn't get off the bus in Aguilar. Leyton and the others are waiting at Walsenberg in case he gets off there."

"It will take us another thirty minutes to reach the third bus stop," Chase said.

Then they went silent for another fifteen minutes.

"The bus stopped. We're watching for any sign of Royce getting off or his cousin getting on at Walsenberg, but just some women got off and some couples got on. We see him sitting next to the window, the second seat to the last on the right-hand side. So it's in your court, Chase. We've got another team headed to the stop in Colorado City, the final destination," Leyton said on a conference call between Demetria, Chase, and him. "We're headed up that way."

"Okay, we're here and I'm parking several blocks from the bus stop. Fisher and Kira are going to stay out of sight. I'm going to the bus stop," Chase said.

"Okay, Tanner and Brock should be there shortly to be your backup," Demetria said. "We'll be there soon also.

"Good," Chase said. "Okay, if I don't see them, I'll be back to tell you what happened."

Fisher and Kira left the deputy's car. "We have to get closer to the bus stop," Fisher said.

"Yeah, I agree," Kira said.

"Just don't let Oscar see you if he's watching for anyone coming after him," Chase said.

"Right. We're going shopping." Kira pulled Fisher toward a clothing shop.

"Super sleuths," Fisher said.

"Yep. Time for a disguise. I've never had to do this before. Oscar would never expect us to be here, believing we're still all tied up back at the cabin. If we are wearing different clothes, he really won't believe it is us."

"Yeah, I agree. We got lucky that we were able to use that man's phone."

"And that you were so clever about being handcuffed in front of your body. You would have made a good con-artist."

Fisher laughed. "Only to do good."

They walked inside the shop and hurried to find what they could use. At least they still had their wallets and that meant they could buy what they needed. It was cold out and it looked like they were getting rain. Their bags were in Kira's car so they didn't have their jackets.

"Jackets and hats, at the very least," he said.

"This would look good on you," she said, pulling out a teal jacket and teal plaid shirt.

He tried them on. She found him a blue jean cap.

"I'm going to try these on." She pulled out a jeans skirt, something she normally wouldn't wear while trying to take down a rogue shifter, and she hoped she looked a little dressier. She picked out a nice olive-green rain jacket with a hood. They picked out a backpack and purchased everything, changed clothes, and put their other clothes in the backpack.

Once they were outside the shop, it started raining.

"Perfect timing," Kira said. "That will help us blend in with our environment." She pulled up her hood.

So did Fisher and they headed toward the bus stop. But then he pulled her into his arms for a moment and kissed her.

"Do you see him?"

He smiled at her. "No, I just needed this after what we've been through. We've been in such a rush to go after him since he took us hostage, that we haven't taken a moment to be there just for each other."

She smiled and kissed him back. "I so agree. Sometimes it's important to take a deep breath and realize what's important in our lives."

"Yeah. And you are definitely that for me."

"So are you." Any moment they could be in another gun battle —one-sided and they needed to share how they felt about each other in the event they lost each other for good.

Then they began walking toward the bus stop again but didn't get close. They saw Chase standing under an overhang of a store where he was putting on a brown rain jacket and pulling up his hood.

Fisher and Kira were looking for Oscar and a boy with him, but they saw no sign of either. They might be at the wrong stop, or Oscar was hiding in a shop near the bus stop, not wanting to show himself in case anyone was here to grab him and Royce, should they try to meet up.

Fisher saw Kira's car parked nearby. "Hell, there's your car over there and we have no phones to tell anyone."

"What if he left the car here and took an earlier bus to meet up with Royce somewhere else? Or he grabbed someone else's car. This guy is sneaky. He might have figured if any of us found it, we would think he was hanging around here," Kira said.

"Possibly a red herring. Sure. There's a store that should sell burner phones." Fisher took Kira's hand and led her to the store. Inside, he purchased one, and she called Demetria.

"Hey, Demetria, this is Kira. We picked up a burner phone. I don't know Chase's cell number, but we found my car here at the bus stop in Colorado City."

"Okay, don't go near your car in case he's watching it," Demetria said, giving her Chase's number. "We'll let the other teams know Oscar was there."

"Right. We figured he might have left it here and took another bus out of here earlier and will meet up with his cousin at another stop or stole another car. I'm going to call Chase now." Then they ended the call. "I wish I could grab my gun," Kira said to Fisher, "if Oscar didn't find it and take it." She called Chase next. "Hey, Chase, Kira here. We found my car. We're not going near it, but we wanted you to know that he has been here."

"I'm on the lookout for him still."

"We saw you. You look nice and casual, not like you're checking people out."

"Good."

"Tell him we're going to start shopping in case Oscar is in one of these shops," Fisher said.

"Did you hear Fisher?"

"Yeah. Just be careful. He's armed with a gun and you're not."

"Right. I want to get my gun out of the car in the glove compartment, but he might be watching the car, and he might have already taken it with him. Talk later." Kira pocketed the phone and took Fisher's hand, and they went into a sandwich shop that had a view of the bus stop. "Let's grab a coffee. I'm cold and wet and—I was thinking we could—ohmigod, there's the boy. Tommy." She hurried toward him. He was sitting in a booth alone, but Fisher slowed her down.

"We don't want to be taken hostage again. Oscar has got a gun," Fisher reminded her, though he was overjoyed to see the boy safe and alone. He hoped the bastard didn't have Kira's gun and use it in the commission of another crime.

"Tommy's alone. He looks scared. He has a plate of food—hamburger, fries—but he's not eating. What if Oscar told him just to sit there for an hour or more and told him not to move or he would kill his family? And Oscar has already gone? You keep a lookout for him. I'm going to grab the boy." Kira handed him the phone. "Call Demetria and Chase and tell them what's up."

Being protective of both Kira and Tommy, Fisher was watching everyone around them while Kira ran for the boy. He immediately called Demetria. "We found Tommy Jones. He's in the Sandwich Shoppe and there's no sign of Oscar. Kira's grabbing the boy."

"Okay, Tanner and Brock said they're there, only a few minutes from the bus stop," Demetria said.

"The restaurant is right across the street from the bus stop." Fisher glanced out the window and saw Tanner and Brock heading toward the bus stop. "I see them. I'll call them." He ended the call with Demetria and called Tanner. "Hey, Kira and I are in the Sandwich Shoppe just behind you. We found Tommy Jones, the kidnapped boy. We need to get him somewhere safe."

"We're headed your way," Tanner said.

Then Fisher called Chase as his brother and cousin entered the restaurant. "We're in the Sandwich Shoppe and found Tommy Jones. Brock and Tanner are here."

"Great. So unless this clown grabs another kid, he's on his own and doesn't have any other hostages for us to worry about," Chase said.

"Yeah, exactly."

Fisher, Tanner, and Brock joined Kira where she was sitting, hugging the boy, who was in tears. "I got his parents' names, their phone number and we need to call them," Kira said.

"On it." Fisher called the number and said, "I'm Fisher Greystoke. May I speak with Mr. or Mrs. Jones?"

"I'm Mrs. Jones."

"I've got good news for you, Mrs. Jones. I'm with a special unit that has been tracking down a kidnapping network and we've found your son, Tommy." The mother was all choked up and then crying hysterically. He was so glad they had good news for her. "Here he is. I'll let you speak with him. It's your momma, Tommy."

"Momma? The bad man grabbed me at the store and then he took the agents hostage too. But they found me. I love you. O-okay." He handed the phone back to Fisher.

"I'm Special Agent Richter with the FBI. Where are you?" a man on the phone said.

"I'm at the Sandwich Shoppe in Colorado City, Colorado." Fisher just hoped that if Oscar was here still, they would take him into custody before the FBI arrived and tried to take over. But they needed to get the boy home to his parents.

"Ohmigod," Kira said, glancing out the window. "Tanner, stay with Tommy. Brock and Fisher, you're with me." She raced for the door, the guys on her heels.

"Got to go," Fisher said to the agent and ended the call. "You saw the cousin?" Fisher's adrenaline was at an all-time high as he kept up with Kira.

"Yeah, and Royce is rushing off the bus. Chase needs backup now."

They were running full out toward Royce, but Fisher didn't see Oscar at first.

"In the wild, colorful maxi skirt!" Kira called out to them. "With the huge sneaker-covered feet."

"Got him," Fisher said, speeding past Kira. But then the person he was targeting turned to face him. It was Oscar wearing a long blond wig and raincoat, the hood up. He'd shaved off his beard, but he wasn't wearing any makeup and he looked like a man wearing a woman's skirt and wig. Fisher figured as soon as Oscar saw him, he would pull out a gun, but instead, he was running as fast as he could toward where he'd parked Kira's car.

Oscar's focus on his goal meant he didn't see Fisher coming in for the tackle.

Chase and Brock went after Royce, who was running after his cousin.

Fisher took Oscar down with a tackle, Kira quickly removing Oscar's guns and a knife from his holsters and pocket. And her car keys! One of the three guns he had on him was Kira's.

"I'm shifting, damn it," Oscar said.

"Let's get him to Chase's vehicle," Fisher said.

Fisher and Kira hauled him to his feet and began running him toward Chase's car. Fisher knew Tanner would let all the other teams know they had apprehended Royce and Oscar.

Fisher saw Chase and Brock rushing Royce in another direction. Brock yelled at Fisher and Kira, "We're taking him to our vehicle. Royce is having wolf issues."

"Same with Oscar. Were taking him to Chase's vehicle," Fisher said.

Chase reached into his pocket and tossed his keys to Kira. She caught them and pocketed them.

"Cute outfit," Kira said to Oscar, "but your whopper-sized shoes ruined the effect."

"How in the hell did the two of you get free and find me here?" Oscar asked. "God, I'm burning up."

"Just hold off on the shift," Fisher growled at him. "How did we find you? We're damn good at our jobs." He smiled at Kira who smiled back at him.

Then they finally reached Chase's sheriff's car and locked him up in the back seat. They didn't have cuffs, but they didn't want to cuff him because he needed to shift.

Fisher called Tanner. "Hey, we got Oscar in Chase's vehicle. Royce is with Brock and Chase and they're putting him in your car."

"I've got a couple of FBI agents and local policemen here. The agents are bringing Tommy's parents here," Tanner said.

"Good. Slip away when you can. The other teams are all coming here to meet up with us." Fisher gave Tanner the location of where Chase's car was.

Then Demetria and Everett arrived. "Thank heavens you got them," Demetria said.

"And Reggie is still on his way to Houston?" Kira asked.

"Yes. We passed him off to the team from Houston. He will be incarcerated by midnight tonight," Everett said.

"Good. Hopefully these two will join him soon after that," Kira said.

Demetria got a call and said, "Yeah, this is Demetria Anderson." She looked at the others and was smiling. "Yes! Thanks so much. Okay, we have a friend, Strom Hart who is a billionaire jaguar and has his own plane in Houston. He's flying here and taking these guys back to Houston. This is the only way we can transport newly turned shifters safely by airplane."

"Too bad he hadn't come for all three of them," Kira said.

"Martin called him to set this up if we caught the last one. If he had come for the first one, he would have been on his way back to Houston by the time we caught the last one. But then we had to update him that we were bringing two of them home," Demetria said.

"Okay, so who's going with them?" Kira asked.

"You've done your job, Kira and Fisher," Everett said. "You're near your home for the holidays. Demetria and I are returning with the prisoners so we'll be back home in Houston for Thanksgiving. Someone will be coming to drive our car home."

Smiling, Kira and Fisher high-fived both Demetria and Everett.

Tanner drove his vehicle with Brock and Chase and Royce to join the rest of them at Chase's car. Chase and Tanner got out of his vehicle, while Brock remained in the car with Royce, who was now a wolf.

"We'll all go to the Colorado City Municipal Airport to make sure they get on their flight," Chase said. "They're not going to get away this time."

"That's for sure," Kira said.

The other teams all showed up and Kira told them what they were doing.

Everyone wanted to follow them to the airport. All the teams got into their cars and Demetria and Everett led the way, while Chase drove his vehicle with Oscar in the backseat and Jack also went with him.

Kira and Fisher followed behind them in their car. Brock and Tanner had Royce in their car, and they were behind Kira's car. The rest of the teams followed behind them in their vehicles. When they arrived at the airport, they parked and Demetria said to the gathered group, "Strom will be here within the hour. Some of you can leave if you want."

But no one made a move to take off.

Brock said, "We'll make sure these guys get on the flight and they're secure before we leave."

Which Kira appreciated after all the trouble they'd had with the men.

As soon as Strom called Demetria to tell her he had landed and was waiting for them, they checked on their prisoners to find them still in their wolf forms.

"I've got crates for them and just in case you needed it, muzzles, leashes, and collars." He had also brought fellow jaguar friends David and his brother, Wade Patterson, Huntley Anderson and his mate Melissa, members of one of the jaguar law enforcement departments. "They insisted on coming and helping Demetria and Everett return home to Houston with these two."

Which was probably a good thing, Fisher was thinking, given all the trouble the two kidnappers had caused.

Demetria introduced them to all the people there. "Strom owns the Clawed and Dangerous Kitty Cat Clubs."

"We'll have to visit one of them when Fisher goes to Houston to take his training," Kira said.

"Drinks are on the house," Strom said.

"Thanks! We'll definitely drop by." Then Fisher collared a growling Oscar.

"We can tase you, if you don't behave," Chase warned Oscar.

Then Oscar settled down and Fisher attached his leash. David Patterson took hold of the leash and shook Fisher's hand. "I'm also with the JAG organization. You had the difficult job. Congratulations on joining the USF."

"Thanks. I'm happy to be part of the organization."

Demetria and Everett had collared Royce and attached the leash and then took him to the private plane. They put the two wolves into the crates and secured them.

Fisher asked, "What about letting the families whose sons had been kidnapped know about us capturing the bad guys?"

"The organization will handle it. We have reporters and FBI agents who are shifters. We'll fix it so that all bases are covered," Everett said.

Which was the issue with shifters getting into trouble and civilian law enforcement and reporters being aware of it.

And then everyone who was returning to Houston said goodbye to those staying in Colorado, including the jaguar who was driving the Anderson's car home.

Fisher pulled Kira into a hug and kissed her. "We did it!"

"We did," she said. "We stayed positive throughout it too."

"Mostly."

She laughed. "Where to now?"

"The town of Greystoke."

"Let's caravan," Tanner said.

"We're headed back to Yuma Town," Chase said.

The wolves from Greystoke said goodbye to the cougars from Yuma Town, and they split off in two separate caravans going in two different directions.

Kira said, "How are you doing?"

"I'm doing great. I was fine when I shifted," Fisher said.

"Okay, so I was thinking you could schedule your training in Houston after Thanksgiving and before Christmas, if you think you can manage it."

"You'll go with me, right?"

"You bet. I'll be on the opposite team, I'm sure."

He laughed. "I would rather love on you instead." He couldn't wait to make love to her.

"When we reach your home, that's exactly what we're going to do." She sounded just as eager, smiling, kissing his cheek.

When they finally arrived home, Fisher grabbed both their bags and they headed into the house.

"Home, sweet home," he said.

"It sure is." She raced for the bedroom, and he dumped their bags and chased after her, loving her spontaneity and fun-loving spirit. He grabbed her up in the hallway before she reached the bedroom and carried her into it.

He set her on the carpeted floor and began pulling off her shirt, kissing her shoulders, her neck, her jaw, and sweeping his mouth across her lips in a lingering kiss. He was so glad they were safe, that neither of them had been hurt and the boy was going home to his family. That the kidnappers would be incarcerated. And that he and Kira could make love and become mated wolves.

She wrapped her arms around his waist and kissed him fully on the mouth, their bodies pressed snuggly against each other. "I've never known a wolf quite like you who would choose a whole new lifestyle to be with a she-wolf he's intrigued with."

"Whom he loves," Fisher said, kissing her nose. "I've never met a she-wolf who would make me want to give up my job to go on risky, but totally worthwhile adventures to take down shifters who could hurt all of us. When I'm with you, I'm on top of the world, seeing a new world view, finding completion in a way I've never done before."

"I love my job, but when I'm with you, I just feel so much more positively about accomplishing the mission. Your brain and mine work together to reach a successful conclusion in the best way possible. Your strength and mine complement each other's in every way possible. And when we're together, I love how we can be more than just USF agents teaming up on an assignment, but lovers who feel the connection that says we're unified as a mated couple."

"I couldn't have said it better," Fisher said. "I felt my whole world change once I met you and I wanted to get to know you even more." Then he cupped her face and began kissing her again and she gave into his kiss and poked her tongue into his mouth to deepen the connection.

"I love you," she said, breaking free from the kiss.

"I love you," he said, pressing his forehead against hers in a gentle way, then nuzzled her cheek in a tender way with his as if they were in their wolf form.

Then they began to slowly remove each other's clothes—his plaid shirt, her jeans skirt, then the rest of their garments until they were perfectly naked and ready to have sex. Every inch of her was beautiful and she smiled as she looked him over in a way that said that she totally approved of his physique. They began kissing again, his fingers combing through her hair and hers running down his back, making him shiver in anticipation.

She lowered her head to lick his nipples and he arched his head back with a groan. He ran his hands over her sides, touching the curve of her breasts, then sliding around to cup them. They fit perfectly in his palms, and he loved the solid feel of them before he leaned down to kiss her nipples.

She slid her hands over his buttocks, murmuring, "So firm."

He loved the sound of her voice when they were making love, the way she complimented him, making him feel that he was the supreme wolf choice among so many she could have chosen from. She was definitely that for him.

He wrapped his arms around her and hugged her tight, just loving the way her full breasts were pressed against his chest, the way her flat belly was firm against his full erection, the way she moved against him increasing the friction while they kissed.

He moved her to the bed, and he was going to pleasure her first, but she had other plans for that. "Behind me," she said, her voice soft, sexy, sultry.

Then she was guiding him to enter her feminine lips from behind while she was on her side, and she guided his hand to stroke her bud at the same time. Perfect. He could kiss her soft skin, her shoulder, neck, back then too.

He was stroking her slowly so he could thrust into her at a slower pace and not come too quickly. But the eroticism of him being behind her and sliding into her from behind and stroking her in front was eliciting more moans, and caught breaths, her heart—and his—beating wildly. Their pheromones were through the roof swirling around each other's saying, "Yes! They were a match."

He had suspected so when he had first met her on the ledge below the cliff, their pheromones had called out to each other, despite the adrenaline flooding his system because of being injured, and had been off the charts.

He was so ready to come, trying to keep things in check until he could bring her to climax, but he was struggling to keep from reaching orgasm. She suddenly kept her body very still and cried out. He knew then she had climaxed, and he continued to thrust until he erupted deep inside her.

He held her close, just hugging on her, their pheromones still in full force, their adrenaline and hearts racing, and he felt in that moment that they were as close to being one as wolves as any two wolves could be. He kissed her shoulder, and she kissed his arm wrapped around her, then looked over her shoulder at him and smiled.

"I love you, Fisher."

"I couldn't love you more, Kira." He just hoped her dad wouldn't want to kill him for mating his only daughter without speaking to him first about a mating!

23

Thanksgiving was going to be super special, Kira thought as they drove to her parents' home in Loveland, hoping they wouldn't be too shocked about her mating Fisher. They had to know that she was serious about her relationship with him since she'd never brought any male wolf to see them for such a special occasion, well ever, really. Though she was sure they would be surprised that she'd actually mated him. They had met her bossy, former USF partner at a hamburger joint in Loveland once, so they knew just how superior he acted toward her. She hadn't planned for them to meet him. It was just by chance while they had been on a mission in the area.

She reached over and patted Fisher's hand. "Just be yourself. They'll love you."

"I sure hope so since we're family forever now."

"They will."

As soon as they reached her parents' split-level house, the siding recently painted a pretty gray and big windows were filled with light, welcoming them to their place, her mom and dad quickly opened the door to greet them. Kira swore she'd seen the curtains move in the living room window as one or both had peeked out to see what Fisher looked like before they hurried outside.

Once they joined them on the porch, the aroma of turkey roasting in the oven, brown gravy, pecan pie, baked bread, and all the other delicious scents of a Thanksgiving feast wafted out the door.

As her parents welcomed them into the house, pumpkin spice candles scented the air. Orange, brown, and beige flowers and pinecones filled ornate filigreed vases, which her mother would change out to Christmas flowers the day after Thanksgiving.

"Happy Thanksgiving!" Kira said to her parents and gave them hugs.

"Happy Thanksgiving," Fisher said.

"Yes, happy Thanksgiving, everyone," Gloria said, Kira's father echoing the sentiment.

"Oh, my, he has a great resemblance to Vaughn. Are you a Navy SEAL also?" her mother asked, hugging Fisher, as if she knew he was part of the family already.

"Army Ranger, ma'am," Fisher said, giving her a hug back and Kira saw the appreciation on her mother's face.

"And just as polite as his cousin," her mother said. "I'm Gloria and this is Russell."

Kira's father shook his hand with a hearty handshake.

"I'm Fisher Greystoke and I owe my life to Kira," he said.

"I owe mine to Fisher. We've had a wild few days of it," Kira said.

"Come on in and we'll get some drinks, and you can tell us all about it," Russell said.

He poured everyone glasses of champagne while Gloria and Kira started to serve up the turkey and sides.

Russell gave everyone their drinks and then took Fisher out back to the deck with a view of Longs Peak and Mt. Meeker.

"Kira has never shown any interest in a guy, and this is the first time she has brought one home to meet us. So you're dating her, right?"

"Uh, well, we're mated," Fisher said.

"Mated? Hell, that was fast, but Gloria said Kira wouldn't wait when she met the right wolf. And she warned me you both might have already mated. How did you meet?" her dad asked.

Kira hurried outside and ushered them inside to eat. "Oh, no, Dad, we'll tell you over the meal. Mom's dying to hear the story also."

They all took seats at the table.

"They're mated already." Russell began carving the turkey while Gloria sat on one side of the table while Kira and Fisher sat on the other, Kira opposite her dad.

Her mother smiled, all knowing like. "Good. I'm not surprised at all once she said she was bringing someone home for the holidays to meet us. I told your dad it would lead to that before long if you hadn't both gone ahead and done it. Which is understandable. Once we meet the wolf of our hearts, it's a done deal. We worried about her not meeting anyone that would suit her while she worked in the jaguar organization."

"Yes, I wasn't sure, but your mom knew just what was going to happen." Russell smiled.

Then Kira told her and Fisher's story of how they met.

"Oh, my," Gloria said. "I thought this job was going to be less dangerous for you than when you worked for the police department."

"It's about the same." Kira served up some mashed potatoes and brown gravy. "I might never have met Fisher if it hadn't been for that."

Both Gloria and Russell eyed Fisher. He smiled at them and told them how he'd just been hired by the USF, but he left out about the training he had to go through.

"Oh, that's just perfect then," Gloria said. "You'll be together on missions."

Then they told her parents how they had protected each other against Reggie. Her parents exchanged glances and she figured they thought they were good for each other.

"So tell us about your family," Russell said. "We know that Vaughn is your cousin and that he's mated to Jillian. What about your parents or siblings?"

"I have three brothers—Heath is the doctor in the family, and Tanner, the eldest is in charge of the tanning manufacturing facility. Shawn also helps to manage it. Tanner is the only one of my brothers who is mated. Devlyn is our pack leader, and he is my cousin. Vaughn has a brother Brock, so he's another cousin and a private investigator. We have another cousin, Aaron, who owns a horse ranch. They're all located in the town of Greystoke. None of our parents are living."

"I'm so sorry to hear that, but even so, you have quite an extended family. It's just the three of us," Gloria said.

"Yes, and"—Fisher glanced at Kira and she nodded—"Kira's joining the Greystoke pack and moving there."

"Yes!" Gloria said, clapping her hands together. "Oh, I'm so glad the two of you mated. No one else would have ever convinced Kira to move back to Colorado from Houston. We were afraid that if she did possibly meet someone there, they would never move here. We've so missed her. And Greystoke is nice and close. This is really a reason to celebrate."

"You could always move to Greystoke. Bella and Devlyn, our pack leaders, and the rest of our pack members would be thrilled," Fisher said. "They're always happy to expand the wolf pack as long as no one who wants to join intends to take over the pack."

Kira and her parents laughed.

"It's certainly something to think about," Gloria said. "Oh, this is the best Thanksgiving ever."

"Yeah, I agree," Russell said, raising his drink to theirs in a cheer.

Fisher smiled and said, "Yeah, the best ever."

Kira kissed Fisher and he kissed her back.

"Well, we didn't have that exciting of a way to meet up," Gloria said. "We just ran into each other at a diner. Russell accidentally got my steak order and when we realized the mix up, he brought my dinner to me, and I invited him to eat with me. We had an instant crush on each other."

"We did. Her dinner looked so good, I wish I'd ordered it, and since I kept eyeing it once I joined her, she ended up giving me some of it," Russell said.

"And Mom *never* shares the food from her plate, so for her to meet some unknown wolf and do that?" Kira said.

"Do they still share food?" Fisher asked.

"You bet," Gloria said. "It's not to say we haven't had some wild adventures over the years. I imagine all of us do, being wolves and dealing with hunters while in our wolf coats, and other life situations."

Russell was quiet for a moment and then finally said, "You have to be a damn brave wolf to fall off a cliff to save your life."

Fisher shook his head. "I'd looked before I did my freefall. I just prayed I wouldn't be injured too badly, but I knew if I had stayed where I was, Royce would have shot me until I was dead. I don't know whether it was brave of me or just I had no other choice."

"Oh, you were brave. I'm not sure I could have done that even with the threat of dying," Kira said.

"I know. Me either," Gloria said. "If you haven't given it any thought, do you have plans for Christmas?"

Kira took hold of Fisher's hand and squeezed. "We would love to be here for Christmas."

Her parents' faces brightened.

Gloria said, "I'm so glad you're going to be here then. Since we're having turkey for Thanksgiving, will prime rib be all right for Christmas?"

"Yeah, that would be great," Fisher said.

As soon as she had spoken, Kira realized she should have asked Fisher about having Christmas with her parents first! She was so used to making decisions about things for just herself, but she had a mate now and they needed to talk about these things. It would take some getting used to, but she was glad that Fisher had gone along with it in such a cheerful way. She loved him.

They finally finished dinner and they visited on the back deck until the sun set, the brilliant reds and golds reflecting off the choppy lake water.

Then Kira said, "We're going to Greystoke tonight and I'll be staying with Fisher at his home. We're going to Houston to pack my belongings and he has got to go through the training that I had done." She smiled. "I get to put him through it too, I think. But then we'll be settled in Greystoke."

"Though we can always get another place that we both love if she doesn't love my place," Fisher said.

"I love his place. You will too. You can visit us anytime," Kira said.

Her parents congratulated them again. "You can't know just how happy we are for both of you," Gloria said.

"Yeah. I always wanted to have a son," Russell said. "I know you'll do us proud."

"And grandkids too," Gloria said.

Fisher and Kira smiled. Then they said good night to her parents and got into her car and left.

"I guess they liked me," Fisher said.

"For my dad to tell anyone that he is brave? He totally admired you. The cherry on top was that you risked your life to protect me from Reggie."

Fisher smiled. "I'm so glad. I really like your parents. They're down-to-earth and fun to talk to. I felt comfortable with them from the beginning. They made me feel welcome to the family. Though I thought you might have been a little worried about your dad talking to me on the back deck before we sat down to eat. I wondered if you were rescuing me when I didn't realize I even needed to be rescued."

She laughed. "Believe me, this is a first for me so I didn't know what to expect, exactly. I was afraid my dad was going to lay down the rules regarding how you treated me. But after telling our stories, he knew you were the right one for me. Will anyone from your family miss you for Christmas? I should have asked you before I said we would see my parents. I felt badly that I hadn't consulted you first after I said we could go there."

"Don't be. My family enjoys having our holidays together, but we can do different things, like having your parents to the Greystoke celebration, or have two celebrations, one with my family and one with yours. But truthfully, my family is so big, they won't miss me as much as your family would miss you. I was fine with that."

She thought the world of Fisher for wanting to make sure her family wasn't left out of the holiday events.

"Now that your parents know we're mated, we need to tell the rest of the family that we are and of course that you're joining the pack," Fisher said.

"Oh, absolutely." She appreciated that he had wanted to tell her parents first.

Then he got on Bluetooth and made a conference call to his brothers and cousins. Since Devlyn was also a cousin, he would let the rest of the pack know the news.

"Congratulations," Devlyn and Bella said first, taking the lead as pack leaders.

His brothers and Tanner's mate, Serena, all congratulated them after that. Then his other cousins and their mates cheered them on.

Devlyn said, "I'm so glad we have a new pack member too."

"Yes," Bella said. "Now we just need to convince your parents to join us here in Greystoke."

"Absolutely," Fisher said.

Kira thought he was so cute to want to have her family living in the same place as they were.

"We'll let the rest of the pack know," Devlyn said. "Expect a celebration in a few days."

Then they all wished each other a Happy Thanksgiving and ended the call.

Fisher asked Kira, "Do you think your parents will want to move to Greystoke?"

"If we end up having little ones? I bet they would. They love that area also and I think if the Greystoke pack encourages it, they'll be interested."

"That would be great."

They finally arrived at his home, and Fisher said, "I want to get this training/testing over with so I'll know that I have a permanent position with the USF. And we need to get your things moved to Greystoke."

"Call Martin."

"It's Thanksgiving."

"We're always available for any mission. He will be glad you're doing well enough to take the test. You are, aren't you?" Kira asked.

"Yeah. I feel just fine. I want to get this over with so I'm a legitimate special agent. I just feel like it's hanging over my head." He got on his phone and called Martin, hoping Kira was right and he wasn't about to annoy his brand-new boss.

"Don't tell me Kira's got another case to take care of," Martin said.

"No, sir. I wanted to schedule my training for Monday and Kira is moving to Greystoke, so we're packing her things and moving them. We mated each other, if Kira didn't tell you yet."

"I'll have you scheduled. Congratulations on the mating," Martin said.

"Thanks, and happy Thanksgiving."

"To the both of you also. We'll see you on Monday."

Then they said goodbye to their boss and Kira hugged Fisher. "You will soon be a genuine special agent with a badge and gun even."

He just hoped he passed the test!

THREE DAYS LATER, Fisher and Kira arrived at the airport in Houston. Everett and Demetria picked them up and took them out to dinner.

"What will happen with the kidnappers?" Fisher asked at the Mexican restaurant where they all ordered beef fajitas.

"They've been charged with shooting you, shooting at both of you with the intent to kill, taking Kira hostage and then again, shooting at the both of you, and all the kidnappings," Everett said. "But they haven't received their sentencing yet."

"We'll do your training test in the morning and get that over with." Demetria smiled. "Everett and I volunteered to help put you through your paces."

"That means you'll go easy on me, right?" Fisher asked, chuckling.

"You wish," Kira said. "They were tough on me. They better not go easy on you."

Fisher laughed. "I know you'll be tough on me."

"You bet. I have to know you're the perfect partner for me."

He smiled at her, knowing she already felt he was the perfect partner for her in all things.

"We're taking you to Strom's club tonight after dinner. Wanting to welcome you to Houston, he said all our drinks are free tonight," Demetria said.

"It's a really fun club," Kira said. "You're going to love it."

Fisher finished his third fajita. "I love this restaurant too."

"Yeah, they have great food," Demetria said.

Then Demetria drove them over to the Clawed and Dangerous Kitty Cat Club for drinks and dancing. A man in a jaguar spotted shirt was blocking a parking space closest to the front door of the club while a driver of a pickup was trying to park in the spot.

"Is that the owner's parking space?" Fisher asked, amused that the pickup driver was trying to still park there. "Hold on. I'm getting out and I'll help the guy deal with this."

"The parking space is being held for us," Everett said, "courtesy of the owner."

"Oh, wow, how nice," Kira said.

"Come on, Fisher. We'll go dissuade the pickup driver to give it up since he isn't getting the message," Everett said.

Fisher was ready to defend their parking spot and help out the club employee who was standing in the parking spot, his arms folded across his broad chest. He looked like a bulldog of a shifter, though he was a jaguar, just challenging the pickup driver to run him over.

The driver was inching into the space, persisting on getting that prime spot. Then Fisher and Everett got involved, joining the club employee in the parking space. Once they did, the employee walked over to the pickup driver's door. "Do you want me to ban you for a week from the club?"

The driver rolled down his window. "You can't do that."

"Move it. The space is saved for a special guest tonight. Move along. Find another parking space or face the ban," the employee said.

The driver pulled forward like he was going to run over Fisher and Everett, but the employee reached in through the driver's window and grabbed the guy's keys. The employee pulled his phone out of his pocket. "I'm calling 911 to get the police out here for threatening us with the pickup."

The driver tried to get out of his truck, but Fisher and Everett made sure he couldn't open the door.

"The police are on their way," the club employee said.

All over a parking spot. Fisher smelled vodka on the guy's breath and figured he was already drunk and hadn't even made it into the club to drink yet.

A couple of patrol cars arrived, and two cops got out to question everyone. The one cop forced the driver out of his pickup and made him do a sobriety test. Then the passenger in the car, who hadn't been drinking, and was a good friend of the driver, was going to take his truck home for him.

In the meantime, the police got Fisher, Everett, and the employee's statements and arrested the drunk pickup driver who had threatened to run them over with the truck. Then the friend drove the truck off, and Demetria, who was waiting for the parking spot, pulled right in.

The employee thanked Fisher and Everett for coming to his aid, and Demetria and Kira joined the guys and were shaking their heads. Before they even went inside, they could hear the beautiful Latin music playing inside. The employee opened the door for them and then they all went inside. It was crowded with club patrons drinking at tables, dancing on the dance floor, colorful lights flashing through live ferns, rubber trees, vining plants, and banana trees. Some club dancers were wearing faux leopard or jaguar skins and dancing high above on platforms.

"This place is amazing," Fisher said.

"Yeah, isn't it?" Kira said. "I knew you would love it. You can smell mostly jaguars in here. Isn't that the coolest thing? A couple of wolves, beside us. And lots of humans."

The guy that had been protecting their parking space led them to a prime table close to the dance floor, which surprised both Fisher and Kira, but he was glad for it because all the tables with seats and the ones for people to stand at were all taken.

Animal sounds from parrots calling to each other, an occasional elephant trumpeting, and monkeys howling added to the ambience. Jaguar print covered the seats they were sitting on, and hibiscus flowers were in vases at each of the tables, giving the setting a South American feel. Jungle scenes had been painted on all the walls featuring every kind of jungle cat there was from jaguars, cougars, ocelots, margays, jaguarundis, and other wild cats of South America.

Everett ordered a drink called a Jaguar made of tequila, Amer Picon, and Chartreuse, but Demetria recommended against it. "Everett likes the slightly bitter drink. Not me. I'm all for nice and sweet."

"That's because you're so sweet," Everett said.

She leaned over and licked his lips. "You see how he says all the right words?" She ordered a peach margarita.

"Or he would be in trouble," Kira said, ordering a Big Bad Wolf made of Curacao, apricot brandy, cream, and grenadine. "I can't believe Strom changed the cocktail menu to include a wolf drink."

"Yeah, but you notice it's the big *bad* wolf," Demetria said.

They all laughed.

Fisher picked the strawberry margarita. Before they were delivered, he rose from the table and asked Kira if she wanted to dance.

Kira smiled and took hold of his hand. "Oh, absolutely. Here we are mated, and we haven't ever danced with each other."

"There are so many things we need to explore about each other." Then he led her to the dance floor and was so glad to be doing this with her. It was crowded, and normally he wouldn't like to dance on a floor this filled with partygoers, but with Kira, it worked just fine as he kept her close and rubbed his body against hers. She leaned against him with her hot little body and danced her heart out. Their hearts were beating like crazy, and he could smell her arousal as they danced nice and close to the sizzling, Latin tunes. He loved dancing with her like this, but he was so ready to take her back to her apartment and make love to her too.

"Now we know something else we can do when we want a night out," Kira said, kissing his cheek and licking his lips.

He nuzzled her behind her ear. "Oh, yeah, there isn't anything quite as wild, fun, and exotic as this in Greystoke. But they have a nice western-themed dance club that would be fun to go to."

His mouth caressed her skin, and she shivered. "That sounds great."

The heat of their bodies pressed together as they danced among the other couples moving on the dance floor. But they had eyes only for each other as they moved across the floor in each other's arms, her head against his shoulder. He kissed the top of her head, sliding his hand over her back in a subtle caress.

She moved her hands to his back and slipped her hands lower until she was enticingly touching his buttocks. At the same time, she began pressing her leg between his and giving a gentle rub. Man, his mate was going to send him over the edge soon, but he loved the way she danced so sexily. The club's atmosphere, the music, the other dancers, the scenery, not to mention just how enticing his mate was—all helped to encourage "misbehaving," he thought, loving this with her.

"Before the ice melts in our drinks, do you want to stop and enjoy them?" Kira asked once they had finished their fourth dance.

"Yeah, and Everett and Demetria are still sitting at the table so they may be waiting for us to return so they can dance. And I need to cool down before I embarrass myself."

Kira laughed. "I love you."

He smiled and kissed her mouth. "I love you too."

They returned to the table to enjoy their drinks topped with colorful parasols and cherries and took their seats.

"We're going to dance if you all are taking a break," Demetria said, snagging Everett's hand. "We didn't want to lose the table if we should all dance at the same time."

"They wouldn't dare," Kira said.

They all laughed, and the jaguars headed to the dance floor.

"This is so much fun," Fisher said.

"I'm glad you like it. It's frequented by jaguars, of course, but I was in here once when a couple of lions were here. That was an experience and a half. I kept thinking that I was mistaken."

"Lions. That's something I would never have imagined."

"Me either. They were just passing through Houston when they saw the club and were drawn to it. They were amazed to see it was a jaguar shifter club."

"I bet."

"So one of the things I want to do is go rock climbing sometime with you. Mountain climbing. You know, after I had to free climb when you were shot, I realized I need to get back into that."

"I would love to do that with you. They have a rock-climbing wall in a gym in Greystoke that we can get a subscription for, and we can go to the national park anytime to get in some climbing."

"That would be great."

They drank from their cocktails when a tall, blond-haired man —a jaguar—came over to the table and smiled at Kira, reaching out his hand. "Dance with me?"

"Uh, no, thanks. We're recently mated."

The jaguar glanced at Fisher as if he suddenly realized Kira had a mate. Fisher smiled, raising his brows, waiting for the guy to honor Kira's words.

"Alright. Your loss," the jaguar said, then headed straight to another table where a couple were sitting, enjoying a conversation and drinks. When he asked the accompanied jaguar woman to dance with him, the guy with her rose from his seat, he didn't speak a word, but pulled back his fist and socked the jaguar in the jaw. The jaguar fell back and raised his fists, ready for a full-on fight.

Neither Fisher nor Kira had seen it coming. The jaguar who had gotten punched, didn't either.

At the same time, the bouncer headed their way, and he hauled the jaguar, who was causing trouble with accompanied ladies, out of the club.

Fisher sighed. "Hell, I should have done that."

"What? Punched the guy?" Kira asked, taking hold of Fisher's hand and leaning over to kiss him.

"Yeah."

"No way. What if the bouncer had tossed out the guy that had thrown the punch instead? Besides, you showed confidence in your masculinity by letting me handle the situation, which I appreciated, by the way. Now if the jaguar hadn't taken no for an answer, we both could have shown him the error of his ways."

Fisher smiled. "Yeah, for sure." Knowing Kira was a USF agent, he felt more comfortable about her being able to deal with someone who was trouble, but even so, he would have gotten between them if the guy had made a move to force Kira to dance with him.

Then Everett and Demetria rejoined them, Everett smiling and shaking his head. "That dude found out the hard way that you don't try to pick up some other guy's date at the club."

Fisher immediately thought Everett might have believed he should have stood up and socked the guy like the jaguar had done.

Demetria and Everett sat down at the table and she said, "It's a good thing you didn't do that, unless you were defending Kira if the guy had put his hand on her, though she would have shown him that was the wrong thing to do. But our boss wouldn't have gone along with how the jaguar had protected his girlfriend or mate."

Then Fisher was relieved he had done the right thing.

"More dancing?" Fisher asked Kira.

"Absolutely. If we didn't have to go in early to have you go through your training, I would say we should stay here until the club closes for the night, but we all have to be at our best tomorrow."

"Besides," Fisher said, pulling her close and working up the heat again, "I want to finish the night off in the best way possible."

She chuckled and rubbed her body against his. "Yeah, me too."

24

After they'd spent a delightful evening together, they finally left right before the club closed. They hadn't planned to stay that late, but they'd all had so much fun. Demetria and Everett drove Fisher and Kira to her apartment.

"We'll pick you up and have breakfast at our place in the morning, and then we'll take you to the headquarters to do the training," Everett said as they wished them a goodnight.

"We had a blast," Kira said.

"We did too," Demetria agreed.

"I agree," Fisher said.

Having breakfast in the morning with the Andersons worked out well for Kira because she had hardly any food in her fridge since she hadn't been home for a while. It was going to be so nice living with her mate now with a stocked fridge and an extended family to enjoy visiting when she and Fisher weren't off on a mission. She loved how beautifully decorated his place was, when hers was really sparse because she hadn't felt settled there and she hadn't even hung pictures yet.

Kira and Fisher carried their bags into the apartment. She had already rented a van and they would pack everything up as soon as Everett finished his training.

Her apartment was a little messy. But not too bad. She always had a clean kitchen, and her laundry was done, but sometimes she was in a hurry to catch a flight when she was on a case, so her bed sheets had been washed, but she hadn't had time to make the bed before she left this last time. She groaned when she saw her bedspread on a chair, and all her pillows on top of it—without their pillowcases.

He laughed and they grabbed her clean fitted sheet and quickly covered the mattress with it. They tugged pillowcases on two of the pillows. Then he began pulling off her dress, and she kicked off her heels. He was trying to unbutton his shirt in a hurry, but she was working on them too.

Then she pulled his shirt off his shoulders and kissed them with tender kisses. "Shower first?"

"Yeah." He unbuckled his belt, and she ran her hand over his arousal.

He was ready for more action this time. He yanked off his pants and the rest of his clothes while she pulled off her panties and bra. They headed into the bathroom, and he took her hand to help her climb into the bathtub and joined her.

"Boy, when I left home and ended up with that last mission, I sure didn't expect to return here with a mate." She started the shower, then poured bodywash out of her bottle and began lathering his body up. She loved the feel of him as she felt his soft skin and hard muscles tense and then relax beneath her fingers. She set the bottle down on a small bath shelf and began running her hands over his taut nipples.

"I know. I never thought I would be leaving Greystoke with my mate and doing shifter training so I could stay with her in my new job!" He grabbed the bottle of bodywash and started running it over her body. His hands lingered on her breasts, fondling them, his fingers circling over her nipples.

His touching her was titillating, making her ache between her legs and grow wet in anticipation.

"You will do stupendously on the mission." She groaned as his fingers continued to play with her nipples.

She rubbed her whole, slippery body against his, feeling the hard planes of his torso and his huge erection against her body and she loved this. She had never imagined being with a mate could be this beautiful.

She rubbed the soap over his back while he wrapped his arms around hers and began soaping her up. This was nice, front to front, washing each other's backs. The next thing she knew, his hand slipped to her front, and he began sliding his hand between her legs.

"Oh," she moaned as he began to stroke her sensitive nub. She thought they would be doing this in bed, but she suspected he didn't want to wait that long and that was fine with her.

His mouth covered hers and she kissed him deeply, but he introduced his finger between her legs and stroked and pumped with it, and she cried out. If she hadn't mated him already, she would have now! He lifted her up so she could wrap her legs around his hips and then he inserted his full erection between her legs and began to thrust.

"Love you so much, honey," he said, then kissed her mouth again, continuing to thrust into her as deeply as he could.

"Love you too, with all my heart."

FISHER TRIED to slow his pace as he pushed into Kira, but she had her hands on his hips, pulling him tighter, encouraging him to keep going and he couldn't stop. He growled with satisfaction as he filled her with his seed. He continued to thrust until he was finished, and he released her to finish their shower. Being with Kira like this was the perfect way to end the great night they'd had. Though cuddling together for the rest of the night was really nice too. They washed and rinsed off.

Even though he loved the job he was doing for the USF, being with Kira made it the perfect job. He loved being with her on the job and off. They dried each other and then returned to the bed to finish making it. They climbed into bed and snuggled together.

"You are going to do great tomorrow," Kira said, kissing Fisher's naked chest.

He smiled at her and wrapped his arm around her back. "I will do my best to prove to Martin that I can do it." No way did Fisher want Kira to have to leave her job if he couldn't hack it. Not that he really thought he couldn't. And if he did fail? He was signing up for the training to do it again—until he got it right.

～

THE NEXT MORNING, Everett and Demetria made breakfast of pancakes and sausages and Kira asked, "Has Martin said anything about any more missions for us?"

"No," Demetria said, bringing them all cups of coffee. "So far, nothing has come up. During the holidays, we always hope things will be quiet."

"Has anyone said anything to you about what roles you'll play in my training?" Fisher asked.

"No. The trainers will tell us when we get there." Everett poured some more maple syrup on his pancakes. "You'll do fine."

After breakfast, Demetria and Everett drove Kira and Fisher over to the jaguar facilities where Fisher would take his test. The place was surrounded by pine woods, and they took quite a drive through them to actually reach a complex of buildings.

"The largest building with all the glass windows is the head-quarters," Everett said.

"The secure building off to the left is the prison. They have room for two-hundred prisoners," Demetria said. "They only have forty-five incarcerated."

When they arrived at the tactical training and testing facility, Demetria parked, and they all got out and headed for the door. Inside, they were met by the instructor in charge, David Patterson. "Since you are an Army Ranger and qualified with the training you had already done and after helping to take down three rogue wolves as an agent—even in your wolf coat, Martin said you only have to do the shifter testing, no training. Otherwise, you would be here for a week of the exercises."

Fisher was glad he wouldn't have to do all the rest of the train-ing, so that he could actively work on missions with Kira.

"You can use the changing room and then once you've shifted, meet me out here and I'll start you on your journey," David said.

Kira went with Demetria, and Everett and Fisher went to a different group of changing rooms connected by a hallway that led to a couple of different doors.

"Wolves have trouble with some of the jaguar course, naturally, because we can leap higher than you can. When wolves began to join our forces, the headquarters added different obstacles that would allow wolves to take different paths to reach their objectives. The courses are designed to test everyone's ability to reach their goals whatever way that works best for them," Everett said while stripping off his clothes. "Which is just like it would be in real life."

"Good. I'm looking forward to it." Though Fisher loved a good challenge, he was a bit worried he wouldn't pass the test, just like anyone might be. This would be a unique challenge that he couldn't have prepared for, but while working on a real-world assignment, he would have just as unique challenges to accomplish.

Both men finished stripping and shifted, then headed out into a small, unfurnished room with a map covering one of the walls showing forests, houses, a river, creeks, and a few roads.

"Your mission, should you accept it, is rescuing a teen jaguar who has been taken hostage. The warehouse is a maze of rooms and obstacles, and you'll have to use your wits to find the teen and rescue him. You have three hours to accomplish the mission." David held a sweatshirt out to Fisher to sniff. "Parker was wearing this shirt the day before he was taken."

Fisher realized that Everett had slipped away. Kira joined Fisher and nuzzled his nose and then she left the room through one of the doorways.

"You'll be able to smell everyone's scents that have been in the building or might be in the building. You'll find water stations to stay hydrated. They are in safe places where no one will bother you. Clocks with the countdown are in every room you go into, so you can keep track of your progress. Do you have any questions?"

Fisher shifted. "Are there any penalties?"

"If you make wrong decisions, you could end up back at the beginning, or worse—failing the mission. If you don't have any further questions, you may begin, and I'll start the timer."

"I'm ready." And anxious to rescue the teen and solve the mission.

"Good luck. I know you can do it. By the way, as a wolf going through this part of the exercise, Kira has the fastest record of solving the mission. You'll have to ask her how she did it."

Fisher smiled. "I'm not surprised."

Then Fisher shifted, David left the room, and Fisher saw the countdown on a clock on the wall. He headed in the direction that he'd seen Kira go and then he smelled she had gone down a hallway to a room that had four doors. Two doors were in one wall, and two more walls each had a door.

Fisher took deep breaths, smelling everyone's scents. Everett had gone to the far-right door. And that's the way the teen hostage had gone also. Fisher suspected he would be attacked anywhere along the way. If that was the most direct route, it could be heavily guarded. Or traps might be set. Then again, guards and traps could be all over the place.

He found Demetria's scent at the middle door, and on the door on the wall the farthest from where the teen's scent was, he found Kira's scent. He figured he would have to shift to open the door Kira went through, but as soon as he approached it, the door automatically and soundlessly opened. Convenient for a shifter.

He noticed cameras were all over and figured he was being monitored to determine if he could take decisive actions under pressure.

He entered the room with a spiral-patterned, tiled floor of blues, oranges, and browns, and could smell chlorinated water beneath the floor. Up above were platforms a big cat could leap on to make his or her way to the opposite side of the room where there was another door. He suspected if he stepped on the wrong tiles, one would open and he would fall into a pool.

He carefully sniffed where Kira had gone. And smiled. She wouldn't lead him astray. He didn't think. He figured if he stepped on one of the tiles that would fall away, it wouldn't move unless he put more of his weight on it. So he just carefully moved from tile to tile, sniffing each before he took a step. He hoped he wouldn't make a mistake, wishing he could just leap across the platforms instead, knowing this was taking longer than he wanted it to. He smelled that other wolves had been this way, but their scents were fainter, as if the wolves had been there a long time ago.

When he was nearly to the floor next to the door that wasn't tiled, strong fans on the ceiling blew across the room, disbursing

Kira's scent and he leapt to a solid rectangular blue tile in front of the door. He believed that was the safe place. When he landed on the tile, nothing happened except that the door opened for him, and relieved, he went inside the room. He wondered if the ones testing him thought that his mate was helping him, and they had to change up the game a bit by turning on the fans.

In this room, there were four doors, the one he had come through and one on each of the other three walls, all painted blue. He could smell the teen had come from the leftmost door and moved across the floor to the opposite door with two jaguars that he didn't know by scent. Or maybe the teen had been moved the opposite way. Fisher could only smell the teen's scent, but he couldn't determine which way he was going.

What if Fisher was being tested on taking the most direct route to the kid? Time was always of the essence in kidnapping cases, but the path that seemed to be the most direct route didn't necessarily mean it was. Again, he smelled Kira's scent and she had gone straight across from the door he had entered, not through one of the two doors that the teen had traveled through. Fisher took a gamble and went through the door she had entered. He figured that the testers were probably amused that he was following his mate's scent instead of the scent of the boy.

But it would be too easy just to do that, he thought. He raced across the floor to the other door and entered. Here, there was a narrow set of stairs, and he went up them. At the landing, he found a narrow walkway suspended two stories high, the chlorinated water rippling way down below. He could imagine falling off the walkway into the water and failing the exercise. He saw a clock telling him twenty minutes had passed. He felt he was wasting too much time, and he began to run across the walkway, feeling sure-footed, but then he realized as soon as he did, it started to sway. He lost his balance, his feet slipping, his heart skipping beats, and he nearly fell below the ropes holding the platform up. He had to be more careful and slowed way down.

When he reached the other side, he took a deep breath, smelling Kira's scent and entered through the doorway. Inside was a maze of stacked wooden boxes at various heights from three feet to twenty. He smelled Kira's and Everett's scents inside the room. Again, jaguars and cougars could leap up on top of boxes to see where they needed to go. Even bears could climb up them, if they ended up with any bear shifters in the organization. As a wolf, Fisher could leap up to a lower box and he did that, but he needed to get to a higher elevation to see which path to take. He could shift and climb as a naked human, he thought.

But then he smelled Kira's scent and she had moved down in the maze rather than climbing on top of the wooden boxes so he jumped down to enter the maze too. When he began to navigate the maze, he discovered some of the boxes were open on one side. Fisher heard movement on top of some of the boxes and saw Everett pacing way up high, with his back to Fisher, waiting for him in case he showed up. With Everett up so high, he wouldn't be able to see Fisher unless Everett was walking on top of a box that was near the maze path Fisher was navigating.

When Everett moved in Fisher's direction, Fisher slipped into an open box to keep from being seen. He had to stay out of Everett's sight at all costs or he might end up in a battle. Everett had been in the middle of the box maze, but he moved off to the right of the boxes. Cats could move quietly, but even so, the boxes creaked no matter how quietly anyone walked, which helped Fisher keep track of the jaguar. Even though he could smell Everett, he had moved all over the crates watching for Fisher so his scent didn't help him keep track of the big cat.

Fisher slipped out of the box and made his move toward the left most path. The advantage he had there was that he could remain quiet on the cement floor as he made his way around the maze. But he didn't know which way to go to get out of the maze to reach another door. Maybe the proper path was to the right where Everett had gone and that's why he was mostly focused on guarding that area.

Fisher kept moving, coming to a dead end that went left or right. He didn't smell Kira's scent this way but maybe more than one path could be taken to reach the door. At least he hoped. He went to the right, suspecting Everett might be watching the middle and right side of the maze to make sure that he caught Fisher if he tried to move in that direction. Why would Everett be there, instead of to the left of the maze, unless the path to the right was the correct path to take?

Fisher heard Everett coming and he took refuge in another box and waited. Everett was moving straight for Fisher's box, except five boxes were stacked on top of the one he was sitting inside. He just hoped Everett couldn't smell his scent down below. For several seconds that felt like minutes, Everett stood way up on top of the box. No more sounds were made. Fisher couldn't hear Everett's heart beating so he knew the cat couldn't hear his either. *Thankfully.*

Then Everett moved away again to the right side of the maze. Fisher breathed a sigh of relief but still he didn't move in case Everett knew Fisher was sitting inside that box, and Everett was waiting for him to leave the spot and move again. Fisher finally moved as stealthily as he could when he heard Everett leaping and landing on a box near him about seven boxes high and Fisher dove into the closest one to him. He waited, afraid Everett had heard or smelled him and knew just where he was. But then after a couple of minutes, Everett walked back to the right side of the maze. Fisher hurried out of the box and headed straight down the path, then to the left, no other option, to the right, to the right again, straight, to the left. All the while, Everett was pacing around the right side of the maze and Fisher thought he was getting closer to the middle of the wooden boxes again.

Then to his guarded relief, Fisher saw a tunnel of boxes with just a missing section in spurts. If he could get through those at a run, it would help him travel faster. But if Everett was anywhere near the open sections, he might be able to catch a glimpse of Fisher. At least Fisher could move through some of the tunnel sections without being seen as long as Everett didn't leap down into the maze.

Then Fisher realized this was probably the section that Everett had been monitoring when he moved back to the middle area. Fisher moved through the tunnel until he came close to the end of this part of the tunnel. He listened, hadn't heard Everett for a few minutes, so figured he was sitting and listening too.

The last he'd heard of Everett, he was still off to Fisher's right. Then a box creaked, but Fisher was certain he could dash through the open area to the next part before Everett could see him. Fisher made it to the next part of the tunnel and navigated to the end of it. Everett was still far enough away that Fisher chanced moving to the next tunnel. He leaped into the tunnel and then moved deeper into it so that Everett couldn't see him. He continued on his way, hearing Everett making his way to where Fisher had been, which gave Fisher the opportunity to continue moving until he was out in the open. The maze had made a right turn and straight ahead was the door. Everett was at the middle of the boxes. Fisher was northeast of him. Fisher ran as fast as a wolf could for the door. Then he heard Everett leaping on top of crates in his direction. Fisher could hide in one of the open boxes to his left or right when they appeared or take the chance to reach the door first.

Once he entered the next room, would Everett just follow him into it? Fisher wouldn't have any choice but to fight him. Fisher was so close to the doorway, he leapt the last few feet, hoping the door would open in time and he could leap through. And with any luck, the door would silently close before Everett knew Fisher had gone into the next room. The door magically opened, and Fisher managed to make it into the next room. He glanced back but didn't see any sign of Everett. The door closed without making a sound.

Fisher took a deep breath and let it out. He smelled Kira's scent in here and he wondered how she had gotten here. He hadn't smelled her scent in the tunnel of boxes. This room was furnished like a bedroom, and he heard a muffled cry behind a dresser. The teen? But Fisher didn't smell the boy's scent in here. An ambush? He didn't think so. At least he had to rescue the person if someone needed rescuing. He hurried to the large chest and behind it, he found Kira gagged and tied to a chair, not in her wolf form, but dressed and in her human form.

His brain couldn't assimilate what was going on at first. Then he shifted and hurried to ungag and untie her.

Kira shook her head. "I'm bait. You've got to hurry and get out of here. Leave me behind."

"Who did this to you?" he asked, his voice hushed.

She spoke in whispered words also. "The trainers. They told me I was supposed to stop you from reaching the teen. I just didn't expect to be a hostage myself.' She smiled up at him, hugging and kissing him.

"My mission just became rescuing my partner and finding the teen. If you're being used as bait, you're now on my side."

"Okay, I'll go for that."

She and Fisher headed for the door on the other side of the dresser. "Do you know your way to where the teen is being held?" he asked.

"No, and they have changed the whole facility since I was here last year so it would be like the blind leading the blind."

"You didn't go toward the boy's scent," he said.

"No. I figured they would have everyone there, waiting for you

to arrive. And I suspected you would know that and go in the opposite direction."

He shifted, then they entered the next room, and it was empty,
save for stairs going down. He went first, since this was his mission,
but also to protect Kira should they run into trouble.

He smelled the boy's scent again, but this time he followed it. A
clock showed an hour and half had passed and he wondered how
that had happened! When they reached the base of the stairs, they
were in a room surrounding a swimming pool that looked to be
about twenty by forty feet. It looked inviting. Across the pool, a teen
was tied up and gagged. Fisher hoped he hadn't been confined for
that long, but he suspected that the trainers would know exactly
where Fisher had been at all times and would set up the hostage
situation when he got close.

He hoped the same had happened for Kira. No guards were
posted anywhere, which surprised Fisher. He could go across the
swimming pool or race around the pool, which would be quicker.
But when he took a step that way, the boy's eyes widened, and he
vigorously shook his head. Fisher glanced up at the walls
surrounding the pool and again saw platforms where jaguars could
leap to and make their way to the hostage from up above. Jaguars
were powerful swimmers though too. But wolves were excellent
swimmers and would cross rivers and large bodies of water in
search of new territories or food.

Fisher didn't see anything that would be an issue around the
pool, but he wasn't chancing it since the boy was indicating that
there was something amiss over there. Fisher jumped into the pool
while Kira waited behind. As a wolf, he could swim five miles per
hour, and he reached the other side of the pool in record time.

He couldn't get out of the pool as a wolf. Since the teen was a
jaguar shifter, Fisher didn't have to worry about shifting in front of
him. He shifted, climbed out of the pool, and removed the teen's
gag and bindings.

"Are you alright?" Fisher asked, knowing this was a simulation, but if it was for real, he would have done the same thing.

The teen smiled at him and rose from the chair. "Yeah, they just tied me up before you got here. They said you were just as quick as Kira and didn't take the long way around."

So the way he took had been the shortcut? Fisher shifted back into his wolf, wondering now if he had to get the teen to safety without getting caught. David hadn't mentioned that part of the equation.

David came through the tunnel entrance and clapped his hands, smiling. "You tied with Kira's winning time to accomplish the mission. You can have a lunch break with your fellow friends and then we have the next part of the exercise. It was a good thing your hostage warned you about walking around the pool to rescue him. Alarms would have sounded, and the guards would have shown up. They're turned off now. You can go through this hidden passage that takes you directly to the changing room, shift, get dressed, and Kira will take you to the lunchroom."

Fisher was glad to have made it in the same time as Kira, which showed they thought a lot alike and that could help when accomplishing missions.

Fisher and Kira went together through the secret passageway then. "They're proud of you," Kira said. "And I'm sure they're glad they hired you. Though because of helping to capture the kidnappers that's a foregone conclusion."

When they reached the changing room, he shifted. "I had a time keeping out of Everett's sight. But that was half the fun." Fisher began getting dressed. "So what's the next part of the test?"

"You'll get to take the teen to safety."

Fisher laughed. "So it will be an escape and evasion exercise with the freed teen hostage." He slipped on his boots.

"Yep."

"As shifters?"

"Yep. You have proven you can do all of that as a human in a real-life situation and also as a wolf, but you'll have the new mission of getting the teen to a safehouse as a shifter."

"Will you be on the mission with us?" Fisher asked.

She smiled. "Probably not, unless I end up being taken hostage again. I don't believe they think I would be on their side."

He kissed her. "If the roles were reversed, I would have broken free and come to your aid."

"That's another reason why I love you."

25

Kira was so proud of Fisher for accomplishing the mission in the same amount of time as she had taken. She'd set the record for wolves, but she was happy to share it with her mate. She had been serious when she had told him to leave her and rescue the boy instead. But she was glad her mate hadn't left her behind in the event the coordinators had decided to use her as bait again.

They headed to the dining room, and she asked, "What made you go in the same direction I had gone in?"

"First, I felt going in the same direction as the teen had was probably the wrong choice because it would make the quest too simple. But also because I had smelled that you had gone the way I had planned to go and I knew you wouldn't try to entrap me."

"What if I had? I would have been obligated to do what they had told me. Even if I had wanted to help you, they had cameras everywhere watching what we did."

"Yeah, right." He sounded like he didn't believe her.

She really would have helped him in any way that she could have if she had been able to if her role had been to thwart him in his mission. She suspected they knew that and would have wanted to see how she had reacted to helping him. But she knew he had to do it alone—unless of course she had needed to jump in and assist him.

They walked into the dining room where Everett and Demetria were sitting at a table waiting for them. A buffet bar was set up and long tables accommodated maybe sixty or seventy people but no one was there eating yet.

"They have a great buffet here, free of charge for new trainees," Demetria said, motioning to the food bar. "Let's get something to eat. Maybe during the next phase of your mission, I can even play."

Everett shook his head, smiling. "I didn't get to play either. I did a lot of pacing, leaping around, and sitting on top of boxes. I thought I heard Fisher going through the maze but when I checked it out, I didn't smell him or see any glimpses of him. I figured I had imagined he had come my way. I never expected him to slip by me without me even noticing. Even when he went through the doorway, I thought that would have alerted me."

"I was sweating it out a few times when I heard you draw close," Fisher said, "and I wasn't really sure I was headed in the right direction." He served up some lasagna and garlic toast, salad, fried chicken wings, and grabbed a bottle of water. "If you had heard me go through the exit door, would you have come after me?"

"No. I would have had to stay in the maze until I was given the okay to move in the event you backtracked. Others were supposed to stop you in the next area," Everett said.

"Where were you, Demetria?" Fisher asked.

"I was in another part of the building where we thought you might go. It was a much longer route and five of us were monitoring various sections there. We should have figured you would take the path that led *away* from where the teen had gone." Demetria got a lunch similar to Fisher's, minus the chicken wings and she added cantaloupe and honeydew melon to her plate.

Everett picked up a hamburger, french fries, and some strawberries and blueberries. Kira dished up haddock and chips, toma-toes, strawberries, and pineapple and they all grabbed bottles of water and returned to their table. Other jaguars began drifting into the lunchroom, looking like they had been having a workout in another part of the facilities while they joked about their successes and failures.

Kira thought everyone looked like they were glad to be here no matter what the rigorous training they were going through entailed.

"Those are jaguar enforcers here for training. Some are new, some are learning to be teachers who train newbies or are retesting for other purposes," Demetria said.

"I never realized how structured your organization is," Fisher said. "So why wasn't anyone in the room with *you*, Kira?"

"Oh, what role did you play?" Demetria asked. "When Martin said you would be helping us, Everett and I figured right away you would be assisting your mate."

"I was the bait," Kira said.

Demetria and Everett chuckled.

"My guard had been complaining about stomach issues and so he told me he had to put a gag on me just so I wouldn't alert Fisher where I was and that I was in trouble, which would have been silly because I was supposed to be the bait. When the guard left to go to the bathroom, several rooms away, I heard Fisher enter the room, or at least I thought it was him. Unless of course it was another guard. I was so proud of Fisher for making it as far as he had in such a short time. I told him to leave me behind, but he wouldn't think of it. But I didn't help him with his mission."

"Unless he had needed assistance." Demetria ate some more of her lasagna.

Kira smiled at her.

"They were testing the two of you in that situation," Everett said.

"That's what we figured." Kira ate another bite of delicious haddock cooked to perfection. "To see how we worked together in a difficult scenario while under observation."

"Where will the next part of the mission be?" Fisher asked.

"You'll have to take Parker out of the facility. Once you reach the door that leads out into the woods, you'll find your way to a safehouse. Fourteen houses are located on the grounds, rock walls concealing the bad guys, tunnels that can be watched or someone could be waiting there for you," Everett said. "We haven't been given our roles yet. I'm sure the trainers knew we would be talking about the course so they wouldn't want anyone to let anything slip during the lunch break."

"But you know the layout? Kira said they've changed a lot of things since she had gone through this last," Fisher said.

"Yeah," Demetria said. "Inside, they change it up every year. Outside, they make some temporary changes—but the houses, forest, major water features, and rock walls have been there from the time they first built the whole outdoor area. We don't know which of the homes is considered the safehouse this time. A map shows the area that you'll be traversing, and you'll have to memorize as much of it as you can before you leave the swimming pool room."

After they finished lunch, Fisher and Kira hugged and kissed, then Kira and Demetria left for their prearranged tasks. Everett escorted Fisher back to the changing room.

"David messaged me to tell you that you'll take the shortcut path you used to get here," Everett said to Fisher as they began undressing. "You'll need to take the door to the north of the pool where Parker was being held hostage. He'll be there, waiting for you, still in his human form. You'll have to find the safehouse. All organization members who are involved in the mission will be given this information. The house is red with a metal roof, and you'll see it in a southeasterly direction on the map. The property consists of ten-thousand acres of jaguar land. But of course, the safehouse won't be that far away.

"You'll want to make your way there as quickly and safely as possible. You have five hours to accomplish the mission. If any of us catch you, the boy would be taken hostage again, and you would be eliminated—in a simulated way. Water obstacles—rivers, streams, lakes, rocky hills, forests, meadows, and houses fill the landscape. Active patrols will be watching for the two of you. When you're on your own, it's easier to keep yourself from being seen. When you must guarantee the safety of a civilian, you never know what to expect. Just a warning, Parker is going to give you some difficulties —just to show you what some freed hostages can be like in the real world—so you'll have to figure out a way to move him without him giving the two of you away. That's about it. Hydration stations are available for the two of you. When you reach them, you can rest, and no one will come for you there. But remember the exercise is timed and you'll need to get Parker to the safe house as fast as you're able to safely. Be sure to study the map in the swimming pool room and pick the way you want to go. It'll show the forest, river, creeks, bridges, trails, roads, and the houses—including the safe-house you need to reach. Good luck, Fisher. We're all rooting for you."

"Thanks, Everett. See you soon, but *after* the mission, hopefully not on the course."

Everett laughed and the two of them shifted. Everett exited through a door to the left, while Fisher headed through the passageway that took him back to the swimming pool where Parker was waiting for him.

Fisher shifted. "We're headed for a red house with a metal roof in a southeasterly direction." He felt it was important to share everything he knew with the teen to make him part of the mission to get there safely. "At all times, watch for my cue. No talking what-soever unless you whisper. Think of this as you being in training and testing just like me. We work together as a team, and I'll get you to the safehouse safely. At the same time, you can help us accomplish the mission."

"But I'm supposed to talk, complain, fuss about going in another direction, and even do so, forcing you to make me behave," Parker said.

"Right. But if you think of this as a test to help us get safely to the house, you'll have the advantage when you go through the training when you're the right age to be a special agent also."

"Oh, okay."

Fisher smiled. "We're going through that door. If you smell the enemy or see one of them and I miss a cue, signal to me. But no talking, or just whisper."

"Yeah, okay." Parker seemed eager to follow the new instructions and be like Fisher rather than try to sabotage the mission like an unruly kid. So far, so good, if it all worked out and Parker didn't go back on his word.

They studied the map first and saw where the house was located. Fisher said, "We won't discuss how we're going to go until we get outside."

Parker glanced at one of the security cameras and nodded.

Fisher shifted into his wolf, and they headed to the door, it opened, and they peered out. He suspected nothing would happen right away, not when they were just exiting the building and they needed to check out their surroundings. Rocky hills, tall wildflower meadows and a river encompassed the area. The river ran from north to south, a forest along the eastern boundary, and extending northwest and a couple of hundred yards due south of the building they were in. A one-story log cabin was sitting in the woods, the front door and patio facing them a few hundred feet from the river to their east.

Fisher pointed in the direction he wanted them to go, and Parker nodded, but before they moved, Parker began removing his clothes. Fisher hadn't expected that, but he figured it might work out better for both of them if Parker was running as a jaguar. No one told Fisher that Parker had to remain in his human form.

As soon as Parker had removed his clothes, he shifted into his jaguar form. Then the two moved low through the wildflowers blooming from goldenrod to purple and white asters and magenta ironweed toward the river. Unless anyone was sitting high above in one of the giant live oak trees scattered all over and could see them, Fisher thought they would be safe. Once they reached the bank of the river, they didn't move to the rocky bank just yet. They listened, smelled the air, and watched for any signs of anyone patrolling the area.

Unlike when he went after Parker to begin with, he was taking a more direct path this time to reach the safehouse. The river turned and headed in a southeasterly direction. The currents could carry them close to the red house, but they would be more exposed while they were in the water. Though he hadn't planned to explain to Parker about his intentions or reasonings, he thought it was a good teaching experience and he wanted to give the boy options to help them find their way.

Fisher shifted. "Swimming down the river would take us closer to the safehouse, rather than us running through the woods but we would be more exposed while swimming."

Parker shifted. "I was thinking the same thing. Should we go around that way? More northeast? And circle around?"

"Yeah, if we go directly southeast, the most direct route to the safehouse, I'm afraid they'll have shifters watching for us. We will still need to cross the river or take one of either of the two bridges that cross it and I'm certain they would be watching for us there."

"Yeah, I agree."

They both shifted and Fisher was glad that Parker was thinking along the same lines. He would make a great agent someday. He was sure that was why Parker was the teen chosen to participate in this exercise.

They waited, watching, making sure no one was nearby. The river's current was swift, and they would have a difficult time crossing it. He wanted them to go one at a time, better not to be seen, but if the boy got into trouble in the water, Fisher wanted to be there for him.

He nudged Parker to go, and the jaguar moved cautiously onto the bank of the river. Fisher quickly joined him. They both went into the water and began to swim across the river to the other side. Despite both being excellent swimmers, they struggled against the strong current.

Fisher suspected they didn't have anyone out here waiting to grab Parker and "eliminate" Fisher as part of the simulated exercise, more concerned that they got across and didn't have a medical emergency.

When they were halfway to the other bank, Parker was struggling to get to shore. Fisher swam up beside him, acting as a barrier against the current until their feet finally touched the rocky bottom and they both managed to climb out of the water. Exhausted, they quickly moved into the trees where Fisher shook off the excess water from his fur. Parker shook off his paws first, then his whole body, and finally, he licked his fur. In the meantime, they took a moment to catch their breaths.

Parker shifted. "Should we head maybe straight east now?"

Fisher shifted. "Northeast, like we first said. They shouldn't expect us to head in that direction. Hopefully."

"Okay."

Fisher led the way through the tangled brush at the base of the oaks and pines. Then he had an idea. With Parker on his side and running as a jaguar, he could leap into trees and see if he could spy anyone off in the distance. He might be able to see the other houses, roads, landmarks, and eventually, the safehouse. He paused and shifted and told Parker the plan.

Parker beamed, nodding. Parker's mission would be even more important during the operation to get them safely "home."

First, they headed northeast for half an hour. The trees were thinning out and they could see hills of rocks with a few scattered trees and shrubs. They would be exposed out there. Now Fisher wondered if they would have had more cover if they had gone straight east like Parker had mentioned earlier.

Fisher shifted. "Can you climb the live oak tree without being seen?"

Parker nodded. With his magnificently muscled jaguar legs, he jumped onto a tree branch, then another, higher and higher, until he could see what he needed to.

Man, what Fisher would give to be able to see the terrain features for himself and plan their next move.

For a long while, Parker observed their surroundings. To Fisher's surprise, Parker shifted in the tree while sitting on a branch high above. "A farm with a white farmhouse and a red barn is to the northeast of us. Trees surround the farm, and the field is filled with crops. A grove of pecan trees borders the north side of the farmhouse. Cattle are in a pasture next to the red barn and lots of haystacks are sitting in huge rolls farther out. Due west are the elevated rock hills and shrubs. Tall flowery meadows lead up to the farmland. To the southeast is a creek and a gravel road. We could possibly go low through the—" Parker stopped whispering and waited.

Fisher was dying to know what he was seeing.

"A farmer is feeding his cows."

Fisher shifted. "Will he be able to see us if we head directly east or southeast?"

"There's a jaguar, oh, it's Demetria Anderson. She's patrolling the rocky hill to the east. If we watch for her, maybe when she goes back to the other side of the hill, we can make a dash for either the pecan grove north of her or go south and keep low among the meadow grasses and the rocky terrain."

"What's the distance to the rocky terrain southeast of us?"

"Maybe sixty yards. The distance to the pecan grove is about a hundred yards."

Fisher so wished he could see the terrain.

"She has gone back to the other side of the rocks."

"Let me leave the woods and have a look. You tell me if you see her returning."

"Alright."

Fisher moved out of the woods cautiously. He looked at the terrain features from a different perspective. The rocky hills were taller than he expected. They would have to move from one rock to another to keep out of sight. Though they would be exposed in some of the areas. Still, he felt there would be more patrols going southeast that way.

He moved back into the woods and shifted. "Let's go to the farmhouse and the pecan grove. Probably there are more patrols the other way."

"Gotcha." Parker shifted and gracefully jumped from branch to branch until he was down on the ground.

"Follow my lead. Unless Demetria heads over to the farmhouse, we can avoid the farm and reach the pecan grove. As long as the farmer doesn't have any dogs and alerts him that we are in the area."

Then they shifted and they sneaked low through the meadow, passing the edge of the farm where bushels of hay were perfect for hiding behind. The wind was blowing in their favor. They could smell the farmer's scent. He was a jaguar—no big surprise. But was he just a farmer, or an agent, pretending to be a farmer?

They moved slowly, cautiously through the meadow, avoiding catching the farmer's eye. He turned in their direction and they immediately crouched down. Parker shifted. "Maybe we could sneak into the house and borrow some of the farmer's clothes. No one would suspect we were traveling as humans. Or at least you and I would be wearing something else."

Fisher shifted. "Were you being tracked?"

"I don't know. They gave me the clothes to wear."

Fisher smiled. "I'm glad you shifted then. Your suggestion of shifting and dressing in different clothes was a good idea, but I'm supposed to accomplish this as a wolf. In a real-world situation, we could sure do that."

"Okay."

They shifted back and headed out again, finally reaching the pecan grove and moved through it with caution. It was clean underneath, no undergrowth that would help hide them, but they didn't smell any scents of jaguars or wolves either if some of them were nearby.

Then they saw a patch of pumpkins and a gray-haired woman in a long sweater tunic, blue jeans and boots, and a cowboy hat crouching down among them. Their scents or movement must have caught her attention because she looked sharply in their direction. They flattened themselves against the ground, but they figured it was too late for that. She smiled and waved at them.

Thinking it might be a trap and that she would call reinforcements, Fisher nudged Parker to move again because she was still smiling at them and watching them so they were no longer undercover.

Parker began moving through the pecan grove at a more cautious pace like they had been doing initially, but Fisher hurried him up. There was no need for secrecy now.

Then they saw a designated water station near the farmhouse with a bench sitting beside it. A freshwater fountain for shifters in his or her fur coat and a water fountain for humans were both set up. Both of them shifted to drink from the human fountain.

"This is a safe zone so no one can come here to bother us," Fisher said.

Then they saw the woman, who had been tending to the pumpkins, head their way. They immediately shifted.

She was carrying terrycloth bathrobes. "Would you like to grab a slice of freshly baked apple pie that I just pulled out of the oven before you continue on your way?"

Fisher shook his head. She might be harmless, but if she wasn't, if they went with her to the farmhouse, they would be out of the safe zone. Wouldn't that be an embarrassing way to fail a mission? Stopping to get a slice of apple pie from an innocent-looking civilian?

She smiled again. "Oh, I see. I'll bring the pie out here and cut it. I'll eat a slice too. That way you know I haven't tampered with it. But you know, this is a safe zone, so I couldn't do anything to you if I was one of the 'bad' guys." She set the bathrobes on the bench. "I'll be right back." Then she went to the farmhouse.

Fisher felt they should just get on their way, but the older woman hurried back with a freshly baked pie still in its glass baking pan and some plates and a pie cutter. She cut them each a slice of pie.

"My husband and I retired from the JAG Corp. We were both Guardians. We loved our job and helping our shifter kind. Who would have ever thought wolf shifters were real and they would help us find bad guys now?"

Fisher knew that eating the pie wasn't part of his mission, and this could mess up his score. But she seemed delighted to meet them and offer them some of her special dessert. Parker looked hopeful that Fisher would agree to eating the pie. She began eating her slice of pie and Fisher shifted, then pulled on a robe. Park hurried to do the same.

Then they saw the farmer coming. He was all smiles and Fisher was afraid that they had made the ultimate mistake.

"Howdy!" the farmer said. "I imagine my mate, Mabel, told you already that we were Guardians in the organization. Training missions are going on here all the time. But we've never visited with any agents-in-training before. We own all the acreage around the farm, about two hundred acres. We retired and they made a deal with us that we could continue to work our farm in retirement because it's in the middle of the ten thousand acres the JAG organization had purchased. If we hadn't been jaguars and part of the organization, they might have forced us out. But we love being here."

"It's beautiful," Fisher said.

"They got right past you, dear," Mabel said, cutting a slice of pie for him. "Not me. I saw them in the pecan grove. It doesn't have any ground cover, but we own it, so no one is supposed to come onto our acreage to capture the good guys."

"What about the water station?" Fisher asked.

"Oh, we copied one that they had created at different areas on their acreage so that any of you knew it was safe to go to and hydrate. We wanted you to know it's safe for you here too. Both Meyers and I use it when we get thirsty out here while working on the farm."

"So all of your land is safe," Fisher said. "And in a way, your farmhouse is a safehouse. We're supposed to go to the red house with a metal roof south of here though."

"Sure, technically, this is as safe as they go," Mabel said. "You're welcome to stay and use our phone to call whoever is in charge to tell them you've gotten your freed hostage to a safehouse."

"They might not count your house as the correct one and then I wouldn't accomplish the mission. They would know just where we are, and we wouldn't be able to leave here without getting stopped."

"I could give you a lift," the farmer said. "I was going to take some pumpkins to market, and I'll be using the road near where the safehouse is located. I'll stop at a discreet spot, let you out, and you can make the rest of your way through the woods. No doubt you'll encounter some trouble the closer you get to the house, but I would love to be part of your adventure like in the good old days. A good agent helping other good agents."

Fisher really liked Meyers and his wife. "You have never done this before for anyone?"

The farmer hurried to eat his piece of pie. "Nope. You're the first we've had the pleasure of meeting. So what do you say?"

"Sure." Again, Fisher hoped he wouldn't regret the decision he was now making, but no one stated there was any rule against it, and as long as the farmer and his wife weren't *really* working with the "bad guys," it couldn't hurt. *Hopefully.*

In a real-life situation, he could have used whatever resource he could to accomplish the mission, after all.

26

Agents were scattered all over, watching for Fisher to show up with Parker while Kira was on the lookout at the red safehouse, trying to see her mate running to safety with his charge. She was supposed to stop him, but she really wanted to pretend she didn't see him. But she had to do her job. She was supposed to be one of the bad guys. She much preferred being a good guy when her mate was. Now if she was working alongside him, and they were both serving as bad guys, that would be fun. Demetria and Everett were totally invested in this and having a blast.

The agents who were acting as the bad guys were just as clueless as to what was going on as Fisher and Parker though. They didn't know where her mate or his charge were. They could be coming from any direction, either close by or far away. The ones setting up the training were the only ones who might know where Fisher and Parker were. She believed Parker would be wearing a tracker in his clothes, that neither Fisher nor Parker would be aware of, so the trainers would have an idea where the two of them were at least. She wondered if Fisher would make the riskier trip to swim across the river with Parker, or head south or north to one of the two bridges, and they could more easily cross either. The bridges were safe zones because the trainers didn't want to lose either Fisher or Parker if they chose to swim across the river and ran into difficulty. But they were a lot farther away.

She paced around the grounds of the safehouse. Woodlands surrounded the house, but it had a grassy area, some rock-bordered flowerbeds, trellises covered by climbing roses, and huge Sunshine Ligustrum that was eight feet tall, providing a beautiful backdrop. But it also would help Fisher to move closer to the house without being seen.

As a jaguar, Everett was stretched out on a branch of a live oak tree at the border of the property, keeping an eye out. He'd been pacing across the roof of a storage building for an hour, but Kira suspected he felt too exposed, so he was trying to sit quietly in the tree now. But he'd moved to different branches several times. Even when he was trying to sit still, his tail was swinging back and forth. Which was great for Fisher! She didn't believe Everett was doing it on purpose to warn Fisher that he was sitting in the tree, waiting for him and he would make his move. He was too competitive for that. She thought he didn't believe Fisher would have had time to reach the red house yet, just like she didn't. She laid down on the long grass that hadn't been mowed in weeks, tired of pacing, worrying that Fisher wouldn't make it safely to the house with Parker in time. They just had to reach the porch, as far as the trainers said and they were safe.

In the Houston area, everything was in flower even after Thanksgiving, the heat having dissipated, giving the flowering plants a chance to rebloom. Which helped Fisher also. Butterflies and bees were still fluttering about the flowers and that was causing a distraction for the ones waiting for Fisher to show up.

The breeze was blowing hard in a northeasterly direction and the branches and leaves were rustling, while birds were twittering and flitting about from one tree to another or around the shrubs, which would help to disguise Fisher and Parker's approach also. But if they were moving up from the south, she and Everett would smell them way before they arrived.

She didn't have any idea about the passage of time. In the other scenario, she had a clock to watch while she was tied up as bait. But here, there were no clocks, so her best guestimate by the position of the sun was that it had been two and a half hours since Fisher left with Parker to find the safehouse. No matter what happened—pass or fail—Fisher wouldn't really fail. She couldn't tell him that. He would learn the truth once he finished. It was a way to teach new agents how to solve problems and change strategies for the next time. Every mission was completely different in real life, so it was a great way to learn from the experience.

She glanced back at Everett who was leaping to a new branch, and she smiled. If anyone was going to alert Fisher that he was watching for him, it would be Everett.

FISHER AND PARKER, and belatedly her mate, thanked Mabel for her delicious pie, left the robes on the bench, and both shifted. Then they ran to the truck and Meyers let them into the cab. They climbed in and he shut the door. "I can't wait to tell some of my retired friends what Mabel and I had done. Believe me, this has been the most excitement we've had in months. They'll want to come and join us the next time something like this happens. Of course, we never know exactly when a mission will take agents this way. The safehouses are located all over the acreage, and they change out the locations for different exercises." He drove down the gravel road for about five miles when a large gray wolf ran across the road in front of the truck and stopped. Meyers slammed on his brakes to avoid hitting the wolf.

Fisher figured their goose was cooked because the agent was

going to examine the truck and learn Fisher and Parker had hitched a ride, but when Meyers opened the door to get out of the cab, the wolf attacked him. Fisher immediately leaped out of the truck and attacked the wolf and smelled it was Reggie. Hell, he had escaped confinement?

The farmer had fallen, his arm bleeding after the wolf had bitten him. Fisher didn't want the teen involved in the fight and the older man either because of his age and since he'd been wounded.

But the teen leapt into the fracas, biting at the wolf's back, not severely and Fisher assumed Parker thought this was part of the exercise and he wasn't supposed to hurt the guy. Fisher didn't have time to tell him otherwise, and bit into the wolf's neck as hard as he could when Reggie turned to attack Parker. Fisher had a hold of Reggie for dear life when someone came up behind him. For a second, Fisher was afraid Reggie's cohorts had escaped also. But it was Meyers, wearing his jaguar coat. Fisher didn't want him to have to fight Reggie and wished instead he had called for help on his cell phone.

Reggie whipped his head around to tear into Fisher, but the farmer bit at the wolf's flank. Parker looked confused. The farmer wasn't biting decisively either. Fisher thought they could wear the wolf down. But he was afraid Reggie might severely injure the two jaguars before they knew what was going on.

Fisher howled for help right before the wolf tried to bite his neck. Then he dodged the snapping, killer jaws.

Kira howled back and Fisher knew she was on her way. She wasn't far away, but he didn't want her hurt either. He needed more backup.

At that point, since Fisher had risked his neck to howl, and another wolf who shouldn't be on his side howled in response, the farmer and Parker probably realized the wolf wasn't playing the game. They both began tearing into the wolf in earnest, which gave Fisher a chance to do the same. Reggie broke free and jumped into the cab of the pickup. Fisher knew he was going to try to drive off. Fisher leaped into the truck and bit at Reggie's neck again, but he had a massive neck, so Fisher wasn't making any headway there.

The passenger door to the cab opened and the farmer was there in his human form, then shifting. But as soon as he shifted and jumped into the cab, Fisher saw Kira and Everett coming to aid them.

Five other jaguars were coming from different directions, and they were all headed straight for the truck. Even though Fisher wanted to take Reggie down, he knew the jaguars could handle the escaped prisoner, while he needed to accomplish his mission.

Then Fisher jumped out of the truck, licked Kira's face in greeting, and nudged Parker to go with him, but the teen was still watching the scene between the jaguars and the wolf in the truck play out. Fisher nipped his shoulder, telling him to move now! Sure, Fisher wanted to see the outcome too, but they still had a mission to accomplish.

Then Parker and Fisher ran off for the red safehouse. They were in the clear now that they had the perfect diversion—one escaped fugitive.

They ran until they saw the treed yard with the rock-bordered flowerbeds and tall shrubs. The sight of the red safehouse would forever be etched in his mind as he and Parker sprinted across the yard to the steps of the house, shifted, opened the door, and went inside.

They found their clothes inside where they'd been delivered, in case they reached the house safely. The tracking device was lying on a table next to the clothes. "Your decision to shift saved us from being tracked," Fisher said, showing Parker the device.

"I never even thought of that. I just believed I could run faster as a jaguar. Who was that guy? I thought he was one of the 'pretend' bad guys overplaying his role."

"An escaped convict we took into custody a short while ago."

"Oh. Wow. No way."

"Yeah. I was afraid to shift and tell the two of you in the event he tried to kill me, but you were biting him so gently, I was afraid he would kill all of us. He did try to kill Kira and me before."

"Wow. You fought well for a wolf."

Fisher smiled. "You did too as a jaguar, once you stopped play biting."

Then Kira came up the steps and into the house, nipping Fisher's pant leg. She disappeared into a room and returned in her human form fully dressed. "I can't believe you tried to recapture Reggie."

"I didn't have any choice. He was trying to steal Meyers's truck and I couldn't let that happen. Then you and I would have been back to chasing down the bastard." Fisher turned to Parker. "He's a newly turned wolf and was kidnapping kids."

"Oh." Then Parker smiled. "We won."

Kira gave Fisher a warm hug and a deeply appreciative kiss, which was totally welcome. "You cheated."

"How's that?"

"You rode in a truck?" she asked.

"We had to," Parker said, "because his wife gave us apple pie and then he wanted to give us a lift and we couldn't say no."

"You stopped to have apple pie?" Kira asked, her brow raised, her voice surprised.

"Nothing in the rule books said that we couldn't," Fisher said.

She laughed. "You were supposed to be in a hurry to beat my time. Instead, you're eating apple pie, riding in a pickup truck, with a hostage that turned into his jaguar coat—"

"We swam in the river too," Fisher said.

"And I was the lookout high in a tree, telling Fisher about all the terrain features and even where Demetria was pacing."

Kira shook her head. "And then Fisher told us your location so we would all be diverted to take care of the threat so you had a free and clear passage to the safehouse."

Fisher kissed her. "Yeah, we were improvising all along the way."

Everett suddenly loomed in the doorway, his jaguar coat a little bloodied. He grunted, headed into the house, dressed, and joined them. "You had to have planned that whole thing."

"What? Reggie's escaping?" Fisher asked.

"Yeah. Here I sat in an old live oak tree forever waiting for you to appear, determined to catch you this time, and the next thing I know, you're howling for help. I was like this was a totally new strategy for a wolf to devise a plan to move us off the property so you could sneak onto it without us catching you," Everett said. "When Kira howled back, telling you she was coming to your aid, I thought you might have bamboozled her, or that even she was somehow helping you out. I couldn't believe you would truly be in trouble. Imagine my surprise to see Reggie in the truck. By the time he was contained, you and Parker were long gone. And Kira was headed back to the house."

Demetria arrived in a car with David, and they entered the house. "Well," David said, "Martin has been apprized of your unique way of handling matters, the ditching of the tracker, running with your charge as a jaguar, meeting up with Mabel and Meyers, and even getting a lift closer to the safehouse."

Fisher was afraid they might take off points for that or add a penalty to his time.

"Well done. You diverted every jaguar and Kira in the area and made it home free," David said.

Demetria hugged Everett. "Aren't you glad we recommended that Martin hire Fisher?"

Everett smiled. "Yeah."

"Oh, and, Fisher, Martin especially liked the way you talked Parker into working with you on the mission and not against you.

We had a camera and audio on you before Parker shifted and the two of you took off. Then of course, we lost you. You didn't cross either bridge, we were told," David said.

"We swam across the river northeast of where the house was," Fisher said.

"And I was the lookout high in a tree, telling Fisher all about the terrain features and even where Demetria was pacing."

Demetria laughed. "Oh, that's really not fair. But ingenious, really."

"Well, Martin said we're going to use your ingenuity in a training session for new recruits. How to ensure a person you're trying to get to safety listens to you and helps you with your mission. No one has ever done that before. When the person who is being tested is told the freed hostage will thwart their efforts to get to the safehouse, they deal with the situation as it arises, which hasn't worked out too well for some trainees. Your idea was the best ever," David said.

"I told Martin he should hire Fisher," Kira said.

Fisher was glad he had done things right then. "How is Meyers?"

"He couldn't be prouder of his wolf bite received in the line of duty, he said. He was taken to our medical facility to be patched up. Reggie probably won't recover from his wounds. The tribunal had already decided he would have the death sentence for trying to kill the two of you. And after what happened with him trying to kill the farmer, you, and Parker? There isn't any doubt he would continue to be a threat to all shifter kind, and humans too," Everett said. "Also, there's no need for either of you to testify against the kidnappers. We have tons of witness statements to verify everything that had happened."

"I can't have missed out on all the action again," Demetria said.

"We did our utmost best to stay out of your sight," Fisher said.

Demetria shook her head. "I never would have envisioned

Parker climbing a tree and spotting me. We thought he would be human throughout the exercise."

Parker and Fisher smiled.

"Yeah, and then we waited until you turned your back and headed out of there before we moved again," Parker said, sounding thrilled they'd been able to get by agents who were really good at their job.

"Next time we do this, I'm going to catch you," Demetria promised, smiling.

Fisher laughed. "I'll have to really be on my toes then."

"Well, if you're ready, Martin wants to meet you in his office," David said. "Kira, he wants to see you also."

When Kira and Fisher finally arrived in Martin's office, it was large and furnished with a big mahogany desk and leather chairs, very rich and showing the importance of his position. On the wall were paintings of jungles and jaguars sitting in trees or hunting. It was just beautiful.

With the way Martin had sounded gruff on the phone in the conversations they'd had, Fisher expected Martin to be in his mid-fifties, maybe a few gray hairs, but Martin was in his early forties with no gray hair and distinguished looking, dark haired and eyed, and welcomed them in.

But then first thing, Martin raised his brows as he motioned for them to take seats in a seating area where he joined them. "Eating apple pie on the mission?"

"That was all my idea," Fisher said, not wanting Parker to get in trouble for it.

"I spoke with Parker, and he said otherwise. He really has your back."

Fisher laughed. He realized then that Martin had a dry sense of humor.

"Usually, I have to tell agents what they've done wrong and could have done better. But you used the resources available to you to accomplish the mission and that's all that matters. If you were truly out in the field and civilians aided you like they did when you had been taken hostage, the more power to you. Most of all, you helped us recapture Reggie. We were planning to end the mission so that no one who was in the field would get hurt when we learned he had escaped. Well done, the both of you." Martin shook their hands and handed Fisher a badge. "You are now officially one of my USF Special Agents. Unless we have a priority mission come up in the meantime, enjoy your Christmas holidays. I understand the two of you just mated so you might want to take some time off for a honeymoon also. Just let me know."

"Thanks so much, sir," Fisher said.

Kira thanked him too, but then Fisher said, "I want to see how Meyers is doing."

"Everett and Demetria are standing by, and they'll run you by the shifter clinic to see Meyers. Again, congratulations for a job well done—both in accomplishing your assigned mission and capturing Reggie with Kira's help. The two of you work together so well, I'm sure you will be partnered up together for the most part."

"Thanks, sir," they both said.

"How, uhm, did Parker fare in the exercise?" Fisher asked, hoping the boy wouldn't be in trouble for siding with Fisher instead of trying to sabotage his efforts in getting him to the safehouse.

"He is receiving a junior commendation for helping the good guy and has a leg up on receiving additional training—both because of your persuasive technique and his own desire to become one of us when he's older. We could use you as a trainer once you've been in the field for a couple of years, if it's something you might be interested in. Though I know you have all your family in Colorado, so you'll probably want to stay there."

"Yeah, though maybe in the future both Kira and I could do that for a year," Fisher said.

"Absolutely. That goes without saying that you two would be together for the venture," Martin said. "Working as a team to solve missions is something we encourage in our training. You and Kira are naturals."

Fisher and Kira smiled at each other. He was so glad Martin saw them in that way. There was just something about Martin that made Fisher want to excel to prove his worth.

Then they left the office, Everett and Demetria took Fisher and Kira to the medical clinic to see Meyers and found Mabel there, holding his hand while the doctor gave him his release orders. Meyers was grinning from ear to ear. "All our friends are going to celebrate my fight with an escaped convict—though they're already giving me grief that a wolf bit me. I keep telling them that it's because I thought he was a good agent pretending to be one of the bad guys."

Fisher smiled. "I'm glad you're going to be alright and thanks for everything."

"You didn't get into trouble for riding in my truck, did you?" Meyers asked as he and Mabel walked out of the clinic with them.

"No," Kira said, introducing herself to Meyers and Mabel and they belatedly told her their names. "He was praised for his ingenuity. But he also has you to thank for that."

Mabel chuckled. "Well, he was so pleasant, and we wanted to help him and the boy."

"Yeah, we're retired Guardians, so it's what we do," Meyers said.

"Anytime you're in the area, be sure and drop by and say hi," Mabel said, "and if you can give me a heads-up, I'll bake something special for you."

"Thanks, we sure will. After this, we're returning to Greystoke, Colorado," Kira said, squeezing Fisher's hand.

Then they said goodbye to the couple and Demetria and Everett drove Kira and Fisher home to have dinner of barbecued ribs and potato salad before they packed up Kira's things into a rental van at her apartment and headed home.

"You're the talk of all the USF organization. You'll be getting a call from your cousin Vaughn who will give you a hard time about cheating, no doubt. But he will only be kidding because he didn't think of it first," Everett said.

"Believe me, I never expected to be presented with everything that happened," Fisher said.

"Exactly. Every mission is completely different. You might have run into hostiles instead of retired Guardian agents. The teen you were trying to take to safety might have given you trouble the whole way there. He might not have been convinced that he should help you and instead worried that in doing so he would have gotten himself into trouble," Everett said.

"Fisher might not have had such a great diversion when Reggie escaped and then we could have easily thwarted Fisher from making it to the safehouse," Kira said.

Everett and Demetria smiled at her.

"What?" she asked, before taking another bite of a rib.

They shook their heads. "I'm sure you would have found a way to help them get to the safehouse should the time have come," Demetria said. "Me? I would done everything I could to stop Everett from reaching the house, if our roles had been reversed."

Fisher and Kira laughed.

Everett raised his glass of champagne to them. "She would have tried for sure."

RETURNING to Greystoke meant a big celebration held by the pack, not only because Fisher was officially a badge-carrying special agent of the USF, but also because Fisher and Kira had mated and joined the Greystoke pack. Even Kira's parents had visited with the pack and were looking forward to buying a home in Greystoke, farther out, which meant they would be expanding the pack's territory out a little bit further and everyone in the wolf pack was thrilled.

Kira and Fisher even managed to get in some rock and mountain climbing the next day. And they went to the western-themed dance club that night. It wasn't quite the same as the exotic jaguar club in Houston, but when Kira and Fisher were dancing—the heat and the beat was just as wildly erotic.

After Kira and Fisher returned home from having a wonderful time at the dance club, they hurried off to the bedroom where a shower and lots more loving was on the schedule for the rest of the night. But coming up?

A honeymoon in Hawaii and they couldn't wait.

EPILOGUE

"We have another mission," Kira said, bringing ice into their honeymoon suite in their hotel room in Hawaii.

"No. Martin couldn't be giving us another assignment while we're on our honeymoon. He said we would have the Christmas holidays off through New Year's, which is why we paid for this extravagant hotel on Waikiki Beach—a dolphin pool, white sand beaches, blue sky, turquoise water, what could be better?" Fisher put the champagne on ice.

Kira laughed. "So you are already tired of the work?"

"No, but on our honeymoon?"

She began stripping off her clothes.

He frowned, thinking they were going to have to get packed in a hurry. "I thought we had a mission."

"Yep, to enjoy our honeymoon without any interruptions. And to send him three boxes of his favorite chocolate-covered macadamia nuts before we leave."

Fisher smiled and began stripping out of his clothes in a hurry. "Now that's more like it. If I hadn't been shot and fallen off that cliff—"

"I wouldn't have fallen in love with a sexy gray wolf, found a mate and a USF partner who is just perfect for me, and a home close to my family," she said.

"And I wouldn't have found the red wolf of my dreams, a new job, and a whole new way of life, which couldn't be better now that you are with me."

They were kissing, naked, the sea breeze blowing through the living room when they got a call and Fisher sighed and answered it.

"Hey, it's Martin. I promised I wouldn't call you and bother you on your honeymoon, but a wolf shifter is causing trouble at a luau close to your location and I wouldn't ask this of you, but a Guardian is there by herself and needs help. The luau is located at a hotel about two miles from yours."

"We're on it," Fisher said. "What do you want us to do about the wolf?"

"I'm having someone pick him up, but he won't be there for another hour or so, and then you'll be free to enjoy the rest of your time there in peace."

"Okay, we're off to check it out," Fisher said.

"He has curly blond hair that reaches his shoulders, he's blue eyed, looks like a surfer, and is wearing a pink Hawaiian shirt, black flipflops, a black watch, and pink board shorts. The Guardian is a redhead wearing a flowery blue dress and she says you can't miss him, but she'll do what she can to try and get him under control until you arrive."

When they ended the call, Kira was already getting dressed and Fisher hurried to dress, and they headed out to their rental car while he filled her in on the details.

"I don't know about you, but it seems too unreal that a Guardian would be here alone and encounter a troublesome wolf shifter—also going solo," Kira said.

"I was thinking the same thing. But I can't imagine Martin is making up the story."

"I know. Which is why we have to take this seriously."

It didn't take them long to arrive at the hotel. They hurried to park, then walked into the lobby, where they heard Hawaiian music playing outside and smelled pork roasting on a spit. They hurried that way, expecting the man causing trouble to be standing on top of a table, being totally out of control.

Instead, they saw Demetria, Everett, Vaughn, and Jillian motioning to them to join them at a table. Everett and Kira smiled.

"This is a setup," Kira said. "I can't believe Martin would tease us like that."

"Yeah, he doesn't seem like the type who would." Fisher and Kira joined the others at the table and a lady brought them flower leis and put them over their heads. "Whose idea was this?" Fisher asked.

"All of us," Demetria said. "Since we worked with you on the last mission and Vaughn and Jillian are your family and also in the USF, we all wanted to come out to see you and enjoy a vacation at the same time. We won't intrude, but we wanted to do the luau with you. And let you know that if anything USF related did come up, we'll take care of it."

"As if we wouldn't be there to help out." Kira ordered a rum cocktail, and so did Fisher.

The Hawaiian dancers began performing, dancing, swallowing fire. Roasted pig was served along with vegetables and fruit. They had a great visit and Fisher and Kira were glad that they had come to see them and enjoy a vacation too.

"So who is managing things if we're all gone?" Kira asked.

"Your former partner. He's healed up and back to duty. Also the group of USF agents in Ely, Minnesota are backing him up," Demetria said.

"Good," Kira said. "I'm glad I'm working with Fisher instead."

They all laughed, knowing just how he and Kira rubbed each other the wrong way.

"Well, we also have some news," Demetria said.

Kira raised her brows.

Demetria took hold of Everett's hand and smiled. "We're finally pregnant and going to have twins in June of next year."

"Oh, wow, that's wonderful," Kira said.

"Yeah, we were waiting until we were ready for it. But I won't be on leave until the babies are born, or if I need to be, a couple of weeks before. By then, Fisher and you will be old pros," Demetria said.

"So that's another reason you wanted Fisher hired," Kira said.

"We had considered it," Everett said, laughing.

After the luau, they all hugged and went on their way to enjoy their own vacations so the honeymooners could have their special time together.

"I can't believe Martin had a hand in this subterfuge," Kira said, stripping her clothes off in their hotel room. "But it was fun to see the others and I know Vaughn and Jillian wanted to welcome you to the USF personally since they hadn't had a chance to before this."

Fisher removed his clothes and slipped his arms around Kira and hugged her tight. "Knowing Vaughn and Jillian, they were the ones who had set this all up. I can't wait for all the family to get together for Christmas in Greystoke."

"But for now, I'm ready for lots of early Christmas presents from you."

He chuckled. "I really lucked out when I met you. And your early Christmas presents are coming right up."

ACKNOWLEDGMENTS

Thanks so much to my wonderful beta readers Darla Taylor and Donna Fournier for taking the time to read my latest novel and find all my typos and other goofs once I was able to send it to them after being without power for days from Tropical Storm/Hurricane Beryl. You both are invaluable! And thanks to Lor Melvin for brainstorming with me anytime I get stuck. It's amazing how we can come up with ideas that make us believe we are identical twins with the same thought process!

ABOUT THE AUTHOR

Bestselling and award-winning author **Terry Spear** has written over a hundred paranormal romance novels and seven medieval Highland historical romances. Her first wolf shifter romance, *Heart of the Wolf,* was named a 2008 *Publishers Weekly*'s Best Book of the Year, and her subsequent titles have garnered high praise and hit the *USA Today* bestseller list. A retired officer of the U.S. Army Reserves, Terry lives in Spring, Texas, where she is working on her next werewolf romance, continuing her new series about shapeshifting jaguars, writing Highland medieval romance, and having fun with her young adult novels. When she's not writing, she's photographing everything that catches her eye, enjoying her grandchildren, making teddy bears, and playing with her Havanese puppies. For more information, please visit www.terryspear.com, or follow her on Twitter, @TerrySpear. She is also on Facebook at http://www.facebook.com/terry.spear. And on Wordpress at:

Terry Spear's Shifters

http://terryspear.wordpress.com/

ALSO BY TERRY SPEAR

Adult Titles

Romantic Suspense: Deadly Fortunes, In the Dead of the Night, Relative Danger, Bound by Danger

***

The Highlanders Series: His Wild Highland Lass (novella), Vexing the Highlander (novella), Winning the Highlander's Heart, The Accidental Highland Hero, Highland Rake, Taming the Wild Highlander, The Highlander, Her Highland Hero, The Viking's Highland Lass, My Highlander

Other historical romances: Lady Caroline & the Egotistical Earl, A Ghost of a Chance at Love

***

Heart of the Wolf Series: Heart of the Wolf, Destiny of the Wolf, To Tempt the Wolf, Legend of the White Wolf, Seduced by the Wolf, Wolf Fever, Heart of the Highland Wolf, Dreaming of the Wolf, A SEAL in Wolf's Clothing, A Howl for a Highlander, A Highland Werewolf Wedding, A SEAL Wolf Christmas, Silence of the Wolf, Hero of a Highland Wolf, A Highland Wolf Christmas; SEAL Wolf Hunting; A Silver Wolf Christmas, SEAL Wolf in Too Deep, Alpha Wolf Need Not Apply, Between a Wolf and a Hard Place, SEAL Wolf Undercover, Dreaming of a White Wolf Christmas, Flight of the White Wolf, All's Fair in Love and Wolf, A Billionaire Wolf for Christmas, SEAL Wolf Surrender, Silver Town Wolf: Home for the Holidays, Night of the Billionaire Wolf, You Had Me at Wolf, Joy to the Wolves, The Wolf Wore Plaid, Jingle Bell Wolf, The Best of Both Wolves, While the Wolf's Away, Christmas Wolf Surprise, Wolf Takes the Lead, Wolf on the Wild Side, Her Wolf for the Holidays, A Good Wolf is

Hard to Find (2024), Dreaming of a Highland Wolf (2024), Mated for Christmas (2024) , The Wolf of My Eye

SEAL Wolves: To Tempt the Wolf, A SEAL in Wolf's Clothing, A SEAL Wolf Christmas; SEAL Wolf Hunting, A SEAL Wolf in Too Deep, SEAL Wolf Undercover, SEAL Wolf Surrender

Silver Town Wolves: Destiny of the Wolf, Wolf Fever, Dreaming of the Wolf, Silence of the Wolf; A Silver Wolf Christmas, Between a Wolf and a Hard Place, Home for the Holidays, Jingle Bell Wolf

Wolff Family Lodge Wolves: You Had Me at Wolf, Wolf on the Wild Side, A Good Wolf is Hard to Find

Highland Wolves: Heart of the Highland Wolf, A Howl for a Highlander, A Highland Werewolf Wedding, Hero of a Highland Wolf, A Highland Wolf Christmas, The Wolf Wore Plaid, Her Wolf for the Holidays, Dreaming of a Highland Wolf, The Wolf of My Eye

Billionaire Wolf Series: A Billionaire in Wolf's Clothing, A Billionaire Wolf for Christmas, Night of the Billionaire Wolf, Wolf Takes the Lead

White Wolf Series: Legend of the White Wolf, Dreaming of a White Wolf Christmas, Flight of the White Wolf, While the Wolf's Away, Mated for Christmas

Red Wolf Series: Seduced by the Wolf, Joy to the Wolves, The Best of Both Wolves, Christmas Wolf Surprise

Wolf Novellas: Day of the Wolf, Seal Wolf Pursuit, Wolf to the Rescue, Night of the Wolf, United Shifter Force

***

Heart of the Jaguar Series: Savage Hunger, Jaguar Fever, Jaguar Hunt, Jaguar Pride, A Very Jaguar Christmas, You Had Me at Jaguar, The Witch and the Jaguar, Dawn of the Jaguar

***

Heart of the Cougar Series: Cougar's Mate, Call of the Cougar, Taming the Wild Cougar, Covert Cougar Christmas, a novella, Double Cougar

Trouble, Cougar Undercover, Cougar Magic, Cougar Halloween Mischief, Falling for the Cougar, Cougar Christmas Calamity, Catch the Cougar (Halloween Novella), You Had Me at Cougar, Saving the White Cougar, Big Cat Magic

***

White Bear Series: Loving the White Bear, Claiming the White Bear, Bear of a Halloween

Grizzly Bear Series: Bear in Mind

***

Wolves of Old: Wolf Pack

Heart of the Huntress Series: Killing the Bloodlust, Deadly Liaisons, Huntress for Hire, Forbidden Love, Deadly Liaisons, Vampire Redemption, Primal Desire, Huntress Unleashed

Vampire Novellas: The Siren's Lure, Vampiric Calling, Seducing the Huntress

***

Comedy Romance: Exchanging Grooms, Marriage, Las Vegas Style

***

Science Fiction: Galaxy Warrior

Young Adult Titles

The World of Fae:

The Dark Fae

The Deadly Fae

The Winged Fae

The Ancient Fae

Dragon Fae

Hawk Fae

Phantom Fae

Golden Fae

Falcon Fae

Woodland Fae

Angel Fae

***

The World of Elf:

The Shadow Elf

The Darkland Elf

Warrior Elf

***

Blood Moon Series:

Kiss of the Vampire

Bite of the Vampire

Night of the Vampire

The Vampire Chronicles Series:

The Vampire in My Dreams

Demon Guardian Series:

The Trouble with Demons

Demon Trouble, Too

Demon Hunter

Non-Series for Now:

Ghostly Liaisons

The Beast Within

Courtly Masquerade

Deidre's Secret

The Magic of Inherian:

The Scepter of Salvation

The Mage of Monrovia

Emerald Isle of Mists

Made in the USA
Middletown, DE
20 January 2025

69843594R00191